VENOM & VICE

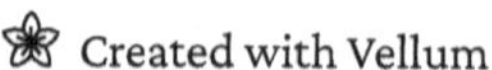 Created with Vellum

BOOKS BY JILL RAMSOWER

THE OF MYTH & MAN SERIES

Curse & Craving

Venom & Vice

Blood & Breath

Siege & Seduction

THE SAVAGE PRIDE DUET

Savage Pride

Silent Prejudice

THE FIVE FAMILIES SERIES

Forever Lies

Never Truth

Blood Always

Where Loyalties Lie

Impossible Odds

Absolute Silence

Perfect Enemies

VENOM AND VICE

JILL RAMSOWER

CHAPTER
ONE

ASHLEY

My awareness of him ate at me like a tumor I couldn't kill.

I didn't have to look behind me to know that Casek was still seated at the same table he'd occupied for the past three hours. Back to the wall. Eyes devouring the room. Cigarette perched casually between two fingers as one end melted slowly into ash. He'd hardly moved from his seat all night.

I'd partied, danced, laughed, and cheered. I'd allowed myself to be swept up in the celebratory current of the packed nightclub, but all the while, his brooding presence remained lassoed around my middle, ensuring I couldn't ignore him completely.

I had tried to tell myself over the past five months of living at the Huntsman that I *didn't* care, but if that were the truth, why did he show up on my radar at all? Why was he the first person I noticed in a room and the only one I couldn't seem to forget when my eyes closed at night? Why did I always gravitate toward him, trying to start conversations and finding ways to coax out the tiniest reactions from him?

Casek wasn't just quiet; he was a hawk high above everyone around him, the embodiment of predatory vigilance. His waters ran so deep that a girl could drown in the undertow. I knew better than to wade into such dangerous territory.

I. Knew. Better.

So why can't I fucking let it go?

Each minute at the party ticked away like drops of Chinese water torture, wearing down my patience. I'd even been so bothered that I'd broken my strict one-drink-an-hour limit. I'd never in my life been more than a little tipsy because I was practically OCD about regulating my alcohol intake. Peer pressure had never remotely tempted me to break my rule, but Casek drove me to a state beyond reason. And when the vodka from my fourth lemon drop martini filtered into my bloodstream, it melted away the last of my restraint. I gave in to the overwhelming need to lash out against the relentless pull toward him.

Slipping from my chair, I drifted away from the table I'd been sitting at with half a dozen other people. They were all too engrossed in conversation to notice my departure, unhindered by the same type of debilitating awareness I'd been enduring. When I zoned in on my intended target, his perceptive stare was already trained on me, despite the steady crisscross of people passing between us.

My heart surged into my throat, attempting to keep pace with the pulsing beat of the music.

Weaving between oblivious clubgoers, I made my way to Casek. He tracked my every movement without betraying a hint of what he might be thinking. I'd yet to see the man succumb to any emotion since I'd known him. He was the most controlled, stoic man I'd ever met, and it made me desperate to rattle him. To see him feel an ounce of the discomposure he caused me on a daily basis.

My unyielding stare speared him through as I approached. A chair sat unoccupied next to him, but I wasn't there to sit and chat. Besides that, I preferred the advantage of higher ground.

I walked straight up where he sat, stopping just inches away, and propped my hands on my hips. "Why did you come tonight if you were going to sit in a corner and ignore everyone?"

God, what a relief it was to say the words that had been burning on my tongue for hours.

Casek held my gaze as he lifted the cigarette to his lips, hollowed out his cheeks with a pull of polluted air, then blew the smoke off to the side while slowly smothering the butt in an ash-filled tray.

When he leaned forward and stood, I retreated a step. I hadn't wanted to concede ground to him without a response from him, but his hulking frame proved too dizzying.

His proximity left me unbalanced and in need of air.

Before I could demand an answer, his hand clamped over my wrist and tugged me toward the back hallway. His pace was determined but reasonable, so I had no trouble keeping up, at least not physically. My emotions, however, were reeling. From relief to worry to excitement to anger and beyond—I struggled to settle on how I felt. With a man like Casek who gave away so little, it was impossible to know my own feelings.

He led me past the office and bathroom doors down to the conference room and pulled me inside, calmly closing the door behind us and releasing me.

The city lights from outside the windows lit the room with a soft glow. Not enough light to detail the flecks of gold in his jade-green eyes, but enough to see a hint of tension in the set of his shoulders. The seemingly benign gesture of pulling me away from the party was an explosive response coming from him. He gave off an unaffected air, but I knew otherwise, and that knowledge kept my lips tightly sealed for once. I'd hopscotched my way into the middle of a minefield and wasn't sure retreat was an option.

Casek rubbed his fingers along his jaw as he considered his words. "For someone having the time of her life, you seem awfully concerned with a man minding his own business." His words slithered through the shadows and crept along my skin, unleashing an army of goose bumps on my bare arms.

I fought to focus on what he'd said rather than the maddening way his voice made me feel.

"Because you're bringing down the entire vibe by brooding in the corner."

"Am I not allowed to celebrate in my own way?"

I crossed my arms over my chest. "No, not if you're going to do it like that." It was a ridiculous thing to say. I knew it. He knew it. He had every right to be as boring as he wanted, but I was too irritated to back down.

"Tell me, Ashley Moore." He stepped closer, his voice softening to a lethal caress. "If there are unspoken rules to this little celebration, why are *you* here?"

Shock hit me in the pit of my stomach.

I knew he didn't like Becca and me around, but I didn't think he would still harbor such resentment after all this time. Did he still see us as just a couple of human tagalongs?

The insinuation touched on a nerve. I'd been turned Fae five months earlier in order to save my life. The feat had never been accomplished before, which meant no one knew exactly what would happen to me. However, I'd been assured that the other Fae could sense my Fae-ness and that my powers would develop with time. I'd been thrilled at the prospect of possessing the ability to wield magic, yet there'd been no sign of these elusive powers. Instead, I'd been trapped in a purgatory of uncertainty for months.

"Are you saying I don't belong because my powers haven't manifested?" My voice shook with barely controlled outrage. "Because they *will*. I have as much right to be here as you do."

Casek stilled. "Don't put words in my mouth," he growled. "I'm asking why you're here tonight when you have just as little desire to celebrate as I do."

My brows shot together in confusion. "I *do* want to celebrate. I'm happy for Becca and everything she accomplished. I want to celebrate her win over Morgan just as much as everyone else out there."

He moved another inch closer. "You want to want it, but your heart isn't in it. I think you desperately wished you'd been the one sitting alone at that table, and that's why you're so damn angry."

I'd never felt so exposed in my life.

I tried to fall back a step but found myself against the wall in more ways than one. I hated that he'd seen past my beaming smile and artificial effervescence. No one else had been remotely aware of the disquiet lurking beneath my shiny surface.

How had he known? Why had he even looked closely enough to see past the illusion?

I'd known he was vigilant, but that kind of intuitive perceptiveness was rare. If he read everyone so easily, it was no wonder he kept to himself.

"You know nothing about me," I whispered, my voice as lost as I felt.

He tilted his head, eyes drifting to my lips. "I know enough." Casek placed his hands on either side of my head and leaned in to bring his cheek close to mine. "I know you want something out of your reach, and no amount of alcohol or dancing will fill that void." The predatory desire in his voice sent my hazy brain spinning.

"You sound like you're familiar with the feeling." So breathless. *Breathe, Ash.*

His body slowly relaxed into mine. "Who says anything is out of my reach?"

Holy. Shit.

Was Casek ... *flirting* with me? Or was the alcohol in my veins making me delusional?

It had to be the alcohol.

He'd never shown me the slightest interest in five months. When I charged over to his table in the club, I had expected him to ignore my existence entirely. This explosion of pent-up desire wafting off him was disorienting.

Maybe it was some kind of sick joke.

Maybe he was getting me riled up before walking away and laughing at my expense. That had to be it because I couldn't reconcile this perceived reality with the man I'd come to know.

I studied him, trying to see behind his mask. To see through to his true intentions. He wasn't the joking type, but none of this made sense. We couldn't have been more different from one another if we'd tried. Could he possibly truly desire me?

It's sex, Ash, not marriage. Maybe this is exactly what you need to get him out of your system.

Shit. Maybe I was right. I was overthinking everything. Sex was sex, and maybe that was all I needed. Then I could scrub Casek from my mind for good. At the very least, it would be an ideal way to relieve some of this nagging tension I'd been trying to manage.

Fuck it.

Tired of fighting with myself, I slammed the door on logic and gave myself over to the moment. I could always blame the alcohol, but I knew, in reality, it had only been a catalyst. This was exactly what I'd wanted for months, and the relief of finally surging forward and pressing my lips to his was all-consuming.

Like a match to kindling, our kiss ignited an inferno.

Our bodies slammed together like magnets free to unite without obstruction. My teeth collided with his, or maybe it was the other way around. It didn't matter. Not even the tang of copper on our tongues slowed our crushing desire.

My hands snaked between us to tug open the button of his pants. He pulled his lips away from mine and lifted his fitted T-shirt over his head, exposing the most exquisite masculine chest I'd ever seen. He wasn't lean muscle and taut skin. Casek was built of solid power—strength hewn from experience and use rather than lifting in a gym.

The sight was almost enough to distract me from the monster cock that sprang free from behind the pants I'd just unzipped. He'd worn nothing beneath his dark-wash jeans, allowing me an unobstructed view of everything he had to offer.

Everything about him was gorgeous—too gorgeous for his personality.

I'd assured myself in the past that he probably had a crooked shlong or trouble getting it up, and that was why he always seemed so moody.

I could unequivocally state now that I'd been wrong.

So incredibly wrong.

My lips parted, but words failed me. I wanted to stare at his majestic perfection for hours, yet my admiration was cut ruthlessly short when he spun me around to face the wall.

I tried to turn in protest, but his large frame caged me in, his lips grazing the top of my ear.

"We do it my way or not at all."

"You have the wrong girl if you think I'm going to beg

for any man's cock." I spoke over my shoulder, catching his dilated gaze from the corner of my eye.

Casek's hand lowered to lift my tight dress above my hips, then caressed the generous globe of my backside while the scalding touch of his hungry gaze seared my skin. Only after he'd seen his fill and coaxed the anticipation in the room to a dizzying level did he return his lips to my ear.

"From you, I would expect nothing less." His murmured words raked across my skin, igniting each tiny nerve ending beneath.

My eyelids drifted shut but flew open again when my lace thong was ripped away in a single swift motion. I was surprised, but most of my shock came from the sudden pressure of the fabric against my core just before the lace gave way. The surge of sensation was overwhelming in the most delicious, mind-bending way.

Casek tore through a foil condom wrapper behind me and sheathed himself as I recovered. He then wrapped one hand around my throat. The gentle pressure of his fingers teased at danger when I swallowed my surprise. He wasn't choking me, but I wasn't sure I approved of the possessive nature of the touch. Before I could protest, however, he was easing himself inside me, rocking forward in smooth, confident strokes. Once he'd buried himself fully inside me, his other hand snaked around my middle and pulled my lower half away from the wall, effectively bending me for better access.

The position was pure domination, and my body purred in approval.

Normally, I liked to be the one in control—life was

easier when I set the tone from the beginning—but Casek wouldn't play by those rules. He made that clear in every fiber of his being.

Just this once, I allowed myself to surrender to a man's touch. To Casek.

He was the architect of this splinter in time, constructing a moment of perfect harmony. Like a master craftsman, even when his pace intensified, he kept perfect control over himself and never once tightened his grip around my throat. He meant to control, not damage or disrespect.

I moaned, overwhelmed with sensation, and felt him thicken inside me.

"*Yes*, Caz. Just like that." I braced my hands on the wall and pushed my ass backward, leaning into his thrusts and reveling in the feel of his touch.

The energy between us buzzed like a live wire. Chaotic and cataclysmic. It built to a maddening peak, both of us lost in the pursuit of what lay on the other side.

This was the release I desperately needed. A biological cocktail of endorphins to lift me out of the funk in which I'd been wallowing for weeks.

I met his movements stride for stride.

Took what he gave.

Demanded more in return.

When Casek's fingers found their way down to my throbbing clit, it only took three swift circles around that swollen bundle before liquid napalm ignited in my veins.

"*Fuck*, woman. You squeeze me so fuckin' tight." His Irish drawl grew heavier as Casek tensed with his own release.

Through the ringing in my ears, the sound of his stunned exclamation sent a flutter of prideful butterflies through my chest. I'd rocked his world just as thoroughly as he'd rocked mine.

Joy tugged upward at the corners of my mouth.

Casek held me close against his chest as we both recovered.

When our breathing slowed to a reasonable pace, he eased away from me. "Don't move," he ordered softly. He fastened his pants and disposed of the condom. At the small minibar built into the wall, he pulled off several sheets from a roll of paper towels and wet them in the sink.

"Leg." He squatted down beside me and patted his shoulder.

It was clear he meant to clean me, but the gesture was so unexpected that I froze. Not until his mossy green gaze lifted to mine did I set my leg over his shoulder. He proceeded to gently wipe me clean, the cool touch of the cloth soothing my swollen, heated flesh.

"Thank you." I chewed at my bottom lip, suddenly at a loss for how to handle the situation. My head still buzzed with the effects of the alcohol, but I was mostly reeling over everything that had just happened. The sex. The domination. The kindness.

Casek stood and took my hand, leading me from the room. "Time for you to go home."

"But everyone's still out there."

"Don't give a shit. You've had enough."

He led us away from the club toward a back stairwell. It couldn't have been past midnight, and the party was still in full swing, but I didn't have the fight in me to challenge his directive. The post-orgasmic flood of dopamine had left me relaxed and pliant. My brain was functioning on such a delay that I didn't begin to question his intent in walking me home until we approached the door of my apartment several floors down from the club.

Was he taking me home for round two? Could I handle a second round with this man?

As if I'd turn down a second chance at the best sex of my life.

When I unlocked the door, though, Casek made no move to follow me inside.

"Did you ... want to come in?" I asked with more uncertainty than I ever let myself show.

"No." His unwavering stare bore into me, not hinting at what he might be thinking. No guilt. No adoration. Nothing to help me understand what was happening between us.

He started to close the door, then paused. "Drink some water before you go to bed. Understood?" He waited for my nod before closing the door and disappearing.

I stared at the lifeless white door for several minutes, processing what had happened and what it all meant.

Holy shit, I just had sex with Casek!

Not just sex. Casek had owned my body and fucked me senseless.

My eyes rounded, and a maniacal grin split my face before I danced my way into my bedroom and fell back onto the bed. I wasn't foolish enough to think anything meaningful would come of it, but the exchange had still felt monumental. Casek was the Fort Knox of men. Even a one-night stand with him felt like stealing a glimpse of the wizard perched behind the curtain. He was made of flesh and bone and carnal desires just like the rest of us, despite the cold-blooded image he projected.

I lay there so long, lost in thought, that the last of my energy drained away before I could take a quick shower. I should have at least removed my makeup, but my veins still thrummed with alcohol and sex.

Giving in to the seductive lure of sleep, I tugged the comforter over me and drifted off with the rich taste of satisfaction still lingering on my tongue.

"Ash, honey. Wake up."

The distant sound of Rebecca's voice penetrated deep into my subconscious. My initial instinct was to swat anything threatening to disrupt my delightfully catatonic state, but a small sliver of rational thought reminded me that this was Becca talking, and she rarely woke me for no reason.

Reluctantly, I coaxed my eyes open and looked blearily at my best friend. "What time is it?" I could have sworn it wasn't a minute later than four or five in the morning from the way I felt, but the light seeping in behind the drapes told a different story.

"It's a little after nine. I'm so sorry to wake you, but I wanted to see you before I left."

"Before you left? Where are you going?" Her words pulled me fully awake, prompting me to sit up and note the formal nature of her dress and hair.

Becca didn't get dolled up for the fun of it like I did. Something was up.

"Lochlan is taking me to Faery to talk to Queen Guin."

"What? Why? Did she summon you?" The queen had warned Becca that once she was fully Fae, Becca would have to live in Faery. We'd both have to face the issue eventually, but I assumed we'd have more time. It hadn't even been twenty-four hours since Morgan had been defeated.

"No. I want to do this on my terms."

My eyes narrowed. "Bec, I'm not sure this is a good idea. Maybe you should let the sleeping dog lie. What if she doesn't let you come back here?"

My heart rate quickened until I could feel it fluttering at the base of my throat.

Becca shrugged. "I don't want her threats hanging over me indefinitely. I know it's a risk, but that's why I wanted to see you before we go. If I'm not able to return, I don't want you to worry about me. Do everything you can to stay here, and if you wouldn't mind horribly, look after my parents." Her brown eyes pleaded with mine as if I would ever tell her no.

"Of course, I will, but that's not happening."

She lifted her hand to stop me from arguing. "I'm just covering all my bases. I have a plan, but nothing is fool-proof." Becca spoke with a commanding confidence she hadn't possessed when she first arrived in Belfast. My best friend had always been kind and generous, but now she radiated self-assurance. Not the puffed-up kind that reeked of arrogance. Inner strength and accomplishment had sculpted her into a woman of power, and I couldn't be prouder.

"Okay, Bec," I said, my voice quavering. "You be careful, and I'll see you when you get back."

We came together in a sisterly hug. Neither of us had any actual sisters, but I was of the opinion that a chosen sister was even better—all of the best parts without the bickering. Bec was my sister from another mister, and I was so glad we were on this adventure together.

She was gone a few minutes later, and I was wide awake.

And worried.

If I didn't find something to do while Becca was gone, I would go crazy with the uncertainty.

I took a long, hot shower. It felt amazing, but I needed to get out of the apartment. I needed a distraction. Once I was dressed and ready for the day, I texted Liam, who had generously been training me in hand-to-hand combat over the past five months. I had no magic to develop, but that wouldn't stop me from learning to protect myself however I could.

Chances were slim that Liam would be up after last night's party, but I tried anyway. Five minutes passed without a response, so I put on a jacket and decided to grab some coffee. Caffeine was the last thing I needed for my nerves, but the comfort of sipping the warm, fragrant nectar sounded too good to pass up.

As always, the common areas of the Huntsman building were near silent before noon. The men of the Wild Hunt led a mostly nocturnal lifestyle. Between running a nightclub and hunting Fae fugitives, their days didn't truly begin until nightfall.

I walked around the corner to a local coffee shop and got a caramel Frappuccino, then headed back home. Hopefully, by the time I got back to the apartment, Liam would text back, and I could occupy myself with training. Stressing out wasn't going to help Becca. Subjecting myself to needless suffering was pointless.

I was contemplating backup plans should Liam still be asleep when the elevator doors opened and brought me face-to-face with Casek. The gears in my head clanged together and ground to a halt at the sight of him. I hadn't had a chance to even stress over a night-after interaction and plan for how I'd handle seeing him again.

"Oh, hey there," I managed to stammer.

He looked incredible. Even more alluring than he had before, but maybe that was because I now knew what lurked beneath the façade.

Casek joined me in the lobby. His impassive eyes were the shadowed green of a pine forest, silent and secretive. "Ashley." He dipped his chin, keeping several feet of space between us. "You're up early."

Was that reluctance I detected in his voice? He wasn't giving off the slightest vibe of acknowledgment that we'd had sex the night before. Casek wasn't the most amiable person on a good day, but he seemed stiff, even for him. Did he regret having sex with me? Was he worried I would expect some kind of commitment from him?

He could be simply having a bad morning, Ash. Not everything is about you.

In theory, that was true. And I could have given him

more slack if his response wasn't so freaking typical. The alpha stud acting aloof and indifferent after sex to discourage us sentimental females from becoming attached. As if. I wasn't the simpering lovestruck type. If he thought I would cling to him in some desperate need for validation, he had another thing coming.

"Becca woke me up to let me know she was heading to Faery," I said nonchalantly.

Casek's full lips thinned. "Lochlan told me."

"He say why they were going?"

"Not exactly."

"I take it you aren't thrilled with them going?"

"Guinevere's a powerful woman."

"Let me guess. You tried to go with them, and Lochlan refused?"

He only scowled in response.

"I suppose as the boss, that's his prerogative." I accented the word boss, a somewhat immature jab at the fact that Casek was an underling, even if he was Lochlan's right hand.

Judging from the way his eyes snapped to mine, he didn't miss the veiled slight.

"And what about the threat she poses to your best friend? You seem awfully indifferent." He gave the steaming cup in my hand a quick glance.

"Rebecca's tough. I trust she knows what she's doing. Women aren't all delicate flowers in need of protection, you know."

He took a small step closer, a move calculated to intimidate. "What's with the attitude?"

My eyes widened innocently. "Attitude? I don't know

what you're talking about." Yes, I was being a little bitchy, but he was being an ass. Why did women always have to take the high road and be accommodating to grumpy men? I would never be so weak as to grovel for scraps of attention.

His only response was a blistering stare that I met head-on.

"Look," I continued, "I'm just doing my thing, making sure you don't get any wrong ideas about last night. Yes, we had sex, but that doesn't change anything. I think that's something we can both agree upon."

Casek didn't move a muscle. Not a twitch or a blink.

He didn't even breathe.

His stillness was disconcerting, but just before I began to wonder if he would argue, he confirmed my suspicions. "What a relief," he said tonelessly. "I'm glad we both agree last night was a mistake."

I kept my features perfectly schooled, but I hadn't been able to control my lungs from rapidly expanding with air.

I'd thought Casek was worried about sending me the wrong message, but calling our night together a mistake was a whole other level of insulting. The insinuation reeked of regret, and that was downright hurtful.

"I think you mean epic," I ground out, anger lacing each word. "It was an *epic* mistake."

CHAPTER
TWO

CASEK

I GOT THE DISTINCT IMPRESSION, HAD ASHLEY POSSESSED THE ability, I would have been reduced to a pile of ash and cinder at her feet. Normally, I didn't give a fuck when I pissed off the people around me. Their anger was their problem, not mine. But something about the ire burning in Ashley's eyes sparked my own temper.

I prowled forward and invaded her space, towering over her curvy little frame. "Why the fuck are you so pissed?"

She didn't give the slightest sign of intimidation. If anything, my actions only fueled her fire. Ashley leaned forward, jabbing her manicured finger into my chest. "*Me?* I'm not the one getting into people's faces and acting like a Neanderthal."

I'd never met someone who crawled beneath my skin the way Ashley did. The second I saw her on the other side of those elevator doors, my hands itched with the need to yank her inside with me and fuck her again.

What was it about the woman that drove me so fucking insane?

She was beautiful, but so were all the other women who wandered in and out of the club on a nightly basis. None of them tested me the way Ashley did. She was the only one who had ever successfully tempted me past the point of restraint.

I hadn't kissed a woman in hundreds of years.

I hadn't wanted to. It was too personal. Intimate. And it sent a message I wasn't interested in conveying.

Until her.

When Ashley's lips pressed against mine in that conference room, I responded on instinct, a starving man at a feast.

Then I'd gone and fucked her as if my life depended upon it.

She crushed my control under her red stiletto heels. I'd kept my distance from her for months for that very reason. I could sense the volatility of my reactions to her and knew she was more dangerous to me than any of the monsters I hunted. Even now, I knew I should be relieved at her anger and use it to reconstruct the wall between us, but I couldn't. It was impossible to ignore her. The need to push back was too overwhelming.

I lowered my face close to hers and whispered. "You weren't complaining about my Neanderthal tendencies last night."

Ashley was livid, though she tried to hide it beneath a mask of impassivity. Like a hungry crocodile lurking beneath the glassy surface of a riverbank, she was poised for attack.

Why did that give me so much damn satisfaction?

Because I wanted her just as fucking off-balance as I was. It was only fair we suffered equally.

"I'd been drinking," she ground out. "I claim temporary insanity because I don't know what else would have convinced me to get anywhere near you."

Depravity clawed at the smile twisting my lips. "I'll bet that was it." I slowly pulled away, a gulf of frigid air filling the chasm between us.

"*Fuck off*, Casek," she hissed, stepping past me to press the elevator call button. The doors immediately opened, allowing her a quick escape.

I let her go, for both of our sakes.

The woman was unreal. From the first day she'd waltzed into our club, I could tell she was different. She wasn't afraid of the darkness surrounding her like most would be. I'd known another woman who was also tenacious to a fault and courageous beyond reason.

That woman had died a horrific death.

Losing Raisa so many lifetimes ago had changed me, leaving me uninterested in maintaining any meaningful female relationships in my life. I'd made it a habit to single out the vapid ones—happy to please and easy to forget.

That had been my life for a long time, and I had no desire to change it. Forming an attachment to a woman—especially one shrouded in danger—was out of the question. I had to get my head on straight and take control of the situation.

I took out my phone and sent a quick text. To my relief,

I received an instant reply. Abandoning my original purpose for leaving the building, I rerouted myself to a nearby apartment building.

I'd fed my magic only days before in preparation for our battle against Morgan, but the magic I'd used since, primarily in healing myself of my battle injuries, had depleted my reserves. I hadn't fed from Ashley like I should have when I'd fucked her. Instead of being practical, I'd refused to diminish her orgasm in any way by siphoning even an ounce of her pleasure. I'd wanted her to come undone and been more than gratified at the result. However, that meant I still hadn't fed, and even more importantly, I needed to remind myself that women were a dime a dozen. The best way to get Ashley out of my head was to lose myself in someone else.

God, I hope so. Because if I can't untangle myself, I'm fucked.

I normally had a few women at any given time available to me, but we'd been so consumed with the Unseelie invasion that I'd been negligent about maintaining my options. When I made arrangements to feed days earlier, I'd found several doors had closed on me, leaving me one avenue available on short notice. I'd told myself after my last visit with Brianna that it was time to cut ties, but here I was, days later, showing up at her doorstep.

Not my finest hour, but it was better than the alternative. I'd rather fend off a clingy Brianna than fall further under Ashley's spell.

At least, that had been my assumption.

When Brianna greeted me, her eyes lit up like a fuckin'

Christmas tree, and I was suddenly questioning all my life's choices.

For fuck's sake.

"Casek! I'm so glad you texted. Come in." She grabbed my hand and pulled me inside her small apartment. She was a knock-out blond with a plump ass and a tiny waist—perfect in every way, except for that telltale gleam in her eyes. The one that told me she had started to make plans and formulate assumptions about the nature of our association.

The gleam meant drama, and I *hated* drama.

Brianna wrapped her arms around me and rose on her toes, seeking out my lips.

I caught her face with my hand, keeping her at a distance. "You know my take on kissing. I'm not your boyfriend, never have been, so don't pretend otherwise."

"It doesn't matter how you label it. It's my bed you keep coming back to."

We definitely had a problem.

I shouldn't have been surprised. For a man who prided himself on well-thought-out decisions, making mistakes seemed to be my new favorite pastime. The worst part was the doubt. I could feel my usual surety becoming soft and amorphous. Ten minutes ago, I'd been confident that fucking Brianna was necessary. Now, I was questioning my ability to see anything clearly.

How else will you get Ashley out of your system? Who cares if Brianna throws an unholy fit? If she's open to being fucked, and that's what you need, do it.

My teeth clenched so tight I could have cracked a tooth.

"Turn around," I ordered.

She didn't hesitate. There was undoubtedly a victorious grin on her face, but as long as I couldn't see it, I didn't care.

I closed in behind her and bent her forward over the kitchen table with a firm hand on her back. She spread her legs and waved her ass in the air, ready for me.

It would have been easy to slide inside her and take what I wanted, but where was the fun in that? With the addictive tang of Ashley's feisty nature still ripe on my tongue, all other flavors paled in comparison.

What was I thinking?

Brianna was so far from measuring up that she had no chance of erasing the memory of last night. Not only would I fail to achieve my goal but I was also about to make everything worse by giving Brianna more ammunition.

"*Fuck*," I roared. "I shouldn't have come here. This isn't going to work anymore."

"You don't mean that." She ran her hands down my chest. "You know you can't get enough of me."

"Think whatever you like, but I'm done. You won't hear from me again." I turned toward the door.

Brianna grabbed my arm and peered up at me from beneath her thick lashes. "Don't leave, Caz. I'm sorry if I upset you. Stay and let me make it up to you."

"I'm not upset. And you're not going to change my mind. It's time to move on." I crossed the room and began to open the door when glass shattered against the wall next to me. The vase of flowers that had been on her kitchen table lay in pieces on the ground, water spreading across the stained linoleum.

"*Fuck you*, Casek," she yelled, chest heaving rapidly.

Twice in one morning. That was impressive, even for me.

At least this time, I felt zero emotional response to the angry woman before me. That was my protocol. That was how it should have been with Ashley, but my reaction to her was visceral. Whether she was simply walking past me or confronting me in a crowded nightclub, her effect on me was absolute and unwavering.

If I was going to free myself from her toxic grasp, I would have to come up with a better plan than Brianna.

I pushed the glass shards and flower stems aside with my foot, opened the door, and walked away. I wasn't two blocks down the road when my phone sounded with an alert. Someone had triggered our wards at the Huntsman.

I wasn't worried about my brothers—they could handle themselves—and Rebecca was away with Lochlan. There was only one vulnerable person in the building, though I doubted she'd ever label herself as such.

Foot slamming on the gas, I raced back home in record time.

THREE

ASHLEY

It was a good thing for Casek that I'd forgotten about the knife I was carrying in my purse, or I might have gone for one of his eyes. He would have stopped me, but I'd have given him a good fight.

What the hell was his problem? Was he truly a grade A caliber asshole, or was he that freaking terrified of people getting close to him?

One-hundred-percent asshole.

Even if he had a reason behind his comments, he still chose to say them. He chose to be plain mean, and that's assholery. His possible excuses were irrelevant.

I slammed the door to my apartment when I returned home, dropping my purse at the door and pacing to the windows and back like a caged tiger. I was so freaking triggered, but at least it was better than drowning helplessly in worry. Casek had successfully distracted me from stressing about Rebecca.

Look at me, appreciating the silver lining.

I turned back for the windows, ready to delve into another mental tirade about Casek when my phone buzzed in my back pocket. Too irritated to pay attention, I answered before I got a look at the screen, committing myself to a call I didn't want to take. It was the very last person I wanted to hear from. He was the reason I was so untrusting—the first person to teach me about the failings of men.

"Hey, Ash. How's everything in Belfast?" My father's voice was full of earnest curiosity, despite my clipped greeting.

The sound only made me angrier.

Matthew Moore had ruined his chance at a relationship with me years ago when he chose alcohol and emotional abuse over his responsibilities as a husband and father. Granted, he'd recovered, but it didn't change things in my eyes. He'd been trying for five years now to worm his way back into my good graces, but it was too little too late. I refused to pretend the past never happened. Civility was the best he'd get from me.

"Everything here is great. How's Mom?" I should have called her more often than I did, but our relationship wasn't great either. Not after she took Dad back when he was a year out of rehab. It had taken her years to finally separate from him, and I couldn't fathom how she'd so quickly fall back into his clutches. I'd been furious. While she was busy playing house, I was still haunted by memories of nights spent crying myself to sleep after witnessing Dad berate her in drunken fits.

You spreading your legs for John next door? Don't fuckin' lie to me! I saw the way you looked at him. I knew you were dumb, but I never took you for a slut. Should have fuckin' known better. Fuckin' white trash.

I could never support their reconciliation. It didn't matter how many AA coins he received or meetings he attended—as far as I was concerned, she was better off without him.

"She's doing really well. They've asked her to continue teaching the watercolor class at the community college through the summer. She's absolutely thrilled."

"That's great news." I was honestly happy for her. Mom had only ever taught recreational painting classes, but when an opening became available at the college to fill in for a professor on maternity leave, Mom went out on a limb and applied. It had been a big step out of her comfort zone, and I was incredibly proud. The fact that she'd been chosen was gravy.

"Yeah, the woman who had the baby decided to put teaching on hold for a bit longer. From what your mother says, she may take a sabbatical for a few years."

"That's awesome. Sounds like a win for everyone involved."

"It really is." His voice trailed off. "Listen, Ash. I've been thinking about this a lot, and I'd like to come visit you. Mom can't get away, but I'd like to see you. Spend some time together."

I couldn't think of anything I wanted less.

Maybe a palm full of fiberglass splinters? Or perhaps a root canal?

"I don't know, Dad. I've been really busy here adjusting to remote work and meeting new people. I'd hate for you to come all this way just to be on your own."

The phone was silent for several seconds, leaving room for a tiny sliver of niggling guilt to wedge its way into the back of my mind.

"I understand," he finally replied. "It's just that ever since we got that mistaken call back in December from the hospital, it's bothered me more than ever that I damaged our relationship so badly. Life can be cut tragically short at any time, and I'd hate to think I didn't do everything I could to show you how sorry I am."

Technically, the hospital's call hadn't been a mistake. I *had* died, but Merlin had saved me by making me Fae. I'd told Mom and Dad the call was a mistake to help explain away my miraculous recovery. Had Merlin not shown up to save me, my parents would still be grieving.

Well, shit.

Deflated, I slumped into one of the bar chairs at the kitchen island.

I wasn't a fan of handing out free passes, but rejecting him now would be plain heartless. He was making an effort to connect, and as far as I knew, he hadn't relapsed once since rehab. Allowing him a visit wasn't the same as sweeping the past under the rug. Would it be so terrible to indulge him this once?

He wasn't always so horrible, remember?

Things hadn't gotten bad until I was around twelve years old. Before that, I'd adored my dad. That had made his fall from grace that much more painful. I spent years desperately hoping to get my daddy back before I finally faced reality. I was terrified of putting him back on that pedestal only to watch him fall again.

But this is one little visit. Surely, that won't kill you.

I sighed heavily. "Yeah, okay. I suppose I can put some thought into when would be a good time for a visit."

"That would be great," he quickly replied. His palpable relief fed the guilt that now had me squirming in my seat.

"I better get going, Dad, but thanks for calling."

"Take care, Ashley."

"You, too," I said in a small voice before hanging up.

Dropping my head back, I sucked in another lungful of air and closed my eyes.

"Sounds like you'll be expecting company soon."

I lurched from my seat, knocking the bar chair to the ground in my hasty retreat.

An unfamiliar man sat on my living room sofa as though he were an invited guest. He lifted his hands to assure me he wasn't a threat, but the gesture was ineffective. Every muscle in my body was coiled in alarm.

"Who the hell are you, and how did you get in here?" The door to my apartment had been locked. He must have traced inside, which meant he was Fae, but he was most certainly not one of the Huntsmen.

I clutched my phone tightly, debating who I could call for help.

"Please, don't be frightened," he said calmly. "My name is Merlin, and I apologize profusely for my unexpected intrusion."

"Merlin?" I whispered, my lips parting in awe.

The Merlin? The man who had saved my life? The man who had theoretically given me Fae powers and started Becca and me on this strange new journey?

"You're Merlin?" I asked incredulously.

His smile twitched with amusement. "I am."

I was going to have words with Rebecca.

She'd failed to tell me the great Fae sorcerer was a total hottie. I'd envisioned a modern-day version of Gandalf, but this man bore nothing in common with the fictional wizard. Merlin looked as if he were no older than forty with perfectly styled white-blond hair and eyes so pale blue I would have assumed they were colored contacts had he been anyone else. He was youthful and fit, dressed in an expensive suit, and gave away absolutely no hint of his vast powers. He could easily have been a Norwegian businessman out for a day of sightseeing.

I stared unabashedly, completely entranced.

Merlin chuckled. "I've been remiss in my introductions. I should never have taken so long to pay you a visit, but I've been exceedingly preoccupied elsewhere. And while I wish we had the time to acquaint ourselves now, I'm afraid we are on somewhat of a deadline. Rebecca will be meeting with Guinevere shortly, and I believe it would be prudent if we were present for that conversation."

In that instant, a pounding fist rattled the door.

I looked between Merlin and the door, unsure what to do.

He nodded once. "Best to let him in."

I got the sense he knew exactly who was on the other side of the door. Sliding the deadbolt, I opened the door to Casek, who looked like he'd sprinted up all four flights of stairs. He immediately barged inside, positioning himself between my guest and me. A second later, two more Huntsmen joined us, remaining close behind me.

"What business do you have here that justifies circumventing our wards?" Casek's threat was inherent in his voice, black and sharp as polished steel.

"It's good to see you, Caz." Merlin bowed his head. "As you are probably aware, Rebecca and Lochlan are on their way to the palace. I believe it would be best if Ashley and I joined them."

I side-stepped Casek as Merlin spoke so that I could remain a part of the conversation. My eyes danced between them, especially curious at Casek's behavior. Merlin acted as though the two were on good terms, yet every aspect of Casek's demeanor called that assumption into question.

"If that's the case," Casek responded coolly, "then I'll accompany you two."

Merlin gave a tight, wary smile. "I'm afraid that won't work. You see, this endeavor will be sensitive as it is, and the more threatened Guin feels, the more resistance we shall encounter. It would be best if you waited here. I promise Ashley will come to no harm."

His assurance struck me as odd. As if Casek cared what happened to me. Though he'd likely be in trouble with Lochlan should I have ended up in danger, but only because Becca would be upset. Casek himself would probably breathe easier if I disappeared forever.

The surly Fae warrior exhaled slowly. "I don't like this, but I doubt I have much of a choice, do I?"

Merlin cocked a single white brow.

"Fine," Casek growled. "But she'd better come back unharmed. She was left in my care, and I take my oaths seriously. If you break my trust, I *will* find you. I don't care how powerful you are."

My shoulders tensed at the overt threat, but Merlin merely bowed respectfully and walked to my side. He held out his elbow as if we were in a Victorian-era romance, and he was escorting me to my carriage.

I followed his lead and clasped his arm. The moment we touched, our surroundings disappeared.

THE NEXT HOUR passed like a dream. That was after I threw up and regained my bearings.

Who knew tracing would be so nauseating?

Merlin took me to a church where he opened a portal to Faery. Our entire journey was surreal. From the female sentries stationed on the other side of the portal to the glittering palace anchored in the center of Avalon, I was in awe of every new sight. My brain stretched and strained to comprehend how an entirely different world could exist so close to our own. I'd known for months about Faery, but seeing the dueling Faery suns and feeling the invigorating pulse of magic in the air made it all that much more real.

So many firsts in one day, including an introduction to the Faery queen, Guinevere. She was the physical embodiment of regal beauty, with waving red hair down to her waist and eyes so green I could see them from the back of her throne room.

She was mesmerizingly gorgeous and utterly terrifying.

What had me the most fascinated, however, was the cunning and confident way in which Rebecca managed her. My best friend was one bad bitch, and I couldn't have been prouder. She argued her way to freedom, using her unique Twilight Realm magic to extract herself from beneath the queen's rule.

Guin wasn't pleased with being strong-armed into a corner, but there was little she could do without appearing outright tyrannical in front of dozens of courtiers.

When the moment was right, Merlin unveiled his reason for bringing me by announcing that I was his new apprentice. I thought it was rather comical, considering I had no magic, but Guin didn't know that.

The ploy worked, and I was given the freedom to stay on Earth under Merlin's protection.

Becca and I both walked away from the palace as free women.

I was pleased, yet my relief was incomplete. I felt just as conflicted as I had the night before while trying to celebrate the end of the Unseelie rebellion. How could I fully embrace our success when I was still stymied in frustration over my nonexistent powers?

I hadn't brought up the subject on our way to the palace because Merlin had clearly been on a mission, but now that the confrontation was over, I decided to make my move. Rebecca and Lochlan had stayed behind just outside the Avalon gates for unknown reasons, so it was only my Faery godfather and me walking through the countryside toward the portal back home. If anyone could help me, it would be him—the man who had given me my powers to begin with. What he'd done was thought to be impossible. I wasn't sure Merlin knew the meaning of the word.

"I really appreciate what you've done for me," I started, easing gently into the subject.

"It's been my pleasure to help. Neither you nor Rebecca would be in this situation if it weren't for me."

"I've been wondering about that, actually. You see, I was told you saved my life by making me Fae, but I'm not so sure. It's been five months since that happened, and I still have no magic."

Merlin's steps slowed, his piercing eyes turning to me. "Is that so? Nothing at all?"

I shook my head.

"Have you felt any different here in Faery than you did back in Ireland?"

"I don't know if *I* feel different, but the air here seems different. Like the way it feels when you rub a balloon against your bare arm and all the hairs stand on end."

"Good, good." He nodded his head and held his hands out for mine. "Let's give something a try."

I placed my hands in his, my eyes quickly closing at the calming sense of warmth that flowed into me at his touch.

"Ah, yes. There it is," he murmured.

As he spoke, I felt a tingling energy shiver outward from my spine.

"Do you feel that?" he asked.

"*Yes*," I breathed. How could I not? It was the most foreign, incredible sensation I'd ever experienced.

"*That* is your magic. I've coaxed it out from its dormancy using my power as a lure. Given that your magic is derived from mine, I had hoped such a tactic might work." Merlin pulled his hands from my grasp, causing the electricity inside me to sputter and fizzle.

"Wait! Not yet." My eyes flew open.

"I'm not done," he assured me with a nod. "I want you to close your eyes again and see if you can identify any remnants of that feeling. Search yourself for its place of origin deep within you."

I did as he asked, centering all my concentration on that place just behind my belly at the base of my spine, and discovered he was right. A residual hum of energy still stirred.

"It's there," I whispered in amazement.

"Good. Now, think of that pool of energy as a ball of yarn and coax a string outward."

I wasn't sure how to do as he asked but found it was easier than I'd expected. Once I identified the energy and concentrated on it, the ball seemed to respond to my wishes, pulsing and growing inside me.

"I think I'm doing it!" I flung my eyes open excitedly.

Merlin grinned, reaching his hand in his jacket pocket and pulling out a mirror that should never have fit in a pocket so small. I was about to question how he'd accomplished the trick when my eyes caught sight of my reflection and derailed my thoughts.

Blue light softly emanated from my eyes.

Becca told me the same thing had happened when

Merlin first saved my life, but I'd seen no trace of it. Not until now.

I was mesmerized.

I'd hated my eyes in the past because they looked just like my father's, but shining with an ethereal glow, they were positively breathtaking. Unique. Powerful.

When Merlin lowered the mirror, I flew at him, wrapping my arms around him in a hug that bordered on assault.

Fortunately, the ancient sorcerer only laughed and patted my back.

"I believe from now on you should have more luck. Most Fae children have years for their power to take seed and sprout. Yours was still burrowed deep, but it looks like we've managed to find a loophole and speed things up a bit."

Grinning somewhat sheepishly, I released him from my hold. "I can't tell you what a relief this is. I was beginning to worry that I wouldn't have powers."

"I suppose it was a possibility. Every bit of this process is experimental. I will be intrigued to hear what powers you develop and if they are identical to my own or if your unique chemistry alters the magic." He studied me almost longingly. "I only wish I could be here to observe."

"You have to leave again?"

"I do. Morgan and her mother both need me. There is still plenty to be done." A somberness shadowed his gaze.

"I understand, but I hope you won't be gone for too long without a visit." I was a bit surprised to realize the sentiment was genuine and not simply a platitude. I'd only just met the man, but he had an endearing quirkiness about him. Not to mention the fact that he'd now come to my rescue on multiple occasions. I was noticeably reluctant to part ways.

"You have nothing to fear in that department. I'm never too far away, and I plan to keep an eye on your progress."

A mischievous twitch of his lips didn't escape my notice. From what I'd heard, the man was endlessly cunning, so there was no telling what he had up his sleeve.

"I have done what I can to see to your safety. However, you are ... one of a kind, and such rarity brings out the covetous nature of both humans and Fae. You'll need to be very careful."

I didn't have to know this enigmatic man long to read the severity of his warning. I nodded with all seriousness. "I will."

"Caution is of the utmost importance, but that's not all. You'll need to trust the Huntsmen to keep you safe. You're still new to this world, and your inexperience will make you vulnerable, regardless of your powers."

"Absolutely," I assured him quickly. "Lochlan and his men have practically become family."

He smiled, but it lacked conviction.

I wondered just how much he knew about me. Yes, I wasn't the most trusting individual, but I understood that the circumstances of my life in Belfast necessitated change. I felt like I'd done a rather admirable job of working with the Huntsmen. Of course, I'd had little choice. Without my magic, I'd been a sitting duck.

But now ... now, I had power of my own.

I could protect myself. I might rely on others to help me, but not out of helplessness.

If I leaned on my friends, it was because I *chose* to do so on my terms. Because someone wanted to help me, and I had no objection. A vast ocean of difference existed between that and the pathetic helplessness I'd experienced for the past five months.

The feeling was reminiscent of being a child seeking purchase on the unsteady ground of a broken family. I'd had no control over my life during those dark days, and I never wanted to feel that powerless again.

CHAPTER
FOUR

CASEK

ONE MINUTE, ASHLEY WAS THERE, AND THE NEXT, SHE WAS GONE.

The men at my back cursed as we all stared at the now empty room.

"That shouldn't be possible," one of them said. "How the hell did he trace with her?"

"It's Merlin," I shot back. "That asshole can do anything. Why the fuck do you think I let him go?" I took one long stride toward the door to Ashley's apartment and punched my fist deep into the wall beside the doorframe.

When Lochlan first told me of Rebecca's plans that morning, I'd insisted on going with them, but Lochlan had given me the same response as Merlin. They thought less was more when it came to persuading the queen. I disagreed, but that didn't seem to matter.

Being sidelined pissed me off anytime it happened, but this instance felt even worse. It wasn't just my pride on the line. Knowing Merlin was taking Ashley into a potential hornet's nest made my skin crawl with helplessness. I'd been charged with her protection while Lochlan was gone. How the fuck could I keep her safe when she'd been taken from me? The whole situation was bullshit, yet I couldn't do a thing about it.

Too pissed to speak, I shouldered past the men and retreated to my apartment before I took out my anger on someone's face rather than the wall. I changed into sweats and spent an hour hitting the heavy bag in the basement gym before I finally got word that Ashley had returned. For once, the time difference between worlds had played in my favor and minimized the agonizing wait.

The tension in my muscles relaxed in a way even the gym hadn't accomplished—a fact I didn't want to examine further, considering Lochlan and Rebecca were delayed and had yet to return. Ashley was an assignment, whereas Lochlan was my commanding officer and best friend. My concern for him should have far outweighed anything I felt for Ashley.

Judging by the sudden lightness of my breathing, I had some wires to untangle in my head.

A CLOYING AGITATION clung to me the rest of the day and into the next, prompting me to keep to myself.

Lochlan stayed with the girls through an impromptu shopping day, but when they planned a girls' night at the club, I had to end my self-imposed isolation. Technically, I wasn't on duty, but I couldn't force myself to stay away when I knew the girls would be drinking around all the fucking perverts who wandered in and out of the club each night. Not when Lochlan would be so caught up in watching Rebecca that he'd likely leave Ashley unprotected.

Chances were slim that anything would happen, but it was a risk I wasn't willing to take.

Much like the celebration a few nights earlier, I sat alone, keeping an eye on the situation from a distance. The girls had invited their red-headed friend, Cat. The three sipped from frosted martini glasses, laughing and talking animatedly, which was a relief. Conversation meant no dancing. No dancing meant less of a chance I'd have to make a scene.

If I had any luck at all, they'd stay right where they were the rest of the night. Though I did have to suffer through watching Liam join their party, entertaining the group with his less than subtle charm that women adored. Had he not been one of my brothers, I would have chased him off the second he set his sights on them. But since he wasn't technically a threat, warning him off would have sparked questions. I took the opportunity to practice restraint and kept my increasingly agitated ass firmly planted in my seat.

Not long into the night, Lochlan lowered himself into the empty chair at my table. He didn't speak at first. Instead, his eyes surveyed the room as mine had done for the past couple of hours.

"You and I both know you don't have to be here," he mused eventually, noting the obvious aberration in my normal behavior. I rarely spent time in the club when I wasn't on duty. Not my scene. Lochlan was telling me he knew something was up.

I took a long drag from my cigarette. "Figured an extra set of eyes might be helpful. Can't imagine after all the chaos of the past six months that everything goes back to normal overnight."

Lochlan grunted. "You don't know the half of it."

I turned to study my one and only friend, waiting silently for him to explain himself.

"Before Merlin brought Ashley back yesterday, he helped unlock her magic." He turned and leveled me with the severity of his stare. "She set a dress on fire while she was out shopping earlier."

Christ.

I sucked on my cigarette until it was nothing but ash.

We had known that if Ashley inherited Merlin's rare abilities, the danger surrounding her would be infinitely worse—especially in the early days before she mastered those abilities enough to protect herself.

Guin would be watching, waiting to learn what Ashley could do. Hoping to conscript her into service.

Of the five forms of elemental magic—one of which almost every Seelie could wield—fire magic was the rarest. It was just one of the many unique gifts Merlin possessed.

My gaze returned to Ashley, laughing with her friends, totally oblivious to the threats closing in around her. "We need to make a plan."

"Agreed. I've been thinking about it all day and have come to a decision. Come with me." He stood and led us over to the pub table where the girls and Liam were gathered, greeting them with a smile. "Liam, it's good to see you've been generous enough to keep the ladies company tonight."

The most lighthearted of my Huntsman brothers grinned. "Ashley here was just telling us about her chat with Merlin yesterday. I, for one, am eager to see what she's capable of."

Ashley grinned and started to speak—no doubt about to share the news of her red-hot shopping experience—when Lochlan cut her off.

"Regardless of the nature of her powers, she'll need someone to guide her learning. After watching Rebecca go through the process, I've realized how difficult this is for someone who wasn't raised around magic." He paused, turning his gaze in my direction. "Now that things have settled down, Caz, I think you'd be a perfect candidate."

If looks could have killed, Lochlan would have become the second Huntsman I'd put in the ground.

What the fuck is he thinking?

I wasn't a goddam teacher. I might have been convinced his decision was based on the need to protect Ashley if it hadn't been for the calculating glint in his eye and the underhanded way he delivered the news of his decision. He'd known that if he told me first while we were still alone, I would have argued. But now, with five sets of eyes all bearing down on me, I had no choice but to capitulate.

I needed out of there, *now*, before I did something I'd regret.

Without a care to the dozens of clubgoers nearby, I traced myself back to my apartment.

Fuck them, and fuck Lochlan.

If he wanted to play dirty, he could damn well deal with the consequences.

A knock on my door woke me the next morning. I wasn't typically a late sleeper, but I'd had trouble quieting my mind the night before. When I saw the source of my restless night's sleep standing outside my apartment, I had to forcibly restrain myself from snarling.

"You're feeling ballsy today," I clipped at Lochlan, my voice still thick with sleep. "First, you order me to play teacher, then you drag me out of bed before the day's even started." I walked back inside, leaving the door wide for him to follow me.

"You know as well as anyone how much danger she'll be in. What better way to protect her than to keep my most trusted brother at her side?"

"If I truly believed that bullshit, we wouldn't be having this conversation." I rested my hip against the kitchen island and crossed my arms over my chest, leveling a challenging stare at him.

He shrugged. "Believe what you like. She'll be safer with you than anyone else I could appoint to the task."

I couldn't argue. I was older than most of the Huntsmen and had wartime experience where they had none. My skepticism and surliness had been well earned. Given the chance to live through what I'd endured, the others would find themselves far less inclined to critique my solemn nature.

"She'll need to get control of her magic and fast." I glowered at him. "She can't go lighting shit on fire and not expect to draw attention."

Lochlan nodded. "Not only that, but she needs to understand the dangers. You saw how eager she was to tell everyone what she'd done."

"As if she'd listen," I scoffed. "That woman has the confidence of Odin's army. Add magic to the mix? She'll think she's unstoppable." The truth of my words settled deep in my gut like a thick ball of mud.

We were both silent for countless seconds.

"She's not Raisa, Caz. You know that, right?"

Lochlan's comment winded me. He was the only one of my brothers who knew about my past, but I was still surprised he'd brought it up.

"You didn't know Raisa, so that's hardly your call to make." My voice grew sharp with warning.

"No, I didn't," he conceded, forging cautiously ahead. "But I know these circumstances are very different. We'll all work together to keep both Rebecca and Ashley safe."

"The only thing that will keep Ashley safe is if her powers are kept secret. Since she's likely to out herself, the best way to go about such a feat would be sending her into hiding."

"For how long?"

"Indefinitely."

Lochlan cringed. "You know the girls would never agree to that."

"I suppose if you're crippled by the need to cater to their whims, that would be a problem."

The shrewd grin that split Lochlan's face sent a surge of tension coiling the muscles at the base of my neck.

"I think I'm going to enjoy watching you complete this assignment even more than I anticipated."

"You're a dick, you know that?"

He threw back his head on a peel of laughter.

Before Lochlan left that morning, I got Ashley's number from him and texted her to meet me in the gym that evening. I spent most of my day trying unsuccessfully not to think about how our first training session would go. Lochlan had informed me that she'd been working with Liam since her transition. I was curious how much she'd learned, which then led to thoughts of what else they might have done together.

The possibilities made me irrationally angry.

I had no right to take that frustration out on her, but there was no escaping my mood. I would have to do my best not to act like the Neanderthal she'd accused me of being. My best bet was to think of this task as clinically as possible. I was training her as I might any other Huntsman who first came to Earth and was unfamiliar with the customs. Except in this scenario, the trainee was a beautiful woman who needed to learn something I'd never actually taught before.

So really, I was completely out of my depths.

I'd never had to show anyone how to use magic because that was something we all naturally developed growing up. Between the uncertainty of how to teach her and my own curiosity about what she'd learned with Liam, I decided to start out in the gym and explore her current abilities. Having a plan, no matter how cursory, eased my nerves.

I arrived at the gym a few minutes before Ashley. Everyone else was preparing for the club to open, so we had the place to ourselves. Normally, the gym was my oasis. A place to work out tension and unwind.

The addition of Ashley's presence engulfed the room in an oppressive tropical heat.

She walked two steps inside the room and paused.

"I appreciate you doing this," she said calmly. "But I can find someone else to work with. I'm sure Lochlan didn't realize how things are between us."

I was surprised at the lack of animosity in her tone. After our elevator encounter and my hasty retreat the night before, I had fully anticipated to be the recipient of her scorn. I wouldn't have blamed her if she had arrived toting a sizable chip on her shoulder. However, that hadn't happened. Ashley was calm, and her comment was made without any aggressive undertones.

"I don't think it's an issue unless you do."

Her brows rose. "I mean, I'm okay if you're okay. At this point, I just want to learn."

If she could pretend nothing had transpired between us, then so could I. Hell, maybe this wouldn't be half as awkward as I'd thought.

A sound resembling a grunt came unbidden from my chest at the absurdity.

"Well, now that we've gotten that out of the way," I grumbled, "let's get started. I've heard you've been training in combat techniques. I thought we'd test your abilities—both physical and magical—then formulate a plan."

With a nod, she followed me onto the grappling mat and lowered her center of gravity with bent knees, lifting her hands to protect her face. She was comfortable in the ready stance. It was a good sign. So was the sleek definition her body had gained over the months. I had intentionally avoided taking in the details of her body whenever she'd been near me. There was only so much temptation a man could take. In her spandex training gear and the bright gym lights, I couldn't miss the way her curvy physique was now taut with lean muscle.

Five months earlier, I'd been the one to carry Ashley's lifeless form out of the alley where she'd almost died. I'd held her on the way to the hospital—a fact she likely didn't know, though it would forever be engrained in my mind. I knew exactly what her soft, feminine body had felt like back then and could testify that she'd come a long way since. Much like Rebecca, Ashley hardly resembled the girl who'd stumbled into our club without a care in the world six months prior. That girl had no idea how to fight and certainly wouldn't have successfully evaded me when I shot out my arm to grab for her hand.

This Ashley was different. Stronger and infinitely more prepared.

She dodged my attack effortlessly.

On my second advance, I pressed forward with my full body, wrapping my arms around her small frame. Lightning fast, she flung her knee up into my crotch, shooting bolts of crippling pain throughout my body. I doubled over instantly.

"*Jesus Christ*, Ashley," I growled through clenched teeth.

"I thought we were testing my skills?" she quipped coyly. Apparently, she wasn't as unaffected as she'd let on.

"If that's how we're playing this—" I said before swiping my leg around and catching both of her ankles.

She hit the mat hard but quickly recovered and rolled. "I'm not playing anything. Liam taught me to fight dirty. I'm just showing you what I've learned."

Before she could return to her feet, I grabbed one of her ankles. Yanking her back toward me, I smacked her ass with a resounding slap. I didn't know what temporary insanity had possessed me and didn't care.

She yelped out in surprise, then glared back at me. "I can't believe you just did that."

"Well, next time you have a problem with me, don't take it out on my balls."

"I was just practicing my defensive techniques. You were the one who wanted to *test* me." She squirmed, wriggling her leg free and kicking me in the chest.

My patience already thinning, I traced over to stand directly in front of where she knelt.

Her face registered shock just before I swept her backward onto the mat, laying my body over hers and pinning her securely beneath me.

"I didn't know you were harboring a secret need to castrate me when I made the suggestion."

"Sounds like you should have been better prepared.

Now let me up. You're suffocating me." She clasped my biceps and struggled against my hold.

"You can breathe just fine right here. In fact, this is great practice. How would you get away right now if I was a real attacker?"

Yeah right, asshole. You just want to keep your dick pressed against her soft curves.

I was abusing my position, but I didn't give two shits. She needed to see that she wasn't as almighty as she thought. Confidence could be a good thing, but it could also get her killed.

"*Ugh!* You make me so crazy." She pressed her hands against my face, a soft blue light brightening her cerulean eyes. "Get. Off. Me. *Now.*"

In a second's time, I was no longer in the gym.

The walls faded away, and a gut-wrenching scene I'd spent years trying to forget played out before my eyes. Every bit was exactly as I'd remembered because what I was seeing was a memory. *My* memory.

The underground cell was damp, the smell of mildew and wet earth permeating the air. As if walking down those rotten wood steps for the first time, I became stymied in the tension and anticipation of knowing I'd found where they'd taken her, just as I'd felt on that horrible day so many lifetimes ago.

I was completely disoriented.

The recollection was so real, so consuming, that I became instantly engulfed in the scene.

When I reached the bottom steps, I could make out her limp form tied to a chair in a dark corner of the room. "*Raisa!* Oh, Gods, Raisa!" I rushed to her side without a care of who might be hiding in the shadows, my fingers entwining in her dark hair, lifting her head from where it had lolled to the side.

I reverently wiped at her filthy face as my world came crashing down around me.

Her sallow skin indicated she had been dead for some time. Her normally soft features were hollow and harsh—I could only imagine the living hell of her last days. She still wore her battle gear, arms bound with iron shackles behind her—the shackles that I would remove from her wasted body and carry with me until the day two years later when I would dole out my brand of justice to the man who had caused her death.

My chest felt like it was being ripped apart from the inside.

I struggled to breathe.

Never had I experienced such a profound sense of loss as when I found my Raisa dead. I had known the chances were slim that she would be alive when I finally tracked her down, but I had still held out hope.

At that moment, I had nothing.

Helpless rage seethed through my veins, and I threw back my head on a murderous howl that rang out in the night.

In a desperate attempt to flee from the pain, I forced myself from the icy depths of the memory. When my eyes refocused in the present, I met Ashley's horrified stare, her face pitying and apologetic.

She knew.

She had seen everything just as I had.

I didn't know how she'd done it, but she had forced

her way into my mind and watched my most closely held memory as if it had been a television program aired for her entertainment.

Lifting myself, I stood, no longer meeting her gaze. "We're done. Get out." My voice bore a tremor that hinted at the storm of emotions raging inside me.

Ashley got up and stilled as if she were going to speak but then reconsidered and left with her head bowed. Her instinct to hold her tongue had been wise. If she had spoken, there was no telling how I would have responded. I knew she hadn't meant to do what she'd done. She was probably equally as clueless about how she'd done it as I was. I didn't even necessarily mind her seeing what she'd seen—the problem was that it had been shared without my consent.

Giving money to a friend was a far cry from having that same money stolen. The memories were mine to share if and when I chose to do so. She might not have meant to steal them, but that was what she had done, and I needed space to regain my bearings.

I had let go of the intense emotions that used to suffocate me after Raisa's death. However, I hadn't relived that moment for a very long time. The forced reality of it was more than unsettling. And to top it off, I found myself envisioning just how easily Ashley could have been bound to that chair instead of Raisa—golden blond hair instead of auburn waves. Raisa had been equally as headstrong and spirited as Ashley. They ran headfirst at life, fearless in a way that both inspired and terrified me.

I'd been too weak to save Raisa, but I wouldn't make that mistake again.

I would have to play my part perfectly because the power Ashley had just exhibited was extraordinary. I'd never known anyone with the ability to push inside the memories of another. I could only imagine what Guin would do if she found out.

Ashley would be hunted until the day she died.

That outcome was simply unacceptable.

She might not like the man I was about to become, but that man would keep her alive, and that was the only thing that mattered.

CHAPTER
FIVE

ASHLEY

GUILT CAST MY GAZE TO THE FLOOR AS I RETREATED TO MY apartment. I felt as though one look into my eyes would give away the horrible transgression I'd committed. What I'd done was an assault in every way that counted, and it made no difference that the intrusion had been unintentional. I'd forced my way into Casek's most guarded memories and made him relive what had to have been the most painful moment of his life.

To have ripped those secrets from him was unforgivable.

I'd seen what he'd lived through. Felt what he'd experienced. I hadn't simply been a curious bystander. My eyes were his, and for a moment, I had lived his heartache. While I couldn't hear any of his thoughts, the experience had felt real in every other way, as if the memory had been my own.

Had this new ability been uncovered in any other manner, I would have been thrilled to have made progress with my magic. Instead, I was mired in shame and mortification.

It wasn't until I was home and curled under my covers that my angst expanded to worry about what such a power entailed. The potential uses were limitless—both helpful and horrific.

For the first time since becoming Fae, the icy hand of fear grazed its fingers along my skin, chilling me to the bone.

I'd hoped to be able to trace and been thrilled when sparks had leaped from my hand. Those were the types of powers I'd expected. I'd never considered I might possess a more sinister ability. Something that might hurt people. A power that could alienate me from everyone around me.

The potential risks made it even more critical that I learned to control my magic.

I had no idea how I'd pushed my way into Casek's head. All I knew was that I was suddenly transported to another time and place. I hadn't even been sure what had happened until I returned to the present and saw Casek's face leached of color. I knew innately what I'd done. That I'd witnessed his deepest sorrow. His greatest regret.

Who had the woman been? Whoever she was, his love for her had been as vast as the deepest ocean, and she'd been brutally killed. His grief left a viscous black residue that I didn't know how to escape or whether I should even try. The least I could do after my intrusion was honor his loss with the sorrow it deserved.

Not that I could have forgotten if I'd wanted to. Each

time I closed my eyes, I saw the lifeless woman. Her auburn hair was mussed and dirty, hanging lifelessly toward the concrete ground.

Or was it wood?

When I focused on the mental picture of the area beneath her chair, it morphed into dark mahogany planks. As I studied the memory, new images surfaced. They were scattered and made little sense. There was a puddle, and next to it ... a glass—a beer pint spilled on its side—and wavy red hair sprawled across the worn wood floor. The thing that stood out the most was the smell. I thought it had been putrid down in that basement, but now it was muskier with a bitter twang.

Everything about the memory seemed to mutate and shift.

I had no idea what was happening and was suddenly too tired to tackle the inconsistencies. I fell asleep cradled in the arms of heartbreak and remorse, hoping morning would bring relief.

I tossed and turned in the night but still woke feeling more like myself. Casek's memory would stick with me until the day I died, but it no longer held me captive. I could see the scene—as it had originally been, not the sleep-muddled version—but I could also lock it away so it didn't control me.

Now, it was time to face what I'd done.

Becca needed to know about this extraordinary new power I'd discovered and help me figure out what to do about it.

I went looking for her in her room, my eyes catching on the hole in our wall next to the front door. I'd noticed it when I'd come back from Faery and known exactly who had left the mark. The why had confounded me. Casek hadn't been thrilled with Merlin stealing me away, but punching a wall was a far more explosive reaction than I would have expected from him.

His memory shed an entirely new light on the outburst.

I pulled my gaze away as a fresh wave of guilt assaulted me.

Becca wasn't in her room. I didn't worry because she spent most nights with Lochlan anymore. I texted her and arranged to get coffee together in an hour, giving me plenty of time to take a scalding shower and mentally prepare for my day. I would see Casek again that evening for my next training session, assuming we were still working together. I'd need all the strength I could summon for our next meeting.

Clean and refreshed, I met Becca in the lobby. "I'm going to need you to tone down the wattage on your smile. It's a bit too early in the morning for so much sunshine," I teased as we left the building for the coffee shop around the corner.

"I can't help it. Life is looking pretty damn great right now."

"I suppose you're right," I conceded.

"Why do I get the feeling there's a but at the end of that?"

"It's not that, exactly. Something happened last night. I discovered a new ability of my magic."

"That seems like something you should be more excited about." She shot me a questioning glance.

I took a deep breath and launched into an explanation of everything that had happened the night before. When I was done, Becca stilled out front of the coffee shop, her eyes wide.

"Holy shit, Ash. I don't even know what to think."

"Tell me about it," I grumbled, leading us inside.

We ordered our drinks and a couple of scones, then found a table once our order was ready.

"First," Becca began quietly. "I'm so excited for you to finally get to explore your … gifts. I know how frustrated you've been these past few months."

"It's a relief for sure. I just wish I hadn't made things so awkward."

"It was an accident. Casek will understand. And now that you know what you can do, you won't make that mistake again."

I appreciated her confidence but wasn't as convinced. "I'll certainly try not to. I'd hate to hurt anyone else, but I'm also a little worried about what this means for me. What if word got out? I'm not sure I want anyone else to know what I can do."

Becca chewed at her cheek. "I think you're right. The fewer people who know, the better. Casek will probably tell Lochlan, but outside of the four of us, no one else needs to know." She studied me, worry creeping into her features. "You're going to have to be careful, Ash. These powers you've been given … they might put you in danger."

"Trust me, I'm beginning to see that. I wanted to show *some* sign of power, but what I did felt wrong. I hated it."

She clasped my hand in hers. "I had my share of awkward accidents when I was learning. It'll get better."

I nodded, hoping she was right. "So are you going to tell me where you disappeared to yesterday? And you still haven't told me what you and Lochlan were up to back in Faery after we talked to the queen."

Becca fidgeted in her seat, taking a second to sip from her steaming coffee. "Just tying up some loose ends. Nothing major."

Okaaaay, that was vague.

She didn't have to tell me every detail of her life, but I thought we'd moved past keeping secrets from one another. I wasn't sure if I was reading into her behavior or not. Either way, my curiosity had been piqued. I'd have to start paying more attention to my friend and make sure she wasn't holding anything back that I should know about. It was a problem we'd already run into once when she first tried to keep her involvement with the Fae a secret. Her attempt to protect me had only made things worse.

"Things with Lochlan going okay?" I figured I'd fish around for information just to be safe.

Becca's answering grin was so effervescent that it left no room for doubt about its authenticity.

She detailed the past few days she'd spent with her boyfriend in the words of a woman hopelessly in love. I was so incredibly happy for her and couldn't help but feel uplifted by the time we returned home. She came back to the apartment with me but retreated to her room for a shower. I got comfortable on the sofa with my laptop and began to get some much-needed work done. My boss had allowed me to work remotely so that I could continue working from Ireland, and I didn't want to piss him off by falling behind.

When a knock sounded at the front door two hours later, I was cross-eyed from staring at the computer and zoned out enough to forget to check the peephole. I opened the door wide, then stumbled backward in surprise, falling on my ass.

"*Shit, shit, shit.*" I shuffled away from the entry, standing as soon as I could get my feet under me, not taking my eyes from the enormous white wolf at Lochlan's side.

"Knight!" Becca cried happily from the kitchen before racing over. She and the beast met in a slobbery reunion, Lochlan smirking at the scene.

"This guy was waiting out front for permission to enter," he explained. "I figured he was here for you."

I suddenly recalled that she'd told me about a dog who'd saved her from Ronan and adopted her briefly. When she mentioned a dog, I'd thought she'd meant a normal dog, but this beast was enormous. He had to weigh two-hundred pounds if he was an ounce.

Becca scratched behind the dog's ears, his lolling tongue evidence of his eternal gratitude. "It's so good to see you, boy. Did Merlin send you?" She looked up at me, eyes bright. "Knight is Merlin's companion. I'm guessing he's here for you now that Merlin has named you his apprentice."

My eyes rounded comically wide. "Me? What do you mean here for me?"

I'd slowly retreated, my legs now plastered against the back of the couch.

We never had pets growing up. I'd wanted one for years, but by the time I was old enough to own one myself, I'd lost interest. They shed and shat and were more trouble than they were worth, and this particular beast was terrifying.

Knight parted from Rebecca and trotted in my direction.

I stopped breathing.

With no time to react, I held perfectly still as he licked my hand, then leaped over the back of the sofa to make himself comfortable on the gray cushions.

My mouth gaped wide.

"Yeah, I'd say he's here to stay." Becca chuckled.

"*What?*" I squeaked.

Lochlan closed the door, joining Rebecca on the loveseat across from the beast. "Agreed. Looks like you have a new housemate. I'll make sure to update the wards and let the others know."

Knight huffed and laid his head on his front paws.

"So he just lives here now?" Was I the only one having trouble with this new development?

Becca smiled softly. "He's not like a normal dog. He kind of does what he wants, so I wouldn't worry about him. This shows us that Merlin is keeping an eye on you. I'm relieved to know you'll have the extra protection."

I eyed the dog warily and stepped around to the front of the sofa, noting that the only place left to sit was inches from an arsenal of claws and fangs. I took a deep breath and eased myself onto the couch, practically draped over the arm of the couch to ensure we didn't touch.

Knight extended his head until his black nose booped my thigh. The affectionate gesture was disarming to say the least.

"Oh, all right," I muttered, placing my hand ever so slowly on the wolf's head and exploring the varied textures of his fur.

"How was your first training session?" Lochlan asked.

My eyes instantly collided with Becca's before looking at him. "Have you talked to Casek at all?"

"No, why?" he asked warily.

"Training didn't go so well."

"There's no one better to teach you to protect yourself. Casek can be rough around the edges, but give him a chance."

"That's not exactly the problem, although his attitude doesn't help. I kind of did something that I didn't know I could do, and now, I'm not sure he'll be willing to work with me anymore." I collected my thoughts, then explained what had happened, knowing Lochlan would find out one way or another.

Lochlan kept himself perfectly impassive while I spoke, collecting his thoughts once I'd finished. "Casek will work with you. I'm sure of that. But if you're truly uncomfortable with the arrangement, I can assign a new instructor. It's your decision."

His concession surprised me. I'd grown used to the unyielding nature of the Huntsmen. They didn't often solicit our opinions.

What did I want to do? Would I prefer to work with someone else?

The instant swell of disappointment in my chest told me my answer. Despite everything that had gone on between us, I was more distraught at the idea of walking away than I was of facing him.

Was this how my mother had felt about my dad?

Don't do that, Ashley. Casek isn't your father. Hell, you're the one who hurt him.

We'd hurt each other ... more than once. Wasn't that enough to show that we'd be better off apart? But how could I walk away from him after seeing what he'd been through? What kind of message would that send? Maybe I was looking for an excuse to justify staying in the arrangement, but I didn't care. It was reason enough.

"I want to try again," I finally answered. "If he's willing, then I am, too." The decision went against everything I'd trained myself to believe through the years. No second chances—not where men were concerned. Everything about our interactions had been contentious, yet I had an inexplicable yearning to explore what else lay beneath his prickly layers.

Growing up, I'd told myself I would never be like my mother. I prayed this wasn't the first step in that direction.

"You're welcome to come to me anytime you have a problem," Lochlan offered graciously.

"Thanks. I'm sure we'll be fine."

Please, please let my instincts be right.

The three of us talked for a few more minutes before Becca and Lochlan spoke privately and left. Becca gave me an odd, apologetic look before going. I assumed she felt bad about leaving me alone with Knight. I locked the door behind them, then returned to the living room, choosing to sit on the loveseat to give us some space.

First, I got out my phone and decided to verify that Casek and I were indeed still working together. If he chose to withdraw as my instructor, despite Lochlan's assurances, I could scratch that worry off my list.

Me: What is the plan for training?

Casek: Tonight. Same time and place.

Well, okay then. Commence stressing.

Knowing I could never concentrate now, I sat cross-legged on the floor and decided to practice summoning my magic. Aside from acting as a distraction, I preferred to test things before our next session that evening. Maybe then we wouldn't end our night in disaster.

One could only hope.

I closed my eyes and focused inward. Quickly locating the pool of energy within me, just as Merlin had instructed, I tugged at the magic, trying to coax it from its resting place. Over and over, I summoned and strained, teased and commanded the elusive energy with zero response. It remained perfectly inert, unaffected by my efforts.

It didn't take long for frustration to well up inside me, cinching tight like a collar around my neck. I tried to assure myself that it was probably the overflow of emotions from last night disrupting my ability to access the magic. Maybe all I needed was an early lunch and a little rest. Then I'd be right as rain.

"I suppose I'm responsible for feeding you as well," I said to Knight.

At the mention of food, his head shot up and tilted to one side as though unsure he'd heard me correctly.

"That's what I figured. Come on, let's see what's in the fridge." I didn't have dog food on hand, but I doubted he'd complain. I put down a mixing bowl full of water, then made us each a charcuterie plate. He managed to inhale his before I'd even sat down with mine.

Looks like I'd be going to the grocery instead of napping.

I spent the afternoon getting work done and running errands. Knight joined me, loping behind me everywhere I went. The comfort of his presence was oddly satisfying. I was never one to prefer being alone—damn extroverted neediness. I loved being independent, but I preferred to be independent with other people. I was a living oxymoron.

I tried one more time to summon my magic later that afternoon but was again unsuccessful. Forcing myself to shrug off the disappointment, I got ready for my evening with Casek. It was time to train, and I needed to figure out what the hell I was going to say.

MY HEART DISAPPEARED down into my stomach in a nauseating game of hide-and-seek on my way to the basement. My hands trembled, and I'd licked my parched lips at least a dozen times on my way downstairs. I'd had less nerves as a teen going out on my first date.

Get your shit together, Moore, before you make a fool of yourself again.

I took a long, deep breath, then opened the gym door.

Casek was mid-pull-up, his legs bent at the knees and muscled arms lifting him effortlessly to the bar and back down in smooth rhythmic motions. He wore a T-shirt and joggers—nothing particularly special—but I'd never seen anything more goddamn sexy in my life.

For a second, I forgot my own name.

When his feet hit the ground and his eyes collided with mine, I had to force my brain back into action.

"Uh, hey. I appreciate you being here. I want to say that I'm really sorry. I know you probably don't want to talk about it, and I totally understand, but I wanted to apologize. I had no idea what I was doing ... or that I was doing anything. I never meant to ... do what I did. So ... yeah."

Fucking phenomenal, Ash. Way to ramble incoherently.

At least it was done. I toyed with the hem of my shirt, unable to contain my nervous energy.

Casek strolled closer. "I know you didn't mean to do it. Let's just move on." He grabbed a hand towel from a nearby bench and wiped his forehead. "We can go straight to testing your magic since that obviously needs attention, and we didn't get to it yesterday." His cool tone was perfectly calm and businesslike. He was showing me in no uncertain terms that he preferred to pretend nothing happened and move on.

Okay, I could do that.

"I tried twice earlier today to summon my magic but couldn't make it budge. I'm not sure what's wrong."

"Could you sense the power at all?"

"Yes, I just couldn't call it to the surface like Merlin had taught me."

He nodded. "I'm sure it's a natural part of the process. Control takes time."

"Yeah, but it seems so weird since it came easily the other day. I don't know why things are different today." As I voiced my concerns, an idea took root. I'd used my magic several times since unlocking it with Merlin. Could those few exercises have depleted my power enough that it needed charging? "Do you think I might need to feed my magic?"

Casek stiffened. "No, not yet. It's only been a couple of days since you started using it."

"Yeah, but what if it's like when kids are growing, and they need extra food and sleep? Maybe the first few uses depleted it more than I realized."

That had to be it.

A deluge of relief came crashing over me. I'd tried to keep myself from getting worked up all day, but subconsciously, I'd been terrified that I'd regressed back to being powerless.

"There's no way you need to feed already, okay? Just let it rest." The normally impassive Huntsman was showing signs of irritation. Why? Did it bother him to think of me needing him to feed my magic? The possibility stung a little.

"It's not like it has to be you," I shot back. "I'm certainly not meaning to force you into something you don't want to do."

"What the fuck is that supposed to mean?" Casek stalked closer, his movements as predatory as a jungle cat.

Alarm bells began to ring in my head that I'd somehow triggered a ticking time bomb.

"I'm not trying to upset you. I just feel strongly that my magic probably needs refueling, and there's no reason you have to do that for me. I can go take care of it tonight, and we can try to train again tomorrow once I'm more able."

"Over my fucking dead body," he growled, walking us backward until my back was against the wall, his large frame caging me in. "Why do you always have to be so damn stubborn?"

His murmured question felt rhetorical, so I didn't answer.

Not that I could have. His violent reaction had rendered me speechless. Over his dead body? What the hell did that mean? Why would he be so adamant against me feeding from someone else? There was no mistaking his irritation and animosity around me. I had no delusions about his feelings for me. But if that was the case, why would he say something that rang of jealousy and possession?

I was starting to think I'd never understand this complicated man.

"I take it you know what this entails?" he asked, face inches from mine.

I nodded, having already learned the foundations of feeding Fae magic with sexual energy. Seelie Fae siphoned the energy created during the sexual release of another person, which meant we could feed from other Fae or humans since the source didn't have to have magic themselves. However, it was impossible to feed from yourself. A partner was required, though penetrative sex was not.

I'd explored the possibility early on that my magic

simply needed to be fed, but without being able to sense the magic at all, my efforts had been pointless. But now, I knew how the energy felt. It was there inside me. All I had to do was give it a little fuel to bring it back to life.

Casek stripped off his shirt and tossed it to the ground but kept the hand towel draped over his shoulder. "Hands on my shoulders." His voice was a husky command that warmed my insides.

I couldn't believe this was happening. I didn't know what I expected from our training session, but this had not been it. Hell, I wasn't even sure what exactly we were doing. Was he planning to fuck me? He clearly had some sort of plan, and I wasn't going to object, whatever it was.

I rested my palms on the round curve of his shoulders, still tight from his workout. Casek placed one hand flat against the wall beside me and used the other to lower the waistband of his joggers, freeing his already engorged cock.

I couldn't look away.

Lips parted, I watched hungrily as his hand clasped firmly around his wide girth and squeezed. My core pulsed with such agonizing need that I debated whether it would be inappropriate for me to slide my own hand down my leggings to ease the ache.

"*No,*" Casek growled.

My eyes flew to his in surprise. "No, what?"

"I want you to concentrate on feeding. That means no touching yourself. Not this time."

He knew what I'd been thinking—had somehow seen it on my face. But the nonjudgmental nature of his response kept embarrassment at bay.

I nodded, still holding his gaze. Each shaky breath I inhaled engulfed me in his dizzying scent—spiced leather and a dash of sweat that only enhanced the masculine nature of the smell.

Casek began to jerk himself in short, angry strokes over the head of his shaft. His muscles beneath my palms coiled and flexed. He'd told me not to touch myself, but he'd said nothing about touching him. From what I'd learned, we only needed a single point of contact for the transfer of energy.

Slowly, with agonizing deliberation, I allowed one hand to migrate down from his shoulder as I kept my eyes trained on his.

The mossy green of his irises flashed with an emerald glow, but he didn't stop me. I drifted shakily over his pectoral, past his rippling abs, and downward to cup his heavily hung balls, careful not to disrupt his movements.

I rolled the delicate organs in my hand, then gave them a gentle tug, testing the waters.

"*Christ*, woman," Casek hissed, eyes shuttering with pleasure.

Seeing him come undone was as much an aphrodisiac as any foreplay. The energy between us buzzed like a live wire—the current climbing to a frenzied state, calling to me.

Casek sought my eyes, his glowing softly. "Are you ready?" he asked breathlessly.

"*Yes*." Desperately ready.

I craved what he offered, and as he growled the start of his release, I took it. My hand clamped down convulsively on his shoulder, my other lifting to his waist. I was a sponge, soaking up every ounce of his proffered power, only vaguely aware of his movements as he used the towel to catch his cum.

For me, the resulting exhilaration from feeding was a release in itself—pure sunshine, scorching and brilliant. Every inch of my body was alive, down to every molecule and atom.

"*Enough.*" His ragged order startled me back to myself.

My eyes flew open, and I could see their blue glow reflected in his. "I'm sorry. Did I get carried away?" I was suddenly horrified that I might have yet again over-stepped my bounds.

"No." He shook his head, eyes falling shut as he leaned against the wall and recovered. Tossing the towel onto the floor, he righted his pants and pulled away.

The loss of his warmth immersed me in an icy chill. Why were things with him always so damn complicated? He hadn't been forced to do what he did, so why did I now feel like he regretted his actions?

Before I could deep dive into an abyss of uncertainty, his phone rang. Grabbing it from a bench, he barked a greeting. The caller was likely another Huntsman. In a deep, severe tone, the man said something about "dead" and "another," but that was all I could glean.

"Be there in five." Casek ended the call in a voice so dark it was almost unrecognizable.

"Is everything okay?"

"It's fine, but our session has been cut short."

"Fine? But what was that about another dead? Did someone die?" I needed to leave it alone, but I couldn't help myself. After everything we'd lived through in recent months, worry came easily.

He spun around and glared at me with piercing green eyes that were weapons in their own right. "It's not your concern. Stay out of it." He collected his things and marched to the door, shooting me one last warning glare before disappearing.

SIX

CASEK

Guilt was a waste of time and energy. Either fix what you fucked up or don't fuck up in the first place. Those were far more effective strategies than wallowing in worthless regret. That had been my philosophy for hundreds of years and had worked well for me up until fourteen hours ago. Ever since the second I blew my wad into a towel to keep Ashley from going near another man.

That wasn't true.

The guilt started another fifteen hours before that when I traced into Ashley's bedroom and put a binding spell on her magic. She would still be able to feel her magic and could feed it, in theory, but she wouldn't be able to access it. She couldn't use the power inside her. The spell was complex. It was one of the many things I'd learned when I was on a mission centuries earlier for revenge. A time when I'd been compelled to seek out dangerous forms of magic, regardless of the consequences.

I'd told myself I'd never utilize such dark practices again, but I'd had no choice. I had to protect Ashley. The binding was the only sure way to protect her. Without unique powers, she would have no enemies. Without enemies, there was no danger.

It was the right thing to do. I knew it with a certainty in my bones, yet that didn't erase the bitter aftertaste of knowing what I'd done. Letting her feed from me when I knew the real reason for her stunted powers was just the squeeze of lime in my cocktail of guilt-riddled emotions.

If my actions had sent her dick-hopping through the Huntsman, my emotions would have pushed me over the edge. I'd had to feed her myself, but if I'd fucked her when I knew the feeding was a manipulation, I never could have forgiven myself. It would have been one step too far, and I couldn't have lived with myself.

Of all the possible outcomes I'd analyzed since the moment she pushed inside my head, her pursuit of energy to fix her loss of power hadn't entered the equation. I'd counted on her being upset. I'd known things would be a little dicey for a bit, but I assumed she'd get over her disappointment and pick up where she left off. The threat to her safety would ebb, and life would go back to normal.

I should have known Ashley would find a way to corrupt my plans.

Whether it was her earnest excitement about her magic, or her bumbling attempt at a rambled apology, or the heady rush of watching her hand wander down my body like the paw of a curious kitten, she found every damn way she could to endear herself. To summon emotions I had no desire to feel, including fucking guilt.

I'd done the right thing. I had to stand by my decision.

If I didn't want to feel bad for what I'd done, then that only left one option. Fix it.

I wouldn't undo the spell, but I could give her a purpose—a sense of control and direction in this new life of hers.

An idea came to me. While I wasn't crazy about drawing her into Hunt business, it was the best thing I could come up with and promised to at least serve as a distraction.

I made Ashley's apartment my first stop the next day. She answered the door in a tiny camisole and pajama bottoms, her hair piled in a sexy blond mess on her head. She was gorgeous without even trying. I had to give myself a stern warning not to make this situation worse than I already had.

"I know it's early, but there was a minor incident yesterday that I need to look into. I thought you might want to come with me." Jesus, I sounded like a pussy now that the words were out.

Maybe next time you can ask if she wants to hold hands and go for a walk.

It was too bad there was no way to strangle my inner voice. That fucker was getting on my last nerve.

"Really?" she asked, her wide eyes reminding me of a rare Irish sky clear of any clouds.

"Apparently," I clipped. "Can you be ready in five?" *Before I change my mind.*

She leaped into motion. "Of course! Let me throw on

some clothes. You're welcome to have a seat while you wait." She disappeared into her room.

I closed the front door and joined Knight in the living room. Lochlan had told me about our newest guest. I'd been lucky he arrived after my break-in or conducting the spell would have proven difficult. Stories abounded about the wolf's mysterious abilities, and I had no desire to test them.

I nodded at the wolf who eyed me curiously. "Name's Casek. Welcome to the Huntsman."

His golden gaze drifted back to where Ashley was busy getting ready, then cut back to me.

"I know you're here to keep her safe," I assured him that I understood his silent message. "We're on the same mission."

Knight huffed, then rolled onto his side. His enormous body took up most of the couch. I chuckled to myself, wondering how the two got along. Ashley didn't strike me as the mothering type.

"Okay, I'm ready. I think." She skipped into the living room, then ran back to her bedroom, then reappeared. "Okay, now I'm really ready."

"We taking the dog?" I asked.

We both looked at Knight sprawled on the sofa.

"Nah," she said, then addressed her furry guardian. "I'm gonna run an errand with Casek. I'll be safe with him and see you back here later." She walked to the door as though she hadn't just spoken to a dog like he was a human and peered at me questioningly.

I didn't know why it amused me. I'd done the same thing minutes before.

Knight made no move to extract himself from the sofa he'd usurped. It appeared we had his blessing.

As we walked to the elevator and then out to the car, I explained the situation. "Yesterday, a jewelry store in town was ransacked and robbed. We have suspicions about the suspect. Belfast police are investigating, but we're also doing our own inquiry. I've been briefed on the scene but haven't had a chance to look over it myself."

She listened intently to every word. I could almost see the gears excitedly whirring away inside her head. "How do you get the police to allow you onto the crime scene?"

"We have contacts on the force. And when needed, we use a touch of persuasive magic."

"Do those contacts inform you when a crime looks suspicious?"

"That and we have someone assigned to police radio at all times. We like to be first on the scene when possible if magic is involved. In the past, instances of Fae crimes were rare, but since Morgan began opening portals, almost every day is a new adventure." I couldn't say I was entirely disappointed when Fae began appearing on Earth in larger numbers. A full-scale invasion would have been a nightmare, but having a few creatures to hunt was a nice change of pace.

I showed Ashley up to the front entrance of the jewelry store, which was untouched aside from the yellow caution tape. She examined every detail, slowly scanning her surroundings as we stepped inside.

"I see they've got cameras. Is there a recording of the intruder?"

"There's a recording, but it didn't capture the thief."

"Rear entrance?"

"None. Access to the back alley had been sealed off years ago after a break-in."

She nodded, taking in the extent of the damage inside. "The only display cases broken are those beyond the reach of the camera."

"A design flaw of their system. The largest, most expensive pieces were kept close to the register in the back."

She nodded absently and then spent the next half hour inspecting every minute detail of the scene. Once she had made a full circle of the room, she turned her bright blue eyes back to me. "The Draug that attacked Rebecca and me months ago. He's never been caught, has he?"

Good girl.

I hadn't been sure if she had enough background knowledge of the Fae to make the connection, but she had put the pieces together exactly as I'd done and come to the same conclusion. "Explain."

"Well, there are no skylights or other way for the intruder to have gotten into the building without being caught on camera, which makes it likely magic was used. After our attack, Rebecca told me how the Draug dissolved into smoke when Lochlan arrived. The creature could have used the same technique to find a way inside, unseen. I'd also say that whoever did this was small—there's a curio cabinet against the wall that had the bottom half shattered, but several expensive-looking pieces were left in the top half untouched. Our research back when that attack had occurred told us that Draugs are known for their penchant to collect jewels. Unless there's some other jewel-hoarding Fae loose, my money is on the Draug." Her face lit up as she walked through her deductions. I could almost envision working alongside her if it wasn't better for both of us to keep our distance.

"Well done—our conclusions were the same. The good news is, Draugs and other Shadow Fae can't stand the sunlight, so the creature can't be on the move during the day. The bad news is, Draugs are exceedingly difficult to catch, so this case will likely be open for a while."

"I'm happy to help anytime you want an extra set of eyes."

I lifted my brow at her. "I'm sure you are. Come on, let's get back home."

She thought I was being kind—extending a sort of offer of friendship. She didn't realize it was more of an apology than anything. Ashley would never understand if she knew what I'd done, but how could I not do everything in my power to keep such passion and innocence safe?

What I'd done was right, but allowing her to think of me as anything but a surly instructor was a mistake because her feelings would be founded on lies. I had to ensure we kept our distance from one another. Guilt was one thing, but I couldn't afford to hate myself more than I already did.

CHAPTER
SEVEN

ASHLEY

When I got home from my outing with Casek, Becca was still gone, and Knight was no longer in the apartment. I could only assume Becca had let him out, though I was a little surprised he would disappear like that if he was supposed to be my guard dog. Wasn't staying close to me somewhat necessary for guarding?

Why do you keep pretending to know anything about anything?

Wasn't that the truth. The more immersed I became in the Fae world, the more clueless I felt. I'd just spent over an hour with Casek investigating a supernatural crime scene. If someone had asked me twenty-four hours earlier, I would have bet my life that scenario would never happen. Zero chance. Casek was too private, and the short history between us too complicated to prompt him to include me in his Huntsmen activities. Yet that's exactly what had just transpired. I was going to have to let go of any notion that I had any ability to predict the future.

Whatever the reason, Casek had given me a behind-the-scenes peek, and I was thrilled. Adrenaline still coursed through my veins. After such an invigorating morning, I couldn't imagine sitting alone in my apartment, so I decided to pack up my computer and work from the coffee shop. I gathered everything I'd need for an afternoon of work, nearly having a heart attack when I spotted Knight lying behind the sofa on my way to the door.

"Where the hell did you come from?" I accused, hand clutching my chest in an attempt to soothe my racing heart. "And don't try to tell me you were here the whole time. I looked for you. It's not like two-hundred pounds of fur can hide that easily." The beast was sent by Merlin, so I'd known he was special, but I hadn't expected him to have tracing abilities.

Knight stared at me blankly, then joined me at the door.

"I'm not sure what's more bizarre," I muttered, "your disappearing act or the fact that I seem to expect an answer from you." I held open the door and shook my head. "Come on, let's go."

A sign in the front window of the shop stated no pets allowed, so I instructed Knight to stay outside. He didn't act overly bothered, melting into a white heap at the entrance. I went in and set my things at a table before ordering a sandwich. The shop's specialty was coffee, but they also offered a few breakfast items and sandwiches at lunch. The atmosphere was cozy. The coffee was divine.

And with the shop's proximity to home, I'd begun to stop in more and more frequently.

"That your dog out front?" A young woman in a shop apron set down my order at my table and motioned to the window.

Knight sat on his haunches looking off in the distance. He was so large that his ears and head could be seen through the window that began halfway up the wall.

"Yeah, more or less."

The girl's eyebrows furrowed together. She was cute. About my age, maybe a tad closer to twenty.

I giggled, realizing how odd my answer must have sounded. "It's a long story, but he sort of adopted me. So yeah. He's mine for the moment."

"Gotcha." She grinned. "Well, he's beautiful."

"Thanks." I returned her smile, looking down at my lunch as she excused herself and returned to the back of the shop. I might not have planned on having a dog, but he was definitely a good conversation starter. In the couple of days that he'd been around, I could hardly go anywhere without strangers asking me about my unusual escort. Lucky for me, I wasn't averse to the attention.

I spent the next two hours going through a manuscript my boss had sent for me to review. The book wasn't my kind of reading, so it had taken all my concentration and willpower to pay attention. By the time I allowed myself a restroom break, I decided it was time to beef up on the caffeine.

I made my way to the tiny single-stall bathroom, where I quickly did my business. As I washed my hands, I started to feel woozy. With my hands firmly planted on the white porcelain sink, I closed my eyes and took a few deep breaths. When I opened them and gazed down at the basin, I yanked my hands away with a gasp and flung myself backward, almost falling into the toilet.

In a writhing ball of legs and furry bodies, hundreds of black spiders poured out of the silver faucet and scurried around the bottom of the sink. Air was racing in and out of my lungs so fast darkness threatened my vision, but the last thing I wanted was to pass out on the floor of a bathroom filled with spiders. I forced my breathing to slow but almost screamed when one of the spiders made it to the top of the basin and leaped onto the floor.

I glanced desperately toward the door, but it was situated right next to the sink, and I was terrified of stepping any closer to the ever-increasing pile of spiders. Needing to defend the small spider-free space I occupied, I stomped my foot on the escapee. When I pulled my foot back, though, I saw no evidence of smashed guts on the ground. Lifting my foot, I discovered my shoe was also squeaky clean.

My heartrate slowed enough for a moment of rational thought.

Lifting my gaze back to the vanity, I surveyed a perfectly ordinary sink. Not a single wriggling spider.

What the hell just happened? Am I hallucinating now?

My head rested back as I took in a lungful of air. Maybe I'd been working a little too intently. Considering all that had gone on in recent days, my brain had to be on overload.

I peered at the sink, deciding to use the hand sanitizer in my purse rather than touch the faucet, just in case.

Once I was back at my table, I packed up my things and decided to head home. The walk would clear my head, and caffeine had lost its appeal. I was already plenty on edge.

Knight accompanied me home, where I was able to get more work done before getting ready for my nightly training session. Becca popped in briefly before giving some cryptic excuse for needing to do some shopping, then left again. I still got the sense she was keeping something from me but was no closer to figuring out what it might be. However, I didn't spend too much time overthinking it because my mind was overrun with curiosity about how my night would go. This was the first session I was approaching with more cautious optimism than dread. Our outing earlier in the day had been comfortable and productive. I was hopeful training might yield the same results.

My eagerness was evident when I showed up at the gym a full ten minutes before Casek arrived. With nothing else to do, I stretched while I waited, greeting him with a smile when he joined me.

He didn't return the gesture.

"You practice any today?" he asked, only briefly making eye contact.

I tried not to let his surliness bother me. "No. I figured if my magic was easily drained, it would be best to conserve my energy until I trained with you." Sound reasoning, in my opinion, but Casek appeared unimpressed.

His lips thinned. "Let's start with some sparring, then we'll see about the magic."

I was disappointed—both in his mood and the delay

in testing my magic—but I didn't argue. Things with Casek had been moving in the right direction, and I didn't want to erase our progress, though it took no small amount of control to keep my normally vocal opinion to myself.

Hoping to catch him off guard while I was leaning down to the floor in a stretch, I swept my leg out toward the back of his knees. He caught on to my strike just in time. I made contact, but he was already on the move, so my attack didn't take him down as I had hoped.

He leaped to the side, and I spun to keep him in my sights. We circled each other, and I wondered if my eyes showed the same feral glint as his. He lunged forward with a clear size advantage and grabbed my hand, pulling my back to his front in a tight bear-hug. I whipped my hips to the side to give my right arm room to swing back into his groin, then I wrenched myself from his grasp. Before I could delight in freeing myself, he swept my legs out and had me pinned to the ground in the span of two seconds.

Our eyes locked as we found ourselves in the same position as two nights earlier. I didn't move a muscle, too terrified I'd repeat the same mistake.

Casek remained equally motionless, though his reasons were a mystery to me. I wouldn't have faulted him for flinching away from me. Instead, the only movement in the room was the push and pull of our ragged breaths.

We teetered on that icy precipice for countless seconds before Casek's phone began to ring. Even then, he didn't move to answer until three urgent tones had broken the silence.

"What is it?" he barked softly into the receiver, rising to his feet.

Just like the night before, the person on the other end rattled off some information, and with an assurance he would be right there, Casek hung up.

"You're leaving *again*?" I blurted, all previous intentions of being agreeable lost in a jumble of emotions.

"Yeah, something came up."

"And that's all the explanation I get?"

"Why the hell do you need to know anything more?"

"Because!" I yelled, all my impatience and frustration bubbling to the surface. "I've been waiting *months* to learn my magic—to have any magic at all—and you seem to be finding every excuse in the book to keep me waiting. Why teach the silly human girl if you can postpone indefinitely." My words were carved in the anger and uncertainty I'd grappled with for the past six months.

A green flash of surging temper lit Casek's eyes. "I don't know what the fuck it is you think I'm doing here—"

"Following orders," I shot back before he could continue. "That's what I think. It was obvious from the minute Lochlan assigned the task that you resented having to work with me. You're doing the bare minimum to keep your ass out of trouble—looking out for yourself, but that's it."

"What exactly is it you want from me?" he roared.

"*Honesty*!" The word echoed off the gym walls and drowned out the sound of my racing heart.

His mouth clamped shut.

Silence stretched out time like honey dripping from a hive.

I sighed, my eyes lifting to the ceiling for guidance. "Look," I said more softly. "This shouldn't be so hard. You and me ... we're like gasoline and an open flame. I really appreciate what you did earlier today, but maybe it's best if Lochlan finds someone else to work with me."

Casek infiltrated my personal space, a roaring inferno of pissed-off energy looming over me. "I told you once, and I won't say it again. Don't you fucking go near any of my brothers."

"You said you didn't want me to feed from them. That's not the same as training," I argued.

"The hell it isn't."

I stomped my foot, so frustrated I was seconds from devolving into a childish tantrum. "You are freaking *impossible*." Why limit who I could work with if he was just going to avoid me and make things difficult? Was this some kind of twisted game to him?

Casek's hand clamped around my neck, his fingers at the back and thumb lifting my chin to bring my gaze to his. "I'm not impossible. I've lost my fucking mind, and it's your goddamn fault."

He stared so intently into my eyes that I swore he could see down to the very depths of my soul. While we waged a silent battle, his lips mouthed silent words, and heat seared the back of my neck. I yanked away from him when the feeling tinged on painful, unsure what had happened.

Panic engulfed me.

Had my magic responded to him? Was it trying to infiltrate his memories again? Why had it hurt so much?

I placed my hand over the heated skin and peered at him warily. "What was that?"

He only lifted his chin defiantly, making me reconsider my assumptions.

Why the fuck did he look so smug?

I rushed to the gym mirror and lifted my hair but was unable to see the back of my neck. "What the hell did you do?"

"I solved a problem. Looking out for myself, remember?"

I grabbed my phone and took a photo of the back of my neck. When I saw what he'd done, words escaped me. My lips parted with wordless huffs of breath. "You ... you..." I brought my incredulous stare back to him. "You fucking *marked* me?"

What looked like a letter in a foreign alphabet was now scrolled in black on the back of my neck. I was speechless. Bewildered and mystified. What could have possibly possessed him to do such a thing?

"Essentially," he said casually. "Now there's no confusion."

Was he serious? I was nothing but a blurry swarm of confusion.

"No confusion about what?" I gaped.

"About who you're working with."

"Take it off, *now*."

"No," he said dryly.

"Does it even come off?" My eyes almost popped straight out of the socket as the question surfaced.

Casek's eyes narrowed dangerously. "It can, but only

by me, and that's not happening. Now that we have that settled, I have to go." He turned for the door.

"You are not seriously going to leave right now."

He kept walking.

"Are you at least going to tell me what the hell you put on my neck?"

He pulled open the door, tossing me one last look over his shoulder before walking away.

Silence descended upon the room yet again.

I looked back down at my phone and the image of the mark I now wore. What did it mean? Why the hell would he do such a thing? Why wouldn't he tell me what it was or where he was going?

At a complete loss, I dialed Rebecca's number and was sent to voicemail.

What the hell was going on with everyone around me? Becca always answered my calls. She was freaky about staying in touch, but for several days now, she was acting like a different person. Was she in on whatever secret was behind Casek's phone calls?

That was it. I was done sitting in the shadows playing good little Ashley, the helpless, hapless female. For five months, I'd been kept in the dark and left home the second things got dangerous. I was sick of it. Sick of being treated like a child. I wanted answers, and I wanted them now.

Glowering at the gym door, I bolted for the hallway and up the stairs.

Before I understood the full impact of what I was doing, I was slipping into the car Becca and I shared and pulling into evening traffic. Normally, I didn't carry the keys with me, but I still had them with me after going out earlier in the day. Off in the distance, I could just barely make out Casek's BMW stopped at a light. I had watched enough movies to know how to remain unseen as I followed him—it wasn't exactly rocket science. The hardest part was whipping the car into an alley to avoid driving right past him when he parked and exited his car.

I had shit luck with alleys in my past, so I made it a habit to avoid them if I could.

With my fingers crossed that I didn't get a ticket or attacked by any monsters, which was the more likely of the two scenarios, I left the car where it was. Peeking around the corner of the building to where Casek had parked, I caught sight of him just as he entered a pub a block down from where I stood.

In my rush to follow him out of the building, I had forgotten I was only wearing a tank top and leggings. We'd only tiptoed into May, and the Belfast nights were still brisk at their warmest. My jaw began to shiver as I nonchalantly walked around the corner and made my way toward the pub.

The Pickled Pig was located in a corner building, and its front entry was angled facing the corner. Both street-facing walls boasted large multi-paned windows surrounded in aged red brick, giving me the perfect opportunity to peek inside. My attempt at looking inconspicuous was most likely pointless as I leaned against the building in my ridiculously inappropriate outfit. Everyone else on the street at that hour wore jackets while I leaned against the freezing wall with my bare arms. Regardless, I played the part of a young woman waiting for a ride, checking her phone, annoyed to be left alone.

A glance inside told me there were two police officers conducting interviews, but I saw little else. Hoping to learn what had happened, I took a second peek inside and forgot all thoughts of being cold. The air outside was nothing compared to the ice that chilled my veins. On the worn wood floor beside the bar lay a dead woman, her face frozen in a look of sheer terror.

Next to her wavy red hair was a spilled pint of beer.

The scene was a perfect replica of the images I had seen days earlier. I had thought my weary, overtaxed brain had muddled Casek's memory with wisps of my own imaginings, but that hadn't been the case. The images my mind had conjured were very real, they simply hadn't happened yet.

My shock at recognizing the scene overrode the horror I would have ordinarily felt at seeing a dead body. All I could think about was how I'd seen all of this before. I abandoned my intentions of staying hidden and pressed my face to the glass, eyes wide and mouth gaping. The scene had come to me in pieces, but once put together, they fit perfectly to form the bigger picture before me.

I was so engrossed with my discovery that I failed to notice I had attracted the attention of everyone inside the pub, Casek included.

CHAPTER

EIGHT

CASEK

"W HAT THE *FUCK* ARE YOU DOING HERE?" M Y ANGER WAS beyond my control. I could see Ashley was upset, but I was too pissed to be gentle as I confronted her outside the pub. Grabbing her arm, I hauled her down the sidewalk away from the windows and curious stares.

She didn't fight me. Instead, guileless blue eyes peered up at me. "She's dead, isn't she?"

"Yes, and the last thing I need is you getting involved. If I had wanted you to come, I would have brought you myself."

Ashley flinched.

For the first time since I spotted her gaping through the window, the suffocating fear I'd experienced eased its vise-like grip on my chest. "It's not safe for you here. You should go," I said with more control, though not as much

93

compassion as I would have liked. She was clearly trauma-tized, and I hadn't helped at all.

"I'm so sorry. I let my suspicions get the better of me—I'll go home now." Her distracted apology was more child-like and lost than I'd ever seen her. She turned to retreat from where she'd come, and I fell into step behind her.

She peered back at me in surprise. "You don't have to follow me. I promise I'll head straight home. I know you're busy back there."

I hated hearing how rattled she was. In a perfect world, nothing would ever diminish the headstrong vibrance with which she charged through life. It was my job to keep that spark in place, and I'd failed. Even worse, being at the scene could have been incredibly dangerous.

"Assholes like this guy enjoy witnessing the chaos they've created. I wouldn't be surprised if he was here watching, soaking up the scene. So yes, I do have to follow you." I'd already fucked up once by not considering she might follow me, so I wasn't going to make things worse by sending her off alone in the dark.

It was a good thing I hadn't because the damn woman had parked hidden in an alley. She might as well have served herself up on a fucking platter.

I clamped down on my irritation, knowing I'd already been harsh enough. "Go straight back. I'll have one of the men wait for you out front."

She nodded, her eyes drawn distractedly to the dark-ened alley, then slid into the car and pulled away. As much as the catastrophe of my night loomed over me, I shoved it aside to dwell on later. For now, I had a killer to catch.

Fᴜᴄᴋ, I needed a cigarette.

When we first bought the Huntsman building, I had insisted on living in this particular apartment. It contained one of the few balconies that had a distant view of the River Lagan. The cold air cleared my head, and I could have a smoke without my place smelling like an ashtray.

Smoking was a shit habit, but that wasn't going to stop me.

I settled into the only chair occupying the space—there was room for another, but I had no interest in encouraging company. The flick of the lighter in the quiet night air coaxed my muscles to relax before I'd even pulled that first puff into my lungs. My body anticipated what was coming and was more than ready. I needed something after the shit day I'd had.

We'd been tracking a rash of murders over the past several weeks. Just a couple at first, but they were increasing in frequency. Always young women. Each time it happened, more work had to go into damage control with the cops and the press. We had to alter memories with plausible stories to make sure anyone involved didn't question the nature of the deaths. The last thing we needed was some reporter spouting off that there was a supernatural creature killing people on the streets of Belfast.

One look at the girls was all it took to be suspicious of their deaths. No visible wounds on any of the bodies, and each of their faces was frozen in a look of abject terror.

That was what happened when you've literally been scared to death. Human investigators wouldn't know what to do with themselves. In order to prevent a panic, we had someone monitoring their call system at all times to ensure we intervened in any incidents that might be abnormal. We hurried to each scene and laid the groundwork for a plausible explanation before conducting our own investigation.

Two deaths in a row had been unexpected when there'd been weeks between the others. I'd been so distracted by the call I'd received that I hadn't given Ashley the proper consideration. It hadn't even occurred to me that she'd follow me. I should have known better, but I'd been too caught up in my emotions to see clearly, which was evident when I lost control and marked her. Even hours later, I showed signs of temporary insanity because I couldn't summon an ounce of regret. Word would get out, and the men would talk, but I didn't give a fuck. No one would go near her with my mark on her, and that was all that mattered.

Hopefully, that knowledge would help me focus on my investigation. There was no way to prove for sure what we were up against, but I would bet my life that a Fear Gorda was loose in the city. This wasn't my first time dealing with their kind. Unlike the other creatures Morgan had allowed onto Earth, Fear Gordas were intelligent. Resourceful and adaptable. They could blend in and disappear with practiced ease. As one of the most civilized castes of Unseelie Fae, they were organized among themselves but rejected outside rule. How could they not? Their natural state was to prey upon those around them.

Anyone outside of their numbers would deem them a threat and respond accordingly.

Going up against a Gorda would be a challenge to say the least.

This one was proving especially crafty, but something was off. Most creatures kept far away from the Hunt if they managed to escape onto Earth. This one seemed to relish toying with us. He was clever and elusive, his kills all made within blocks of our home. It wasn't a coincidence. He knew what he was doing, and I would skin him alive for it. But in order to do that, I would need all my focus, which had been the exact opposite of what had happened. After Ashley left, it had taken me twice as long as normal to accomplish my crime-scene analysis due to my chaotic thoughts.

I had to get a grip on myself.

This hunt would allow for no margin of error—one misstep could lead to disaster. If history found a way to repeat itself ... if I lost another woman to their kind ... the animal I'd become would make the Gorda look like a fucking kitten.

CHAPTER
NINE

Once I was in the car, I called Becca and told her I needed to talk to her as soon as I could get home. Of course, she was with Lochlan, but I assured her that it was probably best if he was present for the conversation anyway. My teeth clanged against each other as my jaw chattered uncontrollably. Between the cold and the shock, I felt like I'd never be warm again.

Becca and Lochlan were waiting for me at our place when I arrived, along with Knight, who huffed at me and nipped at my fingers.

"Hey!" I yanked my hand away, then rolled my eyes. "Of course, you're upset with me, too. I should have known." I squatted down and met his eyes. "I know I messed up, and I'm sorry. I shouldn't have left the building without you."

His irritation only mildly assuaged, he huffed again

then loped away.

Becca took his place before me and scanned me for injuries. "Jesus, Ash, you're freezing! Were you outside without a jacket?" She plucked a hoodie from a nearby chair and thrust it into my arms.

We walked over to where Lochlan had remained seated on the couch and joined him, Becca in the middle, and me angled to see them both. My eyes briefly flitted to Lochlan, and I could tell he was intrigued about why I'd summoned them.

"Two days ago, I had some kind of vision. Actually, I'm not sure if it was a dream or a vision or if the difference really matters. Regardless, I saw a beer spilled on wood floors next to wavy red hair."

Becca still regarded me with confusion, but Lochlan tipped his head back in understanding.

I continued to explain, mostly for her benefit. "Tonight, Casek and I had a bit of an argument that resulted in me following him." I glanced at Lochlan sheepishly. "He'd been cryptic about things, and I might have overreacted a bit. When I got to the pub where he'd gone, I saw the scene from my vision. A red-headed woman was dead, and she lay next to a spilled pint on old wooden floors. It was *exactly* the same as I'd seen days earlier."

Becca whispered in awe, "You saw the future? Are you some kind of oracle?"

I peered at Lochlan again, this time with uncertainty. A part of me still wanted confirmation that I hadn't lost my mind.

His chin lifted as he processed the information. "An oracle is someone who spouts prophetic words given to them from a spiritual plane, so I don't believe that's accurate. We had anticipated visions would be a likely manifestation of your magic, considering your parentage. You derive your powers from Merlin, and he's a legendary Seer. It would make sense that you have inherited his abilities to see possible future outcomes."

Becca's eyes rounded as she turned back to me. "A Seer? What an amazing power!" She was trying to be encouraging, looking on the bright side and celebrating my gains, but after what I'd witnessed, it was hard to feel excited.

"I don't know about that. It's a lot of responsibility. Seeing that girl dead in the pub, I can't help but wonder if I could have figured out the clues early enough to have saved her."

They both regarded me sympathetically, and Becca took hold of my hand. "Think of all the good you may be able to do once your power is fully developed. I can't imagine it's going to be easy, but you could be a huge asset to the Hunt and even the police."

"You wouldn't be the first to help the Hunt in that capacity. Merlin was never a sworn member, but he was a cornerstone of the brotherhood's creation," Lochlan explained.

"The legends say he was a counselor to Arthur," I recalled.

"He counseled a number of individuals. He's the one who foretold the troubles that would come with the progress and expansion of humankind. It was based on those predictions that Guin decided to prohibit the Fae from living on Earth."

"He helped both sides—Guin and Arthur? I thought the two were enemies after Guin's affair with Lancelot," Becca added in confusion.

I wasn't as well informed on Fae history and listened raptly.

"Merlin has always remained neutral in matters of politics, and the Hunt and Court leaders have been inclined to allow it because of his unique gifts. His role in the Hunt was so great that despite not being a member, a seat was always reserved for him at Arthur's table."

"*The* table? The *Round* Table?" I asked with astonishment.

"Yes. Merlin crafted the table himself to foster equality among the Huntsmen. His relationship with Viviene, the Lady of the Lake, was the reason Arthur was given the Sword of Light. Merlin felt the sword would help balance the powers between the Hunt and the Seelie Court. He's had many profound impacts on Fae history. His gifts enable him to see how even small actions could affect the future. It sounds like you may have that ability as well."

The spark of hope he'd lit flickered and fizzled. "I won't be able to help anyone if Casek has anything to say about it. He has bailed on our past two training sessions and has hardly taught me anything. I get the sense he doesn't want me to explore my powers."

"That's absurd." Becca leaned back, her brows drawn tight. "Why wouldn't he be grateful for such an advantageous ally?"

Lochlan cleared his throat. "He's trying to protect you. It wasn't easy for me to accept that Rebecca had to fight

Morgan on her own, but I came around. Try to be patient with him."

"I get why you might have felt that way—you two care deeply for each other. Casek and I aren't like that. We don't have a relationship, and he certainly doesn't care for me. Hell, we fight whenever we're in shouting distance." My hand absently moved to cup the back of my neck.

The corners of Lochlan's lips twitched as though he found something amusing. "Casek's past has made him even more ... risk-averse than most. At least in regard to certain matters. And considering the creature we're after, he's likely to be more on edge than ever." All traces of levity fell from his face.

"Can you tell me more? I'd really like to know what's going on."

"Something has been feeding on women. We suspect an Unseelie creature called a Fear Gorda may have been released onto Earth by Morgan before Rebecca stopped her. The Gorda has been targeting young women, and that's likely why Casek was so upset to have you at the scene of the crime. That, and the fact that I'd assigned him to protect you."

"You did what?"

"I told you he was your teacher, but there's been more to it. We hadn't said anything because we didn't want you to object. Now, I expect you understand how serious the dangers have become. Until you are better equipped to protect yourself, Casek has been assigned to ensure your safety from possible threats by Guin and from the Fear Gorda."

It took a solid minute for me to process what he'd said

and come up with a response. In the end, I couldn't argue. Added protection was a good thing, and I likely would have balked about a bodyguard had I not known about the dangers present. I still wasn't sure the magical tattoo made sense, but I felt awkward mentioning it now.

"What's a Fear Gorda?" I asked, deciding to focus on learning what I could.

"Some Unseelie feed from sexual energy, but many feed from more negative emotions. The Fear Gordas feed on the intense energy released when a person experiences terror. Like the Leannan-Sidhe, they target the opposite sex, lure them close, then feed them horrific nightmares to induce fear. However, Fear Gordas don't have to be touching their victims during this process. There is a certain proximity requirement, but they are one of the only Fae who do not need to have physical contact to feed. They have mental talons that are nearly impossible to defend against if you happen inside their telepathic range. The only way to safely kill them is from a distance. In theory, one could use blood magic, but that kind of power could bring on consequences far worse than the Gorda." Lochlan's tone was grave, making the hair on my arms stand on edge.

"What is blood magic?" The name alone sounded terrible.

"It's an unnatural magic requiring an element of sacrifice—sometimes the sacrifice of a life, but more often, the sacrifice of power. The user must offer up a portion of their own powers via blood to activate the spell. While this may seem a small price to pay at the moment, repeated use of the magic creates a craving for blood.

Before long, blood becomes a requirement for feeding the user's own magic and soon consumes the individual. Blood lust corrupts the mind and is a death sentence in all Fae cultures."

"Using blood magic creates vampires?" I asked in astonishment.

"There are some similarities, though a blood compulsion isn't quite the same as the mythical vampire creatures in human lore. The afflicted don't grow fangs or have an aversion to sunlight, but they do become addicted to blood in order to keep their magic."

"That's definitely not an option," I said defeatedly. "If the Gorda is so dangerous, how will you stop it?"

"The key is tracking it, and fortunately, Casek has had extensive experience hunting them. We are relying heavily on his knowledge. Once he locates the Gorda, it will be a matter of putting an iron bullet or an arrow through its skull so that we can safely get close enough to kill it."

I wanted to ask how they could track such a creature, but I realized I'd already inserted myself enough. Yes, I was a part of the Fae world now, but that didn't mean I was equipped to handle everything. Casek was doing his best not only to help me but to catch one of the very worst sorts of Fae monsters. All I'd done was make his task harder.

Like the swell of the tide, a new wave of guilt pushed in just as the previous had receded.

"I didn't mean to complicate things. I just wish people would tell me what's going on so that I'm not in the dark." I slumped farther into the sofa cushions.

"I'd say that's a reasonable request." Lochlan raised a

brow at Rebecca. "So I'll take the liberty of being up front with you and ask how you'd feel if Rebecca moved in with me. We've discussed it, but she's hesitant to leave you alone."

Becca whacked him on the arm and stood defiantly. "I can't believe you just told her that. It was for me to discuss with her."

That must have been why she'd been so secretive lately. I'd known *something* was up and was relieved to learn there wasn't any real problem.

"You don't have to worry about me." I smiled warmly. "I'd be happy for you guys to move in together. We're in the same building, and I have Knight with me. I'm not remotely alone."

She sat and placed a hand on my knee, her kind eyes filling with affection. "I don't want you to feel forced into it just because Lochlan had to open his big mouth."

"You'll just have to believe me when I tell you that I'm being honest. I am one-hundred percent good on my own."

We both leaned in to hug one another, and when she pulled back, there was excitement brimming in her eyes. This was a step for her, and I was thrilled. Rebecca had never taken well to change. The move to Belfast had affected her in so many ways, and this was yet more evidence of the tremendous strides she'd taken. I was happy to do whatever I could to support her.

The three of us talked for a few more minutes before they returned to Lochlan's apartment. Once they were gone, I changed into flannel pajamas with wool socks. I still hadn't thawed from my unsettling experience at the pub, and Lochlan's words about the mysterious killer hadn't helped.

Hoping Knight would warm me up, I called him over to join me on the couch. I pressed my cold toes under him and put on a TV program as background noise. Once I was situated, I opened up my laptop to see what Google could tell me about Seers. I wasn't sure why I sought such unreliable sources except that I hated to sit in ignorance. Patience was a virtue I'd never quite mastered. I had a magical ability, and I needed to know more about it.

After several searches, I quickly discovered that anything more in depth than "a person who uses supernatural abilities to predict the future" was related to specific fan-fiction sites. I did learn a couple of possible tidbits that might have applied to me. According to one source, the "Sight" was reportedly involuntary, the magic choosing the person who was helplessly subjected to the visions. I hated to think my visions would be without rhyme or reason, but that had certainly been how the first one had appeared.

I also read that a Seer often had telepathic abilities or other mental powers, which went along with my ability to insert myself into other people's memories. Would those two "gifts" be the extent of my mental abilities, or did I have more surprises to uncover? Those two alone felt overwhelming. As much as I liked the idea of being powerful, I hoped I'd seen the extent of my mental superpowers.

Rain began to pound on the large windows of the living room as time drew on, the perfect soundtrack to drown out my racing thoughts. I turned off the television and snuggled up next to Knight. He adjusted himself to make room for me, then gently licked my arm before lowering his head again. Snuggled up next to his warm body, I allowed the rhythmic patter of the rain and his even, deep breaths carry me to sleep.

CHAPTER
TEN

ASHLEY

I LOUNGED IN BED THE NEXT MORNING LONGER THAN NORMAL after moving from the sofa halfway through the night. While I had enjoyed the comfort Knight had provided, he was a little *too* cuddly for my taste. He was also a sofa hog. I'd woken around midnight nearly suffocating in fur and sweating in places I was embarrassed to admit.

After a mostly full night's sleep, I was feeling less overwhelmed by the events of the day before. I lay in bed amazed at the fact that I'd had a prophetic vision. I'd seen the death of a woman before it had happened. What an incredible discovery! Not only was my elusive magic working, but it could be incredibly useful. Think of all the pain and suffering I could help prevent!

Not one to dwell on the negative, I pushed aside thoughts of the psycho killer on the loose and the increasing danger I'd be in if people knew what I could do.

I allowed myself instead to daydream about the good I could do and envisioned all the possibilities. By the time I finally rolled out of bed, I had pruned away the weeds in my garden of optimism and was confident good things were coming.

I took a quick shower and dressed in my favorite blue T-shirt. The color made my eyes pop, so it was a staple in my wardrobe, and this particular shirt was slightly fitted to outline my curves as well. I'd have to wear a jacket over it to start the day, but that was just a fact of life in Ireland.

"Hey, Knight. I'm gonna work from the coffee shop this morning. You want some scones or maybe a croissant?"

Still sprawled on the sofa, he slowly eased to the ground, stretched his back in a classic downward-facing dog, then padded over to me with a toothy smile.

"I'll take that as a yes on both counts. Come on, let's go."

Becca had explained not long after Knight first showed up that he refused to eat dog food. I couldn't blame him. I wouldn't want to eat that crap either. He wasn't a cheap addition to the household, but I was quickly adjusting to ordering for two. Once I set down my coffee and scone, I took a couple of baked goodies outside for Knight. As always, he downed my offering without even chewing.

"I'm not sure why you care what you eat. You don't take the time to taste it."

He answered with a doggy burp and a lolling tongue.

I chuckled and returned to the table I'd set up inside to start working. About a half hour in, after I'd finished my coffee and breakfast, the girl who'd asked me about Knight the day before came over to take my plate away.

"Back again?" she asked with a smile, collecting the dirty dishes.

I got a warm vibe from her the same as I had the day before. It occurred to me that I hadn't really made any friends since coming to Belfast aside from a couple of the Huntsmen, and guy friends weren't the same. Becca was spending more and more time with Lochlan, and while I'd gotten closer with Cat, she was still primarily Rebecca's friend. It would probably do me a world of good to nurture a few new female relationships.

"Yeah, I'm going to have to start paying rent if I'm not careful." I grinned. "My name's Ashley. I live around the corner." I gave a one-handed wave.

The girl's grin spread wider. "I'm Elleree, but everyone calls me Elle."

"I'd ask if you wanted to sit for a minute, but I know you're working."

She set the dishes back down and helped herself to the opposite chair. "They won't mind back there. We're past the morning rush at this point."

"Perfect! I haven't been great about meeting people since I moved here."

"How long have you been in Belfast?"

"About six months. Well, maybe more like five. I came over with a friend just to get her settled but ended up moving here myself."

"That sounds like an interesting story!"

I gave her a tight-lipped smile and nodded. It *was* an interesting story, but one I wouldn't be sharing. "Yeah, so are you a Belfast native?" I redirected the conversation.

She nodded. "Only place I've ever lived, though I plan to travel one of these days."

"Do you have any place in mind?"

"I'm fascinated with the Orient—their customs and lore. It would be a big change, but I'd enjoy the challenge." Her brown eyes glinted with intrigue as she spoke.

"Dang! That would definitely be an adventure. I figured you'd say Paris or New York or some other more typical destination."

"I wasn't allowed to get out much as a kid, so I guess my need to roam is greater than most." Her eyes dropped to her hands for a second, almost sheepishly, before her spine stiffened. "Shite, I think I heard my name being called. I better get back." She quickly stood with the dishes. "It was lovely meeting you!"

"You, too! Oh, wait! Before you go, can I get your number? Maybe we can hang out sometime."

She grinned from ear to ear. I jotted down her number before she rushed away, sitting back to reflect on how well my day had started with a little positive thinking. Maybe that was all I needed to get things going in the right direction. A little determination and a whole lot of optimism. Maybe between the two, I could even talk to Casek without wanting to gouge out his eyes.

Then again, optimism could only take me so far.

My fingers lifted to the back of my neck for what had to have been the hundredth time in the past twelve hours —eight of which I'd spent asleep. I still couldn't believe what he'd done. Pulling out my phone, I looked at the image of his mark again. It looked like an X with lines crossing the tops and one final line descending from the top right of the letter. He'd said it would keep others away, but what did that mean? Was it some form of spell or more of a generalized warning?

"No wonder I haven't seen hide nor hair of you lately." Liam's sudden appearance from behind me caused me to nearly drop my phone.

"Oh! Hey. What are you up to?" Heat scalded my cheeks.

He lowered his lanky form into the café chair across from me and studied me. "Saw your friend outside and thought I'd say hello. Now that you're working with Casek, I don't see you anymore."

My relationship with Liam had been easy and open from the day we met. I valued his friendship and felt bad that I'd neglected him.

"I'm sorry. I've had a lot on my plate lately."

"So I see," he said with just a touch of accusation.

"What do you mean?" My voice lowered warily.

"Well, for starters, I didn't expect to find you here wearing his brand."

Every ounce of the color drained from my face. "His ... what?" I breathed, my eyes wide, hand clamping over the back of my neck.

Liam's eyes narrowed. "What did you think you wore back there?"

My head shook. "A spell ... some kind of warning. He said it would keep others away."

"Aye, that it'll do." He chuckled dryly—an uncharacteristic sound for the normally playful man.

Why did he seem so upset? I understood why I should be appalled. But him? This had nothing to do with him. Any insinuation otherwise made me a tad defensive.

"It's not like I had a choice." I pulled my hair down from the ponytail I'd been wearing to conceal the mark. "He slapped it on there, and I had no way to take it off."

He nodded slowly as though he wasn't quite buying what I was selling, but before I could argue, he waved a hand dismissively. "I didn't mean to rile you. It's probably best you're protected every way possible in the coming days."

"You mean because of the Fear Gorda."

"Aye, but also because the Hunt has chosen its new leader. The vote was unanimous for Lochlan to assume Alberich's role as Erlking. The ceremony will take place outside of Avalon in two days' time, and every Huntsman is to attend. We leave tomorrow."

Rebecca had explained a week earlier, not long after the previous Erlking had been killed by Morgan, that Lochlan would likely be voted into the role. It wasn't a surprise, yet the news still caught me off guard.

"I hadn't realized the vote was happening."

"An hour ago. Now everyone is busy arranging for our absence. It's not a good time for us to leave Belfast unguarded." Again, the gravity of his normally light-hearted demeanor set me on edge.

"How long will you be gone?"

"Two days at most. You and Rebecca seem to be the biggest topic of debate. You aren't allowed at the ceremony, but they aren't sure if you're safer alone in Faery or here at the Huntsman." He paused for a moment, eyes raking over my face. "I didn't mean to worry, ye, Ash. Every precaution will be taken to keep both of you safe."

I smiled and shook my head. "No, I know. It's just been one hell of a week. Care to walk me back home? I don't think I can concentrate at this point."

"Of course." He stood and helped me gather my things but stilled before we could leave the table. "You know, I'm here for you. Anytime you need to talk, or anything at all, you just give me a ring."

Liam was so incredibly sweet, and I'd loved spending time with him, but I suddenly wondered if he hadn't been hoping for more.

My heart contracted painfully. I had never felt more than friendship for Liam. He was funny and clever and thoughtful—I could spend hours entertained in his company—but that spark of desire never existed for me. If it had for him, I'd been unaware and hoped to God I hadn't been leading him on. There was no other man on this planet I'd hate to hurt more than Liam.

I nodded appreciatively at his offer, my throat clogged with emotion.

He led the way out, our conversation light and effortless until we entered the Huntsman lobby and crossed paths with a scowling Casek.

CHAPTER
ELEVEN

CASEK

When I'd called Ashley with no response, then gone by her place and found it empty, I swore that she better not have gone out alone. I realized minutes later when I came across her strolling into the building with Liam at her side that I should have been more specific. I would have been angry if she'd gone out alone, but finding her with Liam made me fucking homicidal.

I knew love-sick when I saw it, and that man had it bad.

If Ashley had been interested in him, they would already be an item, but that didn't stop me from feeling an unholy animosity toward him. She wore my mark, and that bastard was still sniffing around.

"I tried to reach you, but I see you were busy." My eyes never left Liam though I spoke to Ashley. The man had bigger balls than I'd suspected because aside from ignoring my mark, he didn't even flinch at my withering stare.

"I guess my phone was on silent," she explained, her voice an octave higher than normal. "I was working at the coffee shop then got distracted talking. Liam was just telling me about the vote and ceremony." She looked between us, talking quickly and smiling as if trying to draw our attention away from one another.

I gave one last glare, then finally turned to Ashley. "We've decided you girls will stay here. You'll need to remain in the building at all times while we're away. I came to tell you that I have too much to do and won't be able to train this evening, but I'll come by tomorrow morning to run any errands you might have before we leave. Neither you nor Rebecca are permitted to step foot outside of this building once we're gone."

"It's two days. I think we can manage that." She gave a thin smile. "And I just might need to do a bit of shopping if we have a girls' weekend. You think Cat would be allowed to join us?"

"As long as no one leaves, I don't think it would be an issue, but we would need to get Lochlan's approval." I might have refused the Druid girl unchaperoned access to our home if I wasn't already anxious about Ashley complying with our orders. Limit her further, and she was sure to rebel.

"Sweet! I think this would be the perfect opportunity for some girl time." She looked between Liam and me, the lobby settling into a heavy silence. "Yeahhh, so I'm going to head upstairs."

The elevator opened immediately, providing her an

escape and leaving me alone with my brother. Neither of us moved a muscle.

"You think that was really necessary?" Liam said coolly, his chest expanding as broad as his lithe frame would allow. He didn't have to specify what he was talking about. Only one thing would have him so irate. Ashley's mark.

I crossed my arms. "Wouldn't have done it if I didn't."

"She should have the right to make her own decisions. She told me you didn't even ask first."

"That's right, and I'm not interested in anyone's forgiveness either. What I do for Ashley will keep her alive because my decisions aren't compromised by emotion." I took a single step and leaned in close. "You may think you're putting her first, but what you're really doing is thinking with your dick, and *that* is what will get her killed."

Liam's lips pursed tight, his throat swallowing back words he knew were better silenced. He might have been young and a touch brash, but he knew what I'd said was the truth. With nothing left to say, he stormed toward the stairs, letting the door slam behind him.

Fuck me. Why did everything have to be so damn complicated lately?

Shaking my head, I continued outside as I'd originally intended before I'd been intercepted. I had a ceremony to prepare for and errands of my own that needed to be addressed before we left. It was going to be a busy twenty-four hours.

～

"I just have to go a block over to the pharmacy, then I should be done." Ashley put her credit card back in her wallet and grabbed the bag of her purchases from the clerk.

We'd had a perfectly ordinary, uneventful morning of shopping. In fact, Ashley had said very little on our trip, and I had grown more uneasy by the minute. I knew better than to think I'd lucked into snagging Ash on a demure day. Those didn't happen.

"We already hit a pharmacy on our first stop," I noted, not spotting the trap she'd so casually laid.

"Yeah, but the one down the street caries the *brand* of nail polish I like." She shot me a sickly sweet smile. "Brands are important, you see. They mark a product. That way, consumers know what they're getting. If I see that a hair dryer says Dyson on the package, I pass it by because I know it'll be way too expensive for me. Makes life *so* much easier." Every caustic word was dripping with sarcasm.

There it is. I knew there had to be something brewing.

Ashley slowed and looked up at me, her eyes shards of cut glass. "But you know what we can't brand, Casek? *People.* That's what. We don't fucking brand people." She whipped around and kept walking.

I was going to have to thank Liam for this. I had no doubt it was his fault we were having this conversation. Lengthening my stride, I closed the distance between us while Knight stayed behind at a healthy distance. I didn't blame him.

"You're only now upset? I figured you'd gotten over it."

"That was when I thought it was some kind of protection spell—not your personal *brand*. And I didn't want to argue in front of Liam because you two already looked like you were gunning for one another."

"You can call the mark what you want; it achieves the same goal."

"It *does* make a difference, especially when I wasn't asked." She suddenly stopped and glared up at me. "You at least going to tell me what it does? I want to know specifics. I deserve that."

Every muscle in my body prepared for a fight. "Aside from giving everyone notice that they fuck with me when they fuck with you, it also enables me to keep tabs on your location."

Her lips parted. "You put a fucking tracking device on me without my permission?" She jabbed a manicured finger into my chest, accenting her words.

I stepped forward, forcing her to take a reluctant retreat back. "I did, and it stays right where I put it."

"Had you taken the time to ask, you would have learned that I don't have a problem with the functionality, Casek. It's the way you went about it that pisses me off."

Fuck, she was irresistible when she was mad. I couldn't help but imagine her naked, all that energy chan-neled into riding my cock. She'd be magnificent.

The next thing I knew, my lips were devouring hers. I clasped my hand at the nape of her neck, my cock growing impossibly hard at the feel of my mark warming her skin. The Fae rune had linked our energies together. If she had access to her magic, she would have known that the spell worked both ways. It limited either of us from feeding from anyone else and allowed us to sense one another to a degree. Mated couples sometimes exchanged marks as a show of unity, like human wedding bands. Liam had been wise not to share that tidbit. Then I really would have had reason to tear him apart.

I kissed Ashley until the taste of her was seared on my tongue. Until the beast inside me no longer rattled his cage with mindless need.

When I pulled away, we were spared any awkward uncertainty by the menacing rumble of a growl beside us. Knight stepped close, his head tucked low, and a bestial warning reverberated deep in his chest.

I was battle ready in an instant.

Maneuvering Ashley behind me, I looked in the direction Knight was growling. Across the road, a shop door opened, and Durin, the queen's lackey stepped out. He stared at us smugly and meandered with intentional nonchalance across the street toward us.

"We weren't informed you were in town, Durin." My voice and words were a subtle warning. We didn't like to cross the queen, but I wasn't going to cower either.

The bald man with hollowed cheeks flashed a twisted grin and casually stepped forward. "The queen has no obligation to inform you of her business." No, but it was a mutual courtesy both the Hunt and the Crown had observed for centuries.

"And what sort of business has you following us around?"

"Majesty is simply curious about this one," he said, gesturing toward Ashley. "We'd like to know more about her powers, considering where her abilities come from. I don't have to follow her around if she'd prefer to visit with the queen instead." He lifted his head and spoke to Ashley.

"Her Majesty would like to make sure you're aware of all your options. If you were at the palace, you would be treated like royalty—no need for constant bodyguards or threats from the Unseelie."

Ashley's delicate hand gripped my arm with the force of a python subduing its next meal. She was terrified of being taken by Durin. While I wasn't sure if she had seen him before, she had to know that Durin was the name of the man who had kidnapped Rebecca and taken her to Faery. At the very least, she knew the man before her posed a real threat.

When I glanced her way, she gave away none of that fear, and instead, she shot a fierce look of challenge to the man who stood over a foot taller than herself.

I cut my eyes back to Durin. "I don't think the lady wants to take you up on that offer." I began to step menacingly closer to him, leaving Ashley where she stood with Knight. "This is our city, and I'm giving you this one opportunity to get the fuck out. I catch you following her again, and there are no more warnings—you understand?" The last words were spoken inches from his face. I hated that I had to look up at him, but he was a freaking behemoth.

He sneered back at me, enjoying his size advantage. "You think you can threaten me? I represent the queen."

Faster than the man could follow, I slammed an iron cuff around his wrist, preventing him from tracing, grabbed his pinky finger and swung him around, bending back the finger and his arm in a way that forced him to his knees. I then leaned close to speak directly into his ear. "You may have power back at the palace, but around here, you're *nothing.* I'm not telling you again. You come near her, and I will fucking *gut* you."

I let the words soak in nice and deep before releasing the clasp on the iron cuff. The tool was a human thug's equivalent of brass knuckles. I never left home without it.

The second he was able, Durin traced out of sight.

"I remember seeing him at the palace," Ashley said in a hushed voice. "When Merlin convinced the queen to leave me alone." Her cornflower eyes roamed the area for signs of the man.

"She agreed to let you stay on Earth, not necessarily to leave you alone." I rubbed a hand over my head. "*Fuck.* This complicates things." Guin wasn't exactly a woman of her word. And to top it off, I had no doubt she would be well informed of our upcoming induction ceremony. "That's it. I'm staying here."

"What do you mean?"

"The ceremony. I can't leave you here unprotected." I pulled out my phone, trying to figure out what the hell I was going to do.

"I thought it was important you were all there."

"It is, but keeping you alive is important, too."

"What happens if you don't go?"

I looked up to clear blue innocence staring back at me. "A spell is performed when the Erlking is crowned. It bonds him to all of us so that he can connect with us telepathically—a more basic form of Becca's dream walking. If I'm not present, he can conduct a similar rite later in the same way new members are brought into the fold."

"But it's not the same, is it?" She'd read between the lines straight to my most pressing concern.

"The spell is woven into the magic used when the Erlking is named. It can't be replicated outside of the ceremony—not to the full extent." I sighed heavily, knowing how crucial it would be for me to be present. I had been Lochlan's next in command for ages. With all the challenges he would soon face, he needed our bond to be as powerful as possible.

Ashley placed her hand on mine. "Caz, I know you're worried, and I really appreciate your concern for my safety, but it sounds like you need to go," she said softly, her eyes briefly cutting to where Durin had stood. "I know how dangerous it is, and I swear to you that I won't leave the building while you're gone."

If I'd thought feisty Ashley was irresistible, her compassionate counterpart could have sent a man to his grave with a smile on his face.

At a loss for words, a growl of frustration escaped me. "Let's get this shopping shit wrapped up and get home." One more minute alone with her, and I might have said something I'd regret. Something raw and honest and irreversible.

ONLY A HANDFUL of Erlking induction ceremonies had ever been performed, and I'd been present at all of them. Normally, the Hunt spent an entire week gathered in celebration. We had decided to keep events to a minimum this time because of the circumstances, but that still meant almost four days of feasts, politics, and gatherings leading up to the primary ceremony. It would only amount to under forty-eight hours back on Earth since time didn't work the same on both worlds, but it felt like an eternity.

As expected, Lochlan managed to convince me to go. We added extra protections at the Huntsman building, and I waited until the last possible minute to leave, but each second I was gone scratched and clawed at my thoughts until my inner voice screamed in frustration. The only thing that gave me any peace at all was the fact that Rebecca possessed a unique power called dream walking, in which she could communicate with others telepathically. Because of her intense connection with Lochlan, she could perform the feat with him at any distance. Knowing the girls were a telepathic phone call away was the only thing that had felt like sufficient reassurance to justify leaving them. Between the increased wards, an ability to communicate, and minimal time away, our absence shouldn't have left them excessively vulnerable.

"Stop worrying." Lochlan clapped a hand on my shoulder. "They'll be fine."

We'd been preparing for the final ceremony all day, and we're down to the final hour. Huntsman who had been scattered across Faery had been summoned to the hunting lodge Lochlan inherited from Alberich, his adoptive father and predecessor. It was isolated in a remote forest—perfect for a secret ceremony. Everyone was now present. The components of the spell had been gathered. All that remained was the actual ceremony itself before we could get the hell back home.

"I'm surprised you aren't just as on edge." I downed the rest of my wine. "If that Gorda makes a move for them, you know Rebecca will be just as helpless against him as

Ashley." Rebecca had significant powers, but they relied primarily on proximity, which would be useless against a Fear Gorda. Both women were equally vulnerable on that front.

Lochlan sat in the armchair across from me and studied me. "It's not my ideal situation; however, this is nothing compared to what I already had to endure watching Rebecca go up against Morgan. I had no choice but to stand at her side and have faith that she would survive."

"You had a choice. You chose to risk her life to give humans a chance at survival."

"Not at all." His hint of a smile bore a sharp edge. "That was never one of my considerations. Earth could go to hell for all I cared, but it would have broken Rebecca. *That* was the choice I had to make. Give her the freedom to make her own choices or cut her wings and coat her soul with the black tar of hate and regret. For me, that was never truly an option."

And that was why Lochlan was moments away from becoming our newest Erlking. He was ruthless but fair and always logical. He had known that if he gave in to his need to protect Rebecca, he would have lost her regardless.

I reached for the bottle of wine and poured myself another glass to both pass the time and help me swallow the truth I'd just been fed.

Lochlan chuckled, taking a swig from his own glass. "You're a good man, Caz. You'll get through this just as you have every other challenge along the way."

I was quiet for a moment, touched by his confidence, but more than anything, I worried his trust was misplaced. "I'm not so sure. After Raisa..." I met his steely gaze. "I can't go through that again. If something happens to her..." I couldn't finish. I was too embarrassed to admit the things I would do should Ashley come to harm.

"I can't say it won't ever happen, but if it should, I'll be right there beside you. The blood on your hands will coat mine as well." His tone softened to a lethal promise. "We're brothers. You are never alone."

He might have been younger than many of us, but he was easily the best man for the job. Lochlan would lead with honor, justice, and unbridled loyalty.

I dropped my chin in a traditional Fae bow of respect.

Lochlan set down his glass and stood. "All right. Let's get this show over with. I want to get home to my girl." He patted my back as I rose.

His ability to transition an awkward silence back to more comfortable waters was greatly appreciated. I followed him into the main hall, where he inquired about the status of the preparations, urging those in charge to get us started as soon as possible.

A half hour later, we were all gathered in the forest some distance from the house. Over fifty Huntsmen, a blazing fire, and the night sky glittering with distant stars. The profound nature of the ceremony was immensely impactful, despite my incessant anxiety. Pride expanded my chest, and when the bond between Erlking and Huntsman was again in place, I found that a small modicum of comfort returned. It was a layer of unease I hadn't even realized existed. Yet when the spell was performed and our oaths renewed, the tension eased from my muscles.

We were again united, and I felt stronger for it.

Now, the celebration would commence. Cheers and drums reverberated off the surrounding trees and filled the night sky. Men at the back of the circle brought in barrels of Faery wine, and others laughed and joked about the fun that was about to be had.

I grinned, allowing myself to enjoy the celebratory spirit if only for a moment. And that was all I'd be permitted because within minutes of the festivities kicking off, I heard my name thunder in my head.

Lochlan was using his newly bestowed power to summon me, and there was only one reason he would do such a thing.

"Quiet!" I screamed, shoving men aside in search of him.

Curious eyes turned to me, and a pathway cleared.

Lochlan was at my side in an instant, twin blue flames lighting his eyes. "Rebecca's just contacted me. We need to get back at once."

CHAPTER

TWELVE

ASHLEY

"Come on in, ladies! Let's get this party started. I've got margarita mix in the fridge, salt on the glasses, and limes already wedged." I'd been waiting for Rebecca to show up with Cat for what felt like ages. The last-minute decorations I'd snagged on my shopping trip the day before plastered slabs of vibrant color across the living room, and a Spotify party playlist was pumping the room full of energy. I'd missed Cinco de Mayo by a week but figured it worked as well as any theme for our get-together.

Rebecca dropped her work tote by the door and grinned. "That sounds ah-*maze*-ing. Let me get changed, though. I'll just be a minute."

I met Cat's excited green eyes. "You're welcome to use my bathroom if you want to get more comfy."

"I'm fine. I don't have to get dressed up like Becca." She tugged at her shirt self-consciously.

"Either way, you're welcome to make yourself at home since you're stuck here for the next thirty-six hours or so. I got a new deep conditioner and face masks we can try out."

"So that's why you're hair is always so gorgeous. I should really spend more time with mine, but it's such a hassle."

"What?" I gawked at her. "Your curls are adorable, and that color?" I kissed my fingertips in a chef's kiss gesture.

She gave an exaggerated sigh. "It's my burden in life. Never sexy or seductive, but I nail adorable every time." She arched a brow, and we both burst into a fit of giggles.

"What's so funny?" Becca asked as she swept back into the room clad in pajamas and fuzzy slippers.

"I was just telling Cat how *gorgeous* she is." I shot Cat a teasing look.

Becca's eyes widened. "Don't tell me you're unaware of how stunning you are. I bet you've had boys lined up since you were little."

"That shows how little you know. Not only were they not lined up but I've also had exactly two boyfriends, if you could even call them that. I've hardly even fooled around. I'm twenty and still a virgin!"

Becca and I both stared in surprise. She was still young, so it wasn't all that crazy, but she really was lovely and so incredibly sweet that it seemed hard to believe.

"Nothing? Even with the boyfriends?" My mind kept running the math, but the figures didn't add up.

"It's not *that* hard to believe, especially considering the circumstances of my family. I wasn't allowed to socialize with just anyone, and the Druid boys were all ... *eww*." Cat went to the sofa and sat, making me realize we'd made her uncomfortable.

Becca joined her in the living room. "Lochlan said he met with some of your elders yesterday to strengthen trust between the two groups. Well, mostly for the Druids. The Fae didn't even know they existed until recently."

"I think my mom was there. She was in a right awful mood at supper."

"Yeah, he said she wasn't impressed. Hopefully with time, they'll come to accept that the Hunt isn't the enemy."

"Some already have, but there's a group of holdouts like my mom who always fear the worst."

Becca grimaced, turning to me. "Cat's mom is massively overprotective. She's like the exact opposite of your mom."

My nose scrunched. "I'm not sure which is worse."

Cat shrugged. "Well, it just means I'm that much more grateful for you two. You've already made my life infinitely better just knowing we're friends."

"Oh my God, you can't say stuff like that!" I cried, feeling a rush of moisture burn the back of my eyes. "There's no crying on girls' night! I'm going to make the margaritas, and then no more sappy stuff, capisce?" I marched back to the fridge and gathered my supplies.

After witnessing my father's struggles with alcohol, I hadn't gone near the stuff until my junior year of college. Even then, I'd concocted a strict set of rules I followed whenever alcohol was involved.

1. Max one drink an hour.

2. No more than four drinks in a day.
3. No more than one day of drinks a week.
4. No drinking alone. Ever.

I mixed my own drinks whenever I could to keep the alcohol to a single serving per drink. I never ordered doubles. I set a timer on my phone when I started each drink, and if anyone handed out shots or bought me a drink beyond that limit, I was an *expert* at sleight of hand. Pouring drinks into empty cups. Tossing unwanted shots into potted plants. Putting my lips to a glass but not actually taking a sip. I was stricter than a Catholic nun when it came to following my drinking rules, which was why I hardly noticed the girls talking as I measured the tequila.

I was adding the limes to the drink rims when I took in the serious looks on their faces. The two were deep in conversation, Cat nodding as if Becca was offering her the secret to everlasting life.

I had no clue what they were discussing, but it made me glad I'd met Elle at the coffee shop. Becca should have every right to other friends, and unless I had a few other friendships as well, I wouldn't be able to shake off the twinge of jealousy I felt at seeing their private conversation.

"All right, ladies," I called as I walked over with a drink in each hand. "Drinks are served." I gave them each a glass and went back to retrieve my own. "Who's going to toast?"

"Not me," said Cat. "I've never even had a margarita, so I wouldn't know a proper toast."

I grinned mischievously. "Oh, sweet Cat. You're in for a treat."

Becca kicked off our night with a toast to girlfriends. We each took a healthy slug of our drinks, then rolled with laughter when Cat choked on hers.

"It's like acid," she said with watery eyes.

We all laughed some more before Becca explained that I had a heavy hand when it came to mixing drinks, and when it came to making drinks for other people, I did. I was much more conservative with my own. That was why I liked to bartend when possible—better to be the one in control so I knew exactly what was going in my body.

Once the tequila began to warm my belly, and the conversation skipped from one topic to the next, I told the girls about Elle.

"I know it probably wouldn't have worked to invite her since you've never met, but I thought maybe we could give her a call."

Becca gave a lopsided grin. She'd always been quick to feel her alcohol. "Yes! Let's FaceTime her now." She grabbed my phone and thrust it at me.

I giggled and selected Elle's number. The other two scurried around behind me to get a better view.

"Hello?" came the girl's voice seconds before her picture appeared.

"Hey, Elle! I was just having a bit of a girls' night with my friends and was telling them about you. They wanted to meet you, so we figured we'd just give you a ring." I lifted my glass in explanation, belatedly realizing it was now empty. "Oops! Looks like it's time for another."

Elle joined us all in a good laugh. "I'm so glad you did."

She waved at the camera. "I'm Elle. It's lovely to meet you."

The others introduced themselves, and we all chatted excitedly. Although, in reality, it might have been Becca, Cat, and I blabbing excitedly while poor Elle watched in rapt fascination. Who was to say?

"Isn't she sweet?" I asked after we'd hung up. "I definitely think we should try to include her in our next outing." I pulled my hair up into a ponytail and looked for the grocery sack I'd brought home earlier. "And I also think I should go ahead and do my face mask. The alcohol's already convinced me that deep conditioning my hair can wait. Too much hassle."

I located the bag and brought it back to the living room, growing still when I realized both girls were staring at me with wide eyes. "What? Is there a spider? Oh, God. Do I have a spider on me?"

Becca shook her head incredulously. "Ashley Nicole Moore, do you have a tattoo on the back of your neck?"

I sucked my lips between my teeth. "Oh, *that.*"

"Oh, *that?*" Becca squawked. "Are you serious? How do I not know about this?"

Poor Cat sat quietly, her eyes ping-ponging back and forth between us.

Taking a deep breath, I launched into a full explanation of how I'd acquired my new magical ink. The girls absorbed every word, their jaws hanging open by the time I was done.

"I'd say I can't believe he did that," mused Becca. "But really, I can. I'm sorry, honey. At least he can remove it once all this is over. I know he's been difficult to work with."

"It's not so bad." My eyes fell to my hands in my lap. I hadn't gone into my more intimate encounters with Casek. I wasn't quite ready to share the full complexities of our relationship, though by the look on Becca's face, she already knew. I'd told her about our first time together—a night I'd thought would be a simple one-night stand. "The thing that's been the hardest is figuring out this magic business."

Becca's brow scrunched. "What do you mean? I thought all that changed after Merlin helped you."

"So did I, but it hasn't been as easy as I'd hoped. I don't know if it's the way I acquired my power or because of the unique gifts I have, but I'm having trouble accessing it again. This time, I can feel it there, but I can't use it. Not intentionally."

"I'm sorry, Ash. I know that's been so frustrating for you."

I forced a thin smile. "Yeah, but that's exactly why I needed this time with you guys. Great friends, drinks, laughter, and zero troubles. So no more talk about boys or magic."

"Yes, sir, Captain," Becca saluted. "Let me check in for just a second with Lochlan while you get that face mask on, then we can cue up a movie. Sound good?"

"Definitely. Do your thing, and I'll be back in a jiffy."

We had another round of drinks while we watched a romantic comedy, then taught Cat how to play crazy eights, which turned out to be hysterical when tipsy. We had a fabulous night together, and it was exactly what I'd needed.

AFTER SLEEPING off the tequila well into the next morning, we started our day at a nice leisurely pace with coffee and girl talk, transitioning smoothly into nails and chick flicks after lunch. The day sped by at a miraculous rate, considering we did very little. It was the perfect mix of relaxation and friends. Before I knew it, the sun had set, and the first bottle of wine had been opened.

"Next time, I'll bring the Guinness, and we do things my way," said Cat, looking a little green.

Becca smirked. "You don't have to have any if you don't want."

"Please." Cat scoffed. "I'm Irish. If I don't go drink for drink with anyone in the room, I'll let my whole country down."

I laughed and poured her a glass. "What's next on the agenda, ladies? Movie? Cards? Karaoke?"

"Karaoke takes energy," Becca said. "I say we stick with a movie."

"Suggestions?"

"I wish the latest season of *Bridgerton* was out on Netflix, but it doesn't release for a couple of weeks." I scoured my brain for other options.

"What's *Bridgerton*?" Cat asked.

"You haven't watched *Bridgerton*?" I asked incredulously.

She shook her head, and I exchanged an excited look with Rebecca.

"I'll cue up season one." I grinned.

Becca jumped off the couch. "I'm going to check in with Lochlan and run to the restroom before we start." She scurried off, returning minutes later with a beaming grin. "Good news! They're about to start the ceremony and should be home earlier than expected."

We settled in and started the movie. While I'd watched it numerous times before, it felt like the first time since Cat had never watched. We all giggled and swooned in unison.

Near the end, I thought I was nodding off when the room seemed to darken around the edges of my vision, and an entirely new scene unfolded before me. I was outside the building in the shadows across the street from the entrance. Heavy footfalls caught my attention. Casek was jogging down the sidewalk, but before he could reach the lobby doors, he stumbled to a stop and clutched his head. His face twisted in agony as he fell to his knees.

My heart plummeted, its beat hysterical and erratic.

This is a vision. That's all it is.

I pleaded with myself to remain calm and keep watching so I could learn what I needed to prevent whatever was about to unfold.

While Casek was incapacitated, a tall man walked up to him and slapped iron cuffs onto his wrists. Casek acted as though he had no awareness of the man's presence. Lost in his own misery, he made no attempt to fight the man as he hoisted Casek over his shoulder like the Fae warrior weighed nothing. The man never gave me a good look at his face, but I was certain I knew who it was. Durin's enormous frame and bald head were hard to miss.

His swift steps carried Casek away from me. I knew it wasn't real, but the horror of watching him flee and being unable to pursue was torturous. I was powerless to stop him. For seemingly endless minutes, I watched the two disappear farther down the street until, to my shock, Durin turned into a building two blocks away. Once I lost sight of him, flashes of scenes assaulted me. A small square room. A basement. Dirt floors. A chair. Casek bleeding and bruised. Blood dripping onto wet earth. Screams. Agonized, heart-wrenching screams ripped from Casek's throat.

I couldn't take anymore.

My own cries rang out alongside his in my head.

In a flash, the vision was gone, though its vicious claws remained gouged deep in my memories. I gasped and cried out as I came to, a burst of sobs wracking my body.

Becca and Cat rushed to my side, trying to comfort me and frantic to know what had happened. I tried to speak, but the words came out clipped and jumbled. Eventually, I calmed myself enough to explain what I'd seen.

Becca's face hardened. "It was just a vision, Ash. I'll contact Lochlan and warn them. A vision doesn't necessarily mean it's going to happen." She sat back on the sofa and closed her eyes as she tried to dream walk with Lochlan.

One minute passed. Then two and three.

When she finally opened her eyes again, they were shadowed with worry. "I couldn't get through, but that doesn't mean anything. They could be in the middle of his ceremony."

"Would that magic block you from reaching him?" I asked, a spark of hope flickering to life.

Her gaze struggled to meet mine. "I'm not sure."

"Becca, what if they already finished and something happened on their way back? Maybe that was the reason Casek was running to the building alone. It's been, what? An hour and a half since you talked to him? That would be twice as long in Faery, right?"

"Roughly." She nodded.

"So a good three hours had passed for them. Do we know how long it would take for them to travel home?"

She grimaced. "No. Shit, shit, *shit*." Leaping up, she began to pace the living room.

"What if something's happened, Bec? What do we do?"

She walked to the windows and back twice before turning to me, her eyes going jet black. "I'll take Knight and check out the building."

"I'm going with you." My tone was absolute.

"Ash, you haven't learned your magic yet. It's too dangerous."

"First, I'm an adult, and I'll do what I damn well want. And second, you need me to show you the location."

Her lips crooked down in a frown before she grabbed a piece of paper and a pen, scribbling something and handing it to Cat. "This is Lochlan's number. If we haven't checked in every ten minutes at any point, call him. Assuming something hasn't already happened to them, he'll know what to do once he gets back." She swallowed hard. "If they don't come back ... well, I suppose at that point we're all screwed, so we'll just hope it doesn't come to that."

Cat's green eyes watered. "I wish I could help you guys more."

"It's important that you stay safe. If something does happen to us, we'll need you to get word to the others." Becca hugged Cat, then the two of us raced to our rooms to throw on clothes. Two minutes later, she was inserting a knife into one boot and handing me one of my own. "You have your phone?"

"Yeah." Adrenaline burned in my veins. "Knight, you ready?"

Our ghostly protector prowled to the door, his head low and ears back. I'd only ever seen the friendly side of my companion. With his size, even playful Knight was a bit intimidating. Knight on the hunt was a terrifying sight to behold.

He led us out into the night, and when we reached the building I'd seen the man enter, he snapped at Rebecca when she reached for the main door. He sniffed the air, then dropped his head low. With a menacing growl reminiscent of the day before, he traced into the lobby and stalked into the shadows down a dark hallway.

"I think he wants us to stay out here," Becca said quietly.

I nodded, sensing the same. Knight was exceptionally handy to have around, and I wondered what else he was capable of. I'd have to thank Merlin for sending him to us ... if I lived long enough to see him again.

We texted Cat an update and did our best to wait

patiently. It was just after ten at night, so the area was still populated with the occasional person passing by. The club was the primary draw to the area after dark, but notices had been posted on social media announcing that the Huntsman was closed this weekend for "renovations."

Knight was gone for ten eternal minutes before he finally reappeared inside the lobby. He gave us a look, then turned as if to signal for us to follow. Becca texted Cat again to ensure she was kept in the loop, then used her magic to unlock the door. The old building housed various offices for small businesses, with a directory next to the elevator listing its occupants. While the Huntsman building had been renovated from the ground up, others in the area like this one were hanging onto their last days of service like a geriatric gardener desperate for new knees. I wasn't sure when it had been built, but it was long, long ago.

When Knight turned into a dark stairwell, we flicked on a light and followed him down into the basement. My stomach roiled with the sense of familiarity for my surroundings. Would Knight calmly lead us down here if Casek lay at the bottom dead or dying?

Please, God. No.

The stairs opened into the main room, which was currently being used for storage. Knight loped across the space to the back wall containing a single door. I hurried to catch up, my hand shaking as I reached for the knob. It was pitch black inside, the air smelling faintly of gas. The single bulb light fixture overhead illuminated a large boiler to one side, and on the other sat the subject of my vision. Everything was as I'd seen it. Exactly the same, except the person lifeless in the chair wasn't Casek.

My breath caught on a silent sob.

I brought my hand to my lips in an attempt to contain the overwhelming relief. Becca rushed forward to check the young woman for a pulse, then turned back to me grimly. We were too late. The woman was close to our age. Her brown eyes were wide with terror, cast unseeing at the ceiling. I knew I should be horrified, and I was to some extent, but my relief overrode everything else.

Becca handed me her phone. "You text Cat. I'm going to try Lochlan again."

I did as I was told, and while she was still preoccupied, I studied the poor lifeless woman. An eerie sense of unease slithered down my spine. Everything about this reminded me of the woman from Casek's memory—the dark basement room, the auburn waving hair, the way she was shackled to a wooden chair. Could it have been a coincidence?

Something told me it would be unwise to make such an assumption.

I wasn't sure what was going on, but it felt wrong. Why had my vision been off? Was Casek's appearance simply a product of my inexperience, or was there more to it?

"I got through!" Becca called, drawing me from my thoughts. "The guys are fine and on their way. The magic from the ceremony had kept me from contacting him sooner. He said it should be a couple of hours, though, between traveling to the portal and the time difference."

We both peered over at the woman in the chair.

"We can't just leave her," I said.

Becca sighed heavily. "No, we can't. Let Cat know she can call it a night, and we'll wait in the lobby for the guys."

We left the lights on and headed upstairs. With our backs to the far wall of the lobby, we sat on the floor, Knight stationed between us and the door. We talked for a while and messed on our phones to keep ourselves awake. After the crash of adrenaline, sleep was a seductive mistress. But just as Lochlan had said, two hours later, he and Casek, along with several others, appeared at the building's entrance. Each of their brutal expressions was more frightening than the last. Casek didn't have to say a word for me to know he was a tightly wound ball of fury.

As soon as we explained about the woman in the basement, Lochlan barked orders for the others to handle the situation while he and Casek took us home. "We can discuss what exactly happened later once we've all had some rest." His voice bore a ragged edge, making me wonder just how long they'd been awake.

Shoving aside our exhaustion, we all hurried down the street back to the haven of the Huntsman.

Once we reached the elevator, Lochlan pushed the button for the fifth floor where he and Casek had their apartments. I moved to press the button for my floor when Casek's hand shot out and stopped me. He didn't say a word, just guided my hand back to my side and looked back at the closing doors.

"Cat's still at my apartment," I said uneasily.

"Text her," he said in a clipped tone. "Tell her you won't be back until tomorrow."

Okaaay.

We all exited on the fifth floor, Casek corralling me toward his apartment. Tension mounted with each step we took. Once we were alone, I could barely breathe from the oppressive suspense.

The thundering darkness in his apartment made me feel like I'd fallen deep into a volcano on the verge of erupting.

"You told me you wouldn't leave the building. You *promised*," he finally said through barely controlled fury, gouging a dagger deep into my chest. He felt betrayed, and I hated that my actions had brought that about. I felt justified in my decision, but I also didn't want to have hurt him.

"I had to. You don't understand—"

"*What?*" he boomed, all his frustration pouring out. "What could possibly justify putting yourself in that kind of danger?"

His anger rattled my chest, stealing the air from my lungs.

My chin quivered as emotions overwhelmed me.

"You," I finally whispered. "I saw you in that chair. You being taken and tortured. I saw it all, and it broke me."

He stilled, the severity of my pain crashing into him.

I closed my burning eyes and shook my head slowly. "We couldn't get ahold of Lochlan, and I had no way of knowing. I had to go. I had to make sure it wasn't real." Cracked and bleeding, my heart finally revealed the full extent of its injuries. I had to wrap my arms around my middle to keep my insides from spilling onto the floor at my feet.

"*Jesus.*" The rumbling curse was the only warning I had

before I was engulfed in his embrace. One hand cradled my head against his chest and the other held me tight at my back. "You had me so fucking scared."

"I'm sorry." I wrapped my hands around his middle, wishing I could bottle the feeling of comfort he provided and hoard it away for safekeeping.

He breathed deep, my body moving with the motion like a boat coasting over a wave.

I pulled back once I had calmed down. The loss of his touch left me feeling hopelessly adrift, but I forced myself to stay strong because I had something important to say. "When I saw you being taken in the vision, I had no choice but to stand and watch. You were crippled with pain—it was … it was horrific. And I could do nothing but watch. The helplessness I felt was something I thought I'd never feel again. You see, my dad was an alcoholic—*is* an alcoholic. He's technically dry now, but the label stays.

"He was one of those men who always seemed so charismatic to everyone, but once the alcohol had kicked in, he was a different person at home. A horribly mean drunk. I watched my mother take every form of verbal abuse under the sun. He never struck her, but he didn't have to. He broke her spirit instead. I lived in a nightmare, and there was no way out. Mom wasn't strong enough to leave, and I was only a child. All those years, I swore I'd never rely on a man like that and leave myself so vulnerable. I didn't want to have to rely on anyone. Ever. That was why the promise of magic has been so alluring. Magic is power, and power is control."

I paused and wiped at the tear that had trickled down my cheek.

"I know for someone who's lived for centuries, the months it's taken for me to gain access to my magic might have felt like nothing. But to me, it's been an eternity because it's not just magic; it's a promise. An assurance that I'll never feel that helpless again. I know it's not fool-proof, but it's so much more than I had before. Please, I'm begging you. Teach me. Not just for me, but for these women. Help me learn my magic so we can catch this monster and keep me from ever feeling so helpless again."

I shed every barrier I had in those minutes and lay myself bare. No bravado or pretense. No secrets or manip-ulations. I exposed the very worst of my scars and prayed he saw the strength they represented.

Casek listened patiently, giving me his undivided attention. He waited until the last drips of my torrent of words had fallen before cupping his hands on either side of my face. In the room's dim lighting, his turbulent green gaze had darkened to the unfathomable depths of one of Ireland's deepest Lochs. That gaze raked over my face, leaving nothing untouched by the heat of his stare. Then, once he'd consumed his fill, he pressed his lips to mine.

His kiss was a bandage to my gaping wound.

He swathed me in the comfort of his touch, each reverent glide of his tongue a silent vow. He'd heard me, and he understood. And above all, he wanted to do what-ever he could to end my suffering.

My hands found his shoulders as he lifted me into his arms and walked us to his bedroom. He set me on my feet next to the bed and then undressed us unhurriedly, taking his time to relish the reveal of each inch of my body. Nothing about what we were about to do remotely resembled the previous times we'd come together. We'd fucked and fed and fought one another. This was different. So very different.

This ripple in time that we'd fallen into tasted of sacramental wine—rich, ardent, and devout.

I was instantly addicted and terrified at the same time. What did it mean? Where would we go from here? What if I put Casek on a pedestal he could never live up to?

I had no answers except that only time would tell because I couldn't steal this perfection from myself any more than I could pull a curtain of clouds across an empty sky.

Once each stitch of clothing had been removed, Casek laid me down on the bed and covered my body with his. While his gaze was locked with mine, erotic pulses of warmth began to radiate from my core to my breasts and down to the tips of my fingers and toes.

I gasped and arched, savoring the heady sensation. Casek hadn't used magic in an intimate way on me before, that I knew of, but I had no doubt he was doing that now. His powers strummed my body, making it sing. He knew exactly how much to use without overloading me with sensation. Pulses and sparks of pleasure primed my body more thoroughly than any hands, mouth, or toy could have.

Once I was breathless and writhing, he urged my gaze back to his and pressed himself deep inside me. I was so aroused that he had no trouble sliding it in to the hilt, but he remained still once he did to give my body time to adjust. And I needed it. He felt even larger than before if that was even possible.

"That's my good girl," he murmured close to my ear. "Let me all the way in."

I forced my inner muscles to relax and was rewarded when he groaned at the sensation. Slowly, he began to thrust inside me. I spread my knees wide and clutched his shoulders, wanting him to stay close. I needed him close because with Casek inside me, I felt as though the world could crumble, and I'd still manage to get back on my feet.

His lips found mine again while his thrusts continued. And the second his tongue grazed mine, I felt the exact same velvet touch magically caress my swollen bundle of nerves at my center.

"Oh, *God*!" I cried. "It's too much. I'll come too soon."

"No such thing, sweet girl. It just means another one is to follow."

Rather than slow down, he increased his tempo and swirled that magical invisible tongue around my clit, sending my body plummeting into an abyss of pleasure.

He slowed only briefly to allow me to regroup, then started the process again. He conducted an orchestral explosion three times inside me before he gave himself over to the intoxicating pull of release. As the waves of pleasure crashed and ebbed, his face came to rest deep in the hollow of my neck. His heavy breaths warmed my skin while creeping uncertainty chilled me on the inside.

A part of me wanted to clutch him close and refuse to let go, but I would have never allowed myself to be that person. No matter how the rest of our night unfolded, I would survive, with or without him.

Casek eventually rolled to his side and pulled the covers over us before hoisting my back into his front, his heavy arm draped over my middle. Stillness settled over the darkened room.

"I can go back to my place if you'd prefer," I said quietly, unsure what he was thinking. I didn't want him to think I was clingy or unable to manage on my own.

His arm tightened. "Get some sleep, Ash. Everything else can wait."

The sound of my nickname on his lips silenced me. I nodded, and once my mind settled, the overwhelming security of having Casek wrapped around me carried me easily into a deep, dreamless sleep.

CHAPTER
THIRTEEN

CASEK

I lay awake long after Ashley's breathing became slow and steady. I was exhausted and knew I should sleep, but my racing thoughts wouldn't allow it.

From the minute I laid eyes on Ashley, I'd known she was brash and practically fearless. It was easy to see in the way she approached the world with unfettered confidence. But I'd been mistaken about the reason for her boldness. I'd assumed she was simply too young and sheltered to know any better.

I'd been such a fucking idiot.

Her courage wasn't born out of naivete; it was forged out of necessity. And her relentless pursuit of power had nothing to do with vanity and everything to do with survival, or at least, her perception of what she needed in order to survive the harsh realities of this world.

Ashley was a warrior.

She'd been through hell as a child. It was no wonder she'd been so quick to lash out at me after our first encounter at the club. She'd learned to keep men at a distance before they ever had a chance to harm her, and I'd measured up to every one of her meager expectations.

Disgust and reproach burned in my chest.

Good, you've earned it. Own the consequences of your actions.

I considered leaving because I didn't feel like I deserved the comfort of her body pressed against mine, but I would have only harmed her further by disappearing. No other man in her past had been there for her, and I suddenly sensed a conviction deep inside me to be the first.

What did that mean for her magic? Could I be there for her and still keep her magic bound? She might have thought magic was the answer, but her powers would only attract more danger. Wouldn't I be giving her exactly what she wanted by keeping her safe? By protecting her rather than abandoning her to fend for herself?

Considering she'd still had a vision, I had to ask myself whether the binding spell was even working. If she could still access her magic, even if involuntarily, what else might she be capable of doing?

The answers frightened me.

Knowing I'd need to be strong if I was going to keep her safe, I fed my magic while we were together. Too much was going on to risk being weak. Had Ashley's powers not been the source of her danger, I would have said the same for her as well, but that wasn't the case. I would have to be strong enough for us both.

As I wrestled with my thoughts, sleep evaded me until well after sunrise. In fact, I'd been so tired that I didn't hear Ashley slip from my apartment. I woke alone, disappointment my only companion.

Less than an hour later, I was showered and sitting across from Lochlan at his desk. He handed over photos of the scene from the night before. The images crystalized the blood in my veins. If the woman's face hadn't been visible, it could have been Raisa. Everything about the scene looked so similar—too similar.

"This is personal," I said half to myself.

"That would certainly explain the proximity. We've already suspected something was off by the fact that the Gorda hasn't fled. What about this scene gives you that impression?" Lochlan spoke with a calm detachment that I was struggling to maintain.

Setting the photos on the desk, I met his cold stare. "It's Raisa. That woman was selected and positioned specifically to remind me of Raisa."

The lift of his chin was his only reaction. "We need to talk to Ashley and have her describe everything she can about her vision. Maybe there's a clue hidden somewhere that we could use to find this bastard."

"I'm not sure how accurately we can rely on her. She told me last night it was me she saw in the vision. That I'd been the one dead in the chair. It's likely the newness of her power has affected her mind's ability to interpret the visions." That was total bullshit, but I wanted to make sure he knew she was compromised without telling him what I'd done. It was more likely that the binding spell had muddled the vision. As far as I knew, Seers were never wrong.

"Still, I'll send for her to come up and walk us through exactly what she saw." He placed a quick call to Ashley, who answered and agreed to come right up.

Minutes later, she joined us in the office, her eyes only flitting to mine briefly. We would have to address her attempts to push me away, but now wasn't the time. I remained quiet as she walked us through everything she'd seen, including the shocking revelation that Durin had been my captor in her vision.

"It's possible Guin had a hand in this, but then again, she saw me as the victim," I noted as we debated the implications. "Maybe her mind had inserted Durin and I merely because we'd been in a confrontation together just the day before."

"We can't rule out either scenario," Lochlan murmured, his hands steepled together as he always did when he was deep in thought. "Is there anything else you can remember about what you saw?"

"I don't think so," Ashley said apologetically. "But if something comes to mind, I'll let you know immediately."

He nodded. "Thanks for coming up on short notice."

"Of course." She shot him a thin smile as she stood, hardly sparing me a glance. I had to grip the wooden arm of the chair to keep from yanking her back into the room and demanding a kiss.

"You need to handle that?" Lochlan asked as soon as she was out of earshot. His question danced with amusement.

"It can wait." Unfortunately. "We should check out the scene ourselves while the trail is still fresh."

He sobered then stood, and I led us out into the empty club and to the elevators. We spent a couple of hours at the office building two blocks down, ensuring no clue had been missed. Tracking spells had already been performed, but we repeated them to be safe. Aside from Ashley's vision and the obvious reference to Raisa's death, we were no closer to finding the guy than we had been after the first killing months ago.

When we finished, Lochlan decided to stop by the church portal to see if any other clues pointed to Guin's involvement. I went back to the Huntsman with plans to have a cigarette on my balcony but found an unexpected visitor waiting outside.

"Parisa," I said coolly. "What are you doing here?"

"Is that any way to greet me, Caz? Your tone certainly wasn't so frigid when you were in Avalon a few months ago." Parisa was unquestionably beautiful. With sandy-blond hair that glinted in the sunlight and warm brown eyes, she was the perfect Venus Flytrap—all honey and nectar until her teeth clamped shut. For years, she'd been my go-to when I visited Faery. Then I realized that our expectations of the arrangement were no longer aligned. When I'd gone to Faery months earlier on Lochlan's errand to locate a man in the Shadow Lands, I'd run into her at the palace and made the mistake of using her to charge my magic. It appeared that mistake was back to bite me.

"Why are you here, Parisa? Have you been helping

Guin orchestrate the Fear Gorda attacks?" I asked, cutting to the chase.

Parisa was one of the queen's Valkyrie guard, though she'd forgone her usual plated armor in preference of tightly fitted jeans and a black top that drifted off one shoulder. She could have been trying to rekindle things, but it was equally as likely that Guin had sent her to use me for information.

"Don't be absurd. What would I be doing associating with a Gorda?" She slunk forward, her hand teasing at the buttons on my shirt.

"I hear Guin has her sights set on Ashley. Scaring her out of her home might be a good way to get her to consider other living arrangements, maybe even a different allegiance. That was the message Durin sent only days ago."

"Surely, you know me better. If I want something, I take it. I'd be much more direct if I wanted to persuade your pet to serve Guin."

"Then what are you doing here?"

"Just keeping an eye on things. It seems you have a lot going on over here, and the queen simply wanted to be apprised of any new developments."

"No, what are *you* doing here? I find it rather interesting that of all her guard, she happened to choose you for this task after I sent Durin home with his tail tucked."

She gave a small shrug. "Things were quiet, and I needed a change of scenery. Our little reunion reminded me just how good we were together, so when the opportunity arose, I volunteered." She reached out her hand and caressed my arm, peering up at me through her thick lashes. "I missed you—want me to show you how much?"

Her golden hair fell in waves down her back, and her perfectly proportioned Fae features made her exceptionally attractive, but I found all that perfection lacking. When I hadn't cared what was underneath, the outer layer was sufficient. Now, I couldn't avoid seeing how the shallow depths beneath marred the surface irrevocably.

I pulled my arm out of her grasp and gripped her arms firmly, tight enough to get my point across but not leave a mark. "You had no business coming here. I told you my visit was a one-time thing, so you get this through your head. We. Are. Done. You may have committed to staying in Belfast, but you better stay the hell away from me, and we'll have serious problems if I hear about you getting anywhere near Ashley. This is your one and only warning." My words were clipped in an obvious threat, but I could see a light of defiance enter her eyes. Not only was she not going to walk away but she also saw the situation as a challenge.

Fucking hell.

I couldn't catch a single break. Things were strained enough with Ashley. Somehow, I knew Parisa would only make them more difficult. My only shot at avoiding a catastrophe was to be up front with Ashley about my past with Parisa and her reasons for coming here. I was dreading the conversation, but there was no way around it.

CHAPTER

FOURTEEN

T HE ONLY THING THAT COMES CLOSE TO THE MISERY OF helplessness is swimming in a sea of uncertainty. And I was smack in the middle of the Pacific without so much as a life jacket. That was the reason I'd crept from Casek's bed the second I'd woken. It was also why I could hardly meet his gaze in Lochlan's office. I was totally out of my depth, and I knew it.

I'd never opened up to a man the way I'd done with Caz. Hell, I'd never even been quite so open to Rebecca about my past. She knew about my dad, but I hadn't explained things the same way. I felt like I'd bared my soul, and now I was scrambling to find a boulder to hide under.

I was officially a chickenshit. So sue me.

When I got back to my apartment, I collapsed onto the couch and stared at the ceiling with plans of spending the rest of my day counting speckled bumps of texture.

It was better than facing everything else going on in my life.

However, I'd only made it to twenty-five when my phone rang. My father was calling. That made twice in just over a week, which was much more frequent than normal.

I heaved a weary sigh and answered. "Hey, Dad."

"Hey, Ash! What are you up to?"

"Not much at the moment. How are things there?"

"I'm glad I caught you at a good time because there is here. Don't get mad, but I'm downstairs. I'd love to come up and see you." His voice was buoyant with hopeful trep-idation.

I had to roll his words around in my brain to grasp what he was saying. "Wait, you're *here*?" I jumped up and ran to a window that faced the front of the building. My dad stood outside the Huntsman four floors below with his phone to his ear.

He looked up and waved. "I am. I didn't tell you because I knew you'd probably tell me not to come, but I couldn't wait any longer. It doesn't matter how little time you have; I'll take whatever I can get while I'm here."

I stepped back out of view but continued staring blankly at the building across the way. Dad was here. In Belfast.

Shock was a thick soupy fog that muddled my thoughts.

"Ash? You still there?"

"Yeah. Uh, yeah, I'm here. I'll be down in a second." I hung up and numbly made my way to the lobby. I couldn't believe he'd flown to Ireland without warning. Well, mostly. His previous call a week ago didn't exactly count. It was a small mercy he'd called from downstairs and not appeared at my apartment door. At least I had a handful of minutes to compose myself.

"Hey, Dad," I greeted with lackluster enthusiasm when I stepped outside. "This was awfully unexpected." I waved awkwardly, keeping several feet of distance between us. I'd stopped hugging my dad long ago. Even after he got sober, I rarely went near him. It was easier to maintain my emotional barrier with a physical one as well.

He had the decency to look mildly embarrassed. "I know, and I'm sorry. But it sure is great to see you."

I wished I could say the same. Seeing him always brought back memories, and never the good ones.

So fuckin' lazy. Did you even get your fat ass off the couch today while I worked?

Are you telling me how to do my job? You've never even worked a day in your pathetic life. What makes you think you know anything?

This chicken tastes like shit. I don't even know why I come home sometimes.

I could still hear the exact way his words slurred when he spoke. I had to shake my head to keep myself in the present.

"When did you get in?" He didn't have any bags with him, so I had to assume he'd checked into a hotel before coming here.

"This morning. It's already been a long day for me, but I wanted to stop by before I crashed."

"Yeah, okay. Why don't you come up for a few? You can see my place."

His answering smile could have summoned the sun through the thick Irish clouds. "That sounds great."

I led him upstairs to my apartment, relieved when we didn't run into anyone on the way. I wasn't sure how I felt about him meeting my friends.

"Here it is." I held open the door with a thin smile. "You want a bottle of water? I'd offer you something to eat, but I'm terrible about keeping food on hand."

"Water would be great, thanks." He peered around my living area, his eyes bright. "Ashley, this is beautiful. It's so good to know you're doing so well."

I always tried not to let my father's words bear any meaning, but I couldn't ward off a brief swell of pride. "Things are good here. I'm really glad I came." I sat down, handing Dad a water as he joined me on the sofa.

His entire body froze when he spotted Knight on the loveseat. "You got a dog?"

I choked on a laugh. "Yeah, he's a recent addition."

"He's enormous." Dad's eyebrows chased his receding hairline.

"His name is Knight, and he's a softy." Mostly.

Dad's gaze drifted from Knight to the photos of Becca and me framed on a shelf. When his eyes eventually returned to me, they were glassy and red. "I feel like I hardly know you anymore." His voice was tortured, and it did uncomfortable things to my insides. "Ash, I haven't tried to push you for a relationship since recovery because I know ... I know how badly I hurt you. There's nothing I can do that will ever be enough to make up for that. But after we got that phone call. When your mother and I thought we'd lost you—" His words faltered on a shuddered breath. "I realized I couldn't waste the second chance I'd been given. We don't have to be the perfect father-daughter, but I'll hate myself even more if I don't try to at least show you what you mean to me. Show you how sorry I am."

My lungs contracted in an effort for oxygen.

I couldn't breathe, and I certainly didn't know what to say. Dad had always respected my wishes and given me space. He'd never pushed me, and he'd certainly never been so brutally honest about how he felt. His confession summoned emotions that were new and confusing.

"The things you said..." The words tumbled weakly from my lips.

Dad knew what I was referencing. I hadn't meant his most recent plea. I was talking about all the alcohol-infused vitriol he'd spewed at us through the years.

His gaze fell to his hands. "I would say it was the alcohol and not me, but I take full responsibility. I was a sick man. The fact that I would treat the two women I loved most in the world with such horrific disrespect and contempt—it's unforgivable. That's why I've never asked for your forgiveness. I'm not asking now. What I want you to know is that I'm not that man anymore—he's buried and gone—and I'd be forever grateful if you'd give *this* man a chance to prove himself." His hand pressed firmly over his heart.

Was this how it happened? Was this how he'd kept my mom at his side all those years?

It's been five years, Ash. How long does he have to suffer before you'll give him a chance?

Shit. *Shitshitshit.*

I felt like I stood at the top of a skyscraper with someone trying to convince me to step off—that an invisible acrylic floor would catch me. Fear screamed at me to keep my feet safely planted, but what if I didn't? What if I joined the others walking high above the city, happily reveling at the feel or soaring in the sky?

I might fall, but I might not.

You don't have to jump. What if you edged, just a toe at a time?

Getting to know the man I called my father wouldn't be the end of the world. Maybe I could test the waters and just see how it felt.

I lifted my wary gaze, teeth gnawing at my bottom lip. "Okay," I offered quietly.

"Okay?" His wide-open features were stark with disbelief. "Really?"

I nodded.

Dad grinned, sucking in a deep, shaky breath. "Okay," he breathed, wiggling in his seat as if he wanted to pull me into a hug. I was glad he didn't. This was going to take some adjustment.

"So, how long are you in town?" I asked, edging us back to solid ground.

He told me his plans for the week of his stay and then asked me about my schedule. The discussion transitioned smoothly to a short description of my life in Belfast. I told him about the guys we'd befriended who owned the club upstairs—keeping anything Fae related a secret—and how Rebecca was moving in with one of them. I told him about work and the self-defense training I'd been doing and the tourist spots I'd hit since arriving. Dad listened raptly, asking all the right questions and answering the few I posed to him. The conversation was ... good. Surprisingly so.

Before he left, we decided to meet for dinner the next night, then stop in at the club briefly just so he could see it in action and meet the others. It made me wary to take him anywhere near a bar, but he assured me he wasn't remotely tempted. I figured it was as good a test of faith as any.

Once I was alone again, I texted Becca, anxious to tell her what had happened.

Me: You at Lochlan's?

Becca: No, had to take a quick trip out of the city. Be home later.

Me: What are you doing out of the city?

Becca: Nothing important.

Okaaay. It seemed like sticking close to home when a Fear Gorda was on the loose would be a good idea, but what did I know?

Me: Anyone with you?

Becca: No, I'll be back around dinner.

I'd thought Becca's strange behavior was a result of her wanting to move in with Lochlan, but this made me wonder if there wasn't something else going on. Why the hell was she out of the city alone?

Me: Come visit when you get in.

Becca: Will do!

I rolled my eyes and tossed my phone on the sofa. Not

only did her impromptu trip make me uneasy but it also prevented me from talking to her about my dad. This was an in-person conversation, so it would have to wait. However, being the external processor that I was, I needed to talk through everything aloud in order to settle this whirlpool of thoughts and emotions inside me.

I texted Cat and got no response, so I moved on to plan C. I had to be a bit more cryptic with Elle, but it would be better than nothing. "Come on, Knight. Let's grab some coffee and lunch."

I was able to snag Elle to talk for a bit, but she couldn't get away for long because of the lingering lunch rush. It would have felt awkward telling someone I hardly knew about my alcoholic father, so I kept things nice and vague. I explained that my dad had been crap growing up but was looking for a second chance. Walking through what had happened, even in a rudimentary fashion, was still helpful. She encouraged me to spend time with him before I made any decisions. I was fairly certain that's what Becca would have said as well.

Feeling somewhat reassured, I went back home and spent the next few hours working. I received a text from Casek midway through.

We're training tonight.

Anticipation and apprehension combined to make a nauseating cocktail in my stomach. What would he say? How would he act? He'd seemed as though nothing had changed between us while we were in Lochlan's office, but we'd had an audience. Would it be different once we were alone?

Three hours later, I had my answer.

Casek's eyes pinned me in place the second I walked into the gym. He stared but didn't speak until he sauntered closer. "Can't say I was very happy about waking up alone."

"I was worried I'd overstay my welcome. I don't normally share the kinds of things I shared with you last night, and all of it made me uneasy. I didn't want you to feel like you were obligated or anything."

"I ever give you the impression I'd let someone make me feel obligated?"

I sucked my lips between my teeth and shook my head.

"Right. Next time you start feeling overwhelmed, wake me up and tell me." He arched a brow.

Next time? That implied not only that we'd have sex again but that we'd also be *sleeping* together.

Relief spread outward from my chest like warm molasses. "Okay."

"Good, now come sit over here on the mat and tell me about your father." He walked to the mat without waiting for me, but I stood transfixed as I watched his retreating form.

He wanted to hear more about my dad? I'd been caught off guard so many times in a row lately that I was beginning to feel like someone had swapped me with an Ashley from an alternate universe. Everything about this life was strange and unfamiliar.

"Ash," he said in warning, kicking me into gear. How

could I not? The use of my nickname for the second time in so many days hooked in my ears and wouldn't let go.

I hurried to the mat and sat. He occupied a bench a few feet away from me, eyes signaling that he was waiting.

"It's funny you should ask about him," I started. "He actually showed up today unannounced."

An eerie chill wafted over from Casek's location. Not just the emotion; the air literally dropped in temperature. "Your father's here?"

"Yes, but I think it's okay," I said hurriedly, hoping to settle him. "We talked, and I think his visit may be a good thing." I continued, explaining how Dad had gotten sober years earlier and was hoping for a second chance. "I adored my dad when I was little. He didn't develop a problem until I was about twelve, though it may be that he just hid it until then. I think it was the fact that he wasn't always a monster that's made me so reluctant to give him another shot. I know how easy it is to adore him and how heartbreaking it can be to lose him. At first, his recovery was so new that I felt I had good reason to be wary, but it's been five years. I think maybe it's time. If he truly has changed, maybe a do-over is exactly what both of us need."

Casek peered at me warily. "He's only here for a week?"

"Yeah."

He grunted, making me smile. Protective Casek was kind of adorable.

"I'll be fine, I promise. I'm pretty good at protecting myself at this point," I said softly.

"I've noticed." He was quiet for several beats, his eyes studying me. "We're not all like that, you know."

"I know," I assured him softly.

"I don't want you to just know it. I want you to believe it. To see me and be certain that I am not him. I have my own issues that kept me from handling things the way I should have, but I'm not making that mistake again. I'm going to start being up front with you, and I expect the same in return." He looked at me expectantly until I gave him a nod. "A woman arrived today at the Huntsman. Her name is Parisa."

I swallowed hard, wondering where this was going.

"She's one of the queen's guards, but I also have somewhat of a past with her. Nothing serious, but she might imply otherwise. The important part is that it was in the past, and I want you to understand that. I don't know how long she'll be around. Possibly days or even weeks. It's impossible to tell. I don't even know why she's here. She claims Guin sent her to learn about you, but I'm concerned there might be more."

"I get why you'd want to warn me about Guin, but why the rest? Why are you telling me this?"

"Because I know it's easy for you to assume the worst —you've been given good reason. I'd rather give you all the details myself so you have no reason to doubt me. Parisa means nothing to me, and I want you to believe that."

And me? Do I mean something to you?

The possible answers terrified me too much for the question to form on my lips.

"Is she dangerous?" I asked instead.

"Unquestionably."

I took a controlled breath, deep and even, pleased to find that the addition of yet another enemy had only a marginal effect on me. "I suppose it's a good idea to train then."

Casek's lips twisted in a wolfish grin. "Let's begin."

FIFTEEN

ASHLEY

Dinner with my father flowed seamlessly. He was a bit taken aback when I showed up with Knight at my side but took it in stride. What he didn't know was that we were also being watched by Casek. While it was still early in the evening, night was the Gorda's preferred feeding time, and Caz wasn't willing to send me out alone. I think he was also being overly cautious about my dad.

I liked to think of myself as capable and independent, but I couldn't deny that I appreciated being the recipient of his protective instincts.

Casek waited until we entered the club to approach, maintaining an austere façade when he did. "Ashley, I see you've brought a guest." He positioned himself to my side but just enough behind me that he could rest his hand possessively at the nape of my neck.

Not one to feel pressure to look a certain way, he often

arrived at the club in casual jeans and T-shirts—no patterns or graphics—he was a no-nonsense type of guy. However, tonight he'd seen fit to don a perfectly tailored suit. All black. Shirt and tie included. It was striking, and his message of power was unmistakable.

Heat radiated across my cheeks. "Uh, yeah. Casek, this is my dad, Steven Moore."

The two shook hands, my dad looking a bit over-whelmed.

I didn't blame him. Casek had that effect on people.

"It's a pleasure," Dad said, smiling.

Casek only nodded. "Why don't you two have a seat?" He motioned to a reserved booth on the back wall as far from the bar as possible. I doubted it was a coin-cidence.

The club nightlife was just warming up, so we didn't have to weave through people or worry about getting separated. Dad asked Casek to join us, and I was pleased when he agreed. Minutes later, Rebecca and Lochlan appeared, squeezing into the booth and rounding out our party.

"It's lovely to see you again, Rebecca." Dad grinned as he scooted to make room. "I think the last time was college graduation."

"I think you're right. I'm glad you were able to come all the way over for a visit."

A server appeared, smiling brightly, and nodded when Casek instructed her to bring a round of club sodas.

Dad gave a thin smile. "You really don't have to do that. Get what you want."

I felt a pang of embarrassment for him. It couldn't be

easy knowing everyone around you knew that you were an addict.

"Actually, I do have to do that. Ensuring we all have a good time tonight is a hell of a lot more important than a drink."

Dad smiled appreciatively, and I found my hand sliding under the table to squeeze Casek's hand beside me. The gesture was more intimate and familiar than I was used to giving a man. Flirting was easy and sex was no problem, but an earnest token of my appreciation felt foreign.

When I tried to pull away, his grip held firm, refusing to set me free. Without making a show of it, he brought his other hand down and clasped my hand between his two, swaddling me in reassurance.

The fluttering butterflies that filled my chest were so distracting I lost track of the conversation.

We sipped our virgin drinks over the next hour and talked about a broad spectrum of topics. When Liam appeared, Rebecca and Lochlan excused themselves, giving him room at the table to join us. I hadn't expected us to stay so long, but everyone seemed to be having a good time, so I made no move to call it a night. Liam was in the middle of one of his classic stories when he suddenly stilled, then cut his eyes to Casek.

"If you'll excuse us, we're going to have to run and check on something." Liam smiled reassuringly, but my stomach bottomed out. Something was wrong.

"Yeah, we should probably call it a night anyway," I said, scooting over to allow Casek out of the booth.

He gave my hand one last squeeze. "I'll text you when I can."

Nodding, I watched his form disappear into the now crowded room.

"He seems like a good man," Dad said close to my ear over the music.

"Yeah, I think so, too. It's all kind of new, but it's good."

The happiness shining in his eyes was laced with a tinge of bitter regret. "This may sound crazy, but I missed my chance at father-daughter dances. I'd love it if you'd indulge me in a song before we go."

How could I say no?

We'd had such a perfect night, considering our tumultuous past. I didn't care that the music was all wrong. The little girl still buried deep inside me preened at the chance to steal back a piece of my childhood.

"Yeah," I nodded. "We can do that."

We made our way to a corner of the dance floor, which was starting to fill up. Dad held out his hand for mine, then pulled me in as though it was Frank Sinatra rather than EDM blasting over the speakers. He left an appropriate amount of space between us, a smile tugging at the corners of his mouth. The moment was surreal. I was certain it would be etched into my memory banks forever.

When the song came to a close, he twirled me out of his hold, making me giggle.

"This has been a dream, Ashley. Thank you."

I grinned and leaned in to make sure he heard my reply. "I'm glad you came, Dad." I opened my mouth to suggest we headed to the elevator when a horror-movie-style scream rang out over the music.

We both stilled, looking around to see what had happened. Several others craned their necks to look over the crowd, but many of the inebriated guests continued dancing and mingling as if nothing had happened. I started to think it had been a fluke when more screams sounded, this time from the back hallway that led to the offices.

People collided in an intoxicated chaos as they surged away from the back of the room. Dad yanked me toward our table out of the fray. We watched in horror as one girl stumbled to her knees and was trampled by the crowd pushing past her. I started to go help her but froze when I caught sight of what had the mob on the run.

A large black dog with glowing red eyes snarled and gnashed its sharp teeth at the terrified individuals nearest him. The mass of people was too thick to exit the area, so instead, they pressed as close as they could get to those in front of them.

The music suddenly disappeared, but the confused cries wailed on. Hearing them without the music was even more terrifying.

For a suspended second, everyone seemed to still, unsure what was wrong or what to do. Even the dog held motionless.

Like a gunshot going off at the start of a race, someone hollered near the club entrance for people to evacuate down a stairwell. The room instantly burst into frenzied action, but Dad and I made no move to enter the fray. We were already near the back of the crowd and had a better chance of escaping safely down the back hallway exit if we could get behind the dog.

The woman who had been forced to the floor scrambled to stand, seizing the dog's attention. Like lightning, his jaw clamped tightly around her throat, throwing her to the ground while the crowd screamed with hysteria. I couldn't take my eyes from the grotesque scene unfolding before me. The woman's arms feebly batted at the dog as blood pooled beneath her.

Dad and I clung to one another, speechless, unable to turn away.

As if the nightmare hadn't been bad enough, a second dog prowled out from the back hallway, blocking our escape.

Their bestial bodies were broad and rippled with muscle coated in sleek black fur. They weren't as tall as Knight, but they were much stockier. Bowling balls with teeth.

Many of the club goers were now filtering out of the room, but plenty were left in the crosshairs. The new arrival slinked around to the other side of the crowd, which was pushing its way toward the front exits. He didn't simply lunge at the first victim in reach. He appeared more interested in hunting his prey, possibly singling out a straggler from the herd.

I spotted Liam shuffling people into the stairwell just before two other Huntsmen with guns raised worked their way around to the flanks of the first dog, who was still grasping the woman. It lifted its head, the woman's body now hanging limp from its jowls, and growled at the Fae hunters. As soon as one of the men had a clear shot, he unloaded what had to be an entire clip into the beast. It staggered backward a few steps before falling to the ground, the woman still clenched in its grip.

I heaved a shaky breath and lowered my face into my hands. Dad pulled me against his chest, then lurched, a strangled cry wrenched from his throat. "*Go*, Ashley. Get out of here."

Horror coated my insides in a suffocating black sludge.

One of the dogs had my father's lower leg clamped tight in his mouth.

More screams sounded from the people closest to me. I jerked my head up as adrenaline and terror shot from my head down to my toes.

No. I refused to let this happen.

Thinking as fast as I could, I grabbed a beer bottle off a table, smashed the bottom off, then lunged at the dog, impaling the jagged glass straight into its eye. The animal reared back with a ferocious roar, releasing my dad. I grabbed him and pulled us back into the booth. The moment we were free, a gun unloaded a hailstorm of bullets into the injured dog.

When the explosive blasts quieted, my eyes flicked from the dying dog over to the shooter ... Casek.

Hardly skipping a beat, he slipped the gun into the back of his pants and rushed toward us. "Were you hurt?" He looked me over, eyes scouring me for signs of blood.

"Not me, just Dad." I scooted us out of the booth, clasping my father's hand to help support him. Blood stained the fabric of his left pant leg and dripped onto the floor. "We need to get him help."

"What the hell were those things?" Dad's words were

growing slurred. Shock and blood loss were on the verge of pulling him under to unconsciousness.

"Rabid dogs," Casek said, then called Liam over, instructing him to get my father medical attention.

"Where are you taking him?" Panic clutched tight around my chest.

"Relax, Ash. We'll get a doctor over here and have him stitched up." He leaned in close to my ear. "Then we'll fix his memories so he'll remember this as a much less traumatic dog bite incident."

"Okay, but don't steal this night from him. Leave the rest."

Casek nodded, then motioned Liam to proceed with my father.

"What were those things?"

"Hell Hounds."

"Are they dead?"

"No, but they will be soon. No point in keeping them alive; they can't tell us how they got in here. One of the guys will finish the job once everyone's out of here."

The last of the crowd was vacating the room. All that was left were the Huntsmen along with the dead woman and several wounded. I forced my eyes away from the mutilated corpse. Her fate could have so easily been my father's. Or mine.

Shock began to set in, and my whole body shook like the legs of a newborn fawn. Casek lifted me in one smooth motion, and I gladly wrapped my arms around his neck.

"Let's get you home," he murmured against my forehead.

I closed my eyes, taking in his spicy scent and

attempting to push out all thoughts of what I'd just witnessed. I considered the club an extension of my home and had expected both to be impenetrable. Not only had my dad nearly been killed, but my absolute confidence in our safety inside the Huntsman had been profoundly shaken.

Casek took me down a back stairwell to my apartment and didn't set me down until we were in the bathroom. I leaned against the vanity as he turned on the shower. Once steam rose over the curtain, he carefully undressed me, reassuring himself that I had no hidden injuries.

He helped me into the warm spray, disappearing only briefly to retrieve my pajamas.

"You don't have to stay. I'm okay."

He leaned his hip against the vanity counter, arms crossed. "Yes. I do." He spoke with absolute authority. He was telling me that he needed to be here to assure himself I was all right. He checked his phone while I soaked, not rushing me. When his gaze did fall on me through the glass shower door, I never felt ogled. The gentle touch of his stare was comforting. Protective.

Once I was finished, he handed me a towel and then stripped to take his own shower. He washed in record time, finishing as I wrapped up my bedtime routine. He dried off and put his briefs back on, then led me to bed. Instead of curling his body around mine, he lay on his back and pulled me into his side. Being close to him was beginning to feel natural. As though I was more at home there in his arms than anywhere else. Home was sanctuary. Home was peace. At least, that's what I'd always wanted my home to be. And here with Caz, I had that.

A single tear slid from the corner of my eye and landed on his chest.

He trailed the backs of his fingers over my arm, his heartbeat strong and steady. "The woman you saw in my memories was my twin sister, Raisa, and she was killed by a Fear Gorda."

CHAPTER
SIXTEEN

Who knows what moves a person to shed their skin in front of another. It certainly wasn't something I expected to do. Not at that moment, anyway. But after all that had happened. After learning the club had been invaded and that Ashley's life was in jeopardy, yet again, the words demanded to be said.

"Raisa and I were as close as any two siblings ever were. I think our bond freaked people out. If I were to guess, I'd say that's why neither of us ever settled down. When we were young, we were inseparable. My father would teach me to spar and wield a sword, and despite my mother's objections, Raisa insisted on participating in the lessons. She possessed a natural gift and excelled at every skill he taught us. As far as I was concerned, the training was merely a step toward taking over my father's role as Lord of our estate. Raisa's aspirations far exceeded mine.

"I tried daily to persuade her to stay with me on the estate and lead a simple life. She could marry and have children. I'd happily give them lands and do whatever I could to keep her close, but she wouldn't be swayed. She insisted her purpose in life was to become an elite soldier in the queen's guard. The Valkyrie had not yet been formed. At the time, the elite guard consisted primarily of men, but there was no prohibition against women. Perhaps because magic could equalize a man and a woman's strength, the division between the sexes had never been as strong among the Fae as with humans.

"I knew how desperately she wanted to enlist, so when the time came, I joined along with her. There was no way I could have let her go off alone. Over the years, we became accomplished warriors, and our unique twin abilities garnered us the favor of the queen. We became her most prized assassins. Pregnancies don't come as easily to Fae as they do humans, and twins are even more rare. Our ability to communicate with each other and our deadly combination of skills made us unstoppable.

"When The Great War began, we were ordered to participate in a number of dangerous missions. Always together. Until the queen insisted that we were needed on two fronts and would need be to split up. I refused up until the night before I was supposed to leave. Raisa came to me and pleaded, saying that if we both executed our missions, we could end the war, and so many lives would be saved. I could never say no to her.

"Raisa went with a small battalion of soldiers on a dangerous mission inside the Unseelie Wilds to infiltrate enemy lines while I went the opposite direction toward the mountains along with a separate battalion. It was one of the handful of times I wasn't with my sister—a decision I will forever regret.

"One of their own, a man who was supposed to be on night-watch duty, slipped away from his post. His absence allowed a host of Unseelie to ambush the camp. They killed all who were inside, some more quickly than others. Raisa was captured and taken to that underground cell. She was held there for two weeks before I could locate her. In that time, she was tortured mercilessly. The only reason it didn't take me longer to find her was because I used blood magic to track down and kill the Unseelie bastards responsible. A clan of Fear Gordas had taken her to their commune—four cabins in the woods, and they had stashed her away in a hole in the ground to feed off like their own personal larder. I killed every last one of them. The risk of using blood magic was high, but my fear of losing her outweighed any possible consequences. The magic helped keep me alive and helped me find where she'd been taken, but I was too late.

"I knew there was no way her battalion would have been so easily defeated had there not been a betrayal from within. I spent years tracking down who had been responsible. During that time, I left the queen's service and followed Arthur after he formed the Hunt. When I finally located the culprit, I was horrified to discover he was also a Huntsman. That man and I were sworn brothers. Our laws state that disputes among members are to be sorted by the Erlking. Arthur was a good leader, but he was also soft when it came to disciplining his men. I didn't trust him to serve out justice as I would see fit, so I took matters into my own hands.

"I'm telling you this because I want you to know who I am—see every black mark on my soul—so that you know what you're getting into. I live my life unapologetically according to my own compass of right and wrong. Lochlan and the others know about the Unseelie I killed to find Raisa, but they don't know how I accomplished it or that I killed a brother as part of that vengeance. What I've done, these things could get me exiled or killed—not only for murdering a brother but for the prohibited use of the worst kind of magic."

Her breaths fell in shaky puffs against my chest as she nodded.

"I'm also telling you so that you understand why ... why it terrifies me that something will happen to you. Every aspect of our world is dangerous, and you're just like her—you race headfirst into danger with blind courage. I couldn't stand to live through that again." I had to stop because my throat had tightened beyond my capacity to speak.

Ashley scooted even further against me, clinging tightly to my chest. "Thank you, Caz. For sharing that with me," she whispered into the dark.

I kissed the top of her head and gave her a squeeze. "Go to sleep, sweet girl."

Within minutes, her body relaxed, and her breathing grew steady and even.

I had no intention of sleeping.

Not yet. I had a decision to make.

No. I'd already made my decision. I just needed to come to terms with it.

I'd felt the switch flip inside me when I'd watched from a distance as Ashley took a broken beer bottle and fended off a Hell Hound. A fucking Hell Hound with her bare hands.

I'd done that. I'd forced her into a position where she couldn't trace to escape. She'd had no tools at her disposal except a makeshift blade and her exceptional courage. For today, it had been enough. Tomorrow? She might not be so lucky.

Lochlan's words about his faith in Rebecca had haunted me ever since we'd spoken. Between that and the close calls we'd had, I knew I'd made the wrong choice. I'd chosen to clip her wings rather than protect her—they weren't the same, though I'd tried to convince myself they were.

I wanted Ashley to have everything she ever wanted. I didn't want her chained and defeated, and I certainly didn't want to live with the fact that I was the man responsible.

I was utterly terrified, yet I knew this was the right thing to do. I had to remove the block on her magic. I had to set her free.

Waiting until I was confident she was deeply asleep, I slipped from the bed and retrieved my wallet from my pants. Inside one of the compartments was a thin band of woven grass. It looked inconspicuous enough if you didn't know what it was. Any Fae would know that one of these circlets was the key to a binding. Often, they were simple spells such as ensuring a gate stayed locked, or a promise was kept. An ordinary spell that normally wouldn't have the power to lock away someone's powers, but this spell was slightly different.

The secret lay in the crusted red blood dried on either end of the grass stalks.

It had been centuries since I'd called on the use of blood magic, but it was still a risk I'd weighed carefully before taking. No other form of magic could accomplish what I'd needed. It had been necessary to protect her ... or so I'd thought.

As it turned out, I'd only fucked things up worse.

Thank the gods the spell could be undone. So as long as the circle remained intact, the spell would hold, but all it took to break the spell was to sever the circle.

With one sharp tug, the binding spell I'd created ceased to exist.

As much as it pained me, I would never be able to keep every danger away from her. The best chance I could give her at life was the ability to defend herself and my arsenal at her side. I would have to hope it was enough. Because if not, the entire world would know my pain.

SEVENTEEN

CASEK

Faery, Year 1 of the Wild Hunt
325 AD on Earth

BELLY TO THE GROUND IN THE KNEE-HIGH GRASSES, I SILENTLY inched closer to the scum I had been following for hours. It was nothing compared to the two years I had spent tracking him and biding my time for this perfect opportunity.

He had deviated from the woods where it had been easier to stalk unnoticed. Making matters more challenging, the Wilds of Faery were perpetually blanketed in an unsettling silence. The creatures that inhabited the dangerous landscape knew better than to draw attention to themselves. There were no chirping or rustling leaves—even the trees kept from swaying in the passing breeze. The slightest sound would announce my presence, and that was not an option.

Tracing to his location would be equally foolish. He would only transport himself away just as quickly as I had appeared. No. Success hinged on stealth.

With the sun setting behind me, I dragged myself bit by bit beneath the cover of the grass. As I neared, the Fae man's back came into view just ahead of me. He wore the ridiculous formal attire of the haughty Seelie Court—what he was doing dressed like an imbecile out in the Wilds was anyone's guess. Despite my years at Court, I had always hated the absurd pomp and circumstance of formal dinners and other inane events. This man obviously did not feel the same. I hoped he liked his burgundy long-tail suit because it was going to be the last thing he ever wore.

That thought put a smile on my face or as much of a smile as I'd managed in the past two years.

The man sat on a boulder, a trail of smoke from a small campfire rising into the cool evening air in front of him.

Even more of a fool than I had believed.

There was nothing more half-witted you could do in the Wilds than light a fire. It was a beacon to every vile creature in the area. In a place where even birds stayed silent, the last thing you wanted to do was become an easy target. I was relieved that nothing had beaten me to the opportunity to end his life.

The pleasure would be all mine.

As he poked at the fire, I eased my hand into a pocket

and withdrew one of the darts I had prepared for this exact situation. Placing it into the blow tube, I rose just enough to aim properly and launched the dart into his neck with a sharp puff of air. He hardly had time to swipe at the sting in his neck before he slumped to the ground beside the boulder. The sedative did its job quickly, but it would also process through his system at a rapid rate. I needed to act with haste.

I hauled myself up to my feet and warily scanned the horizon before dousing his smoldering campfire with dirt. I had not come this far just to have something bigger and nastier than myself deny me my right to vengeance.

Hefting the man onto my shoulder, I left his belongings behind. I hoped they would be sufficient distraction to any inhabitants who had taken notice of the man and wandered over in curiosity. Once I had located a secluded spot some distance away, I dropped his limp body onto the hard ground. It was a relief to physically remove his weight from my shoulders, but it was the burden on my subconscious I was most interested in easing.

Listening to his head land on the rocky soil was a welcome bonus.

I took out the iron shackles I'd brought with me. I had held on to them for two years and carried them with me at all times in hopes of vengeance. The beast inside me roared to finally cuff the man who had set this manhunt into motion. Of course, there were practical reasons the shackles were needed as well. Not only would the metal bindings keep him from using his hands but they would also stop him from using any magic.

He would be waking up any minute, and I was more

than ready to enjoy the show. I lowered myself onto a nearby log and gathered a handful of pebbles. One at a time, I tossed them at the man until he stirred groggily. He tried to lift himself up to a sitting position but quickly discovered that his hands were bound at his back. His head whipped around until he spotted me where I sat watching him.

"What are you doing? What is this?" Shaking off his stupor from the dart, he managed to hoist himself upright but stayed seated on the ground.

"This is justice. This is retribution," I answered.

"What the hell are you talking about?" he spat with a sneer on his pretty face. Everything about him was aristocratic and worthless. I could not imagine how he had ever been a soldier.

"The Battle of Tirath during The Great War. You recall it, do you not?"

"Of course, what about it?"

"Before the battle took place, a small encampment of soldiers was ordered to infiltrate enemy lines. They set out on their own for weeks on a dangerous mission that could have ended the war before the famous battle of Tirath ever took place. You were one of the few who knew about that mission, were you not?" I bit out the last words, already knowing the answer to my question.

His brows narrowed in feigned confusion, but I knew better than to believe his lies. It had taken me months to track down each morsel of information that had finally led me to Cormac Doyle, and I was confident I had the right man.

"Not only did you know about the operation, but

you were a *member* of that honorable team," I said casually while I felt anything but inside. "I use the word 'member' loosely because, as I understand, your father's rank had more to do with your place on the team than skill or merit. Judging by your pathetic survival skills here in the Wilds, I would say that rumor was true."

"I earned my spot on that team, just like the rest," he shot back defensively.

"Then you would have known how important it was to be able to rely on every member of your battalion when a part of such an elite operation."

"It was not our fault we were not able to accomplish the mission. We were ambushed in the night by scores of Unseelie," he said indignantly.

I crossed my arms over my chest and narrowed my eyes at him. "And why exactly was that? Did you not have guards posted around the camp perimeter? Surely everyone was equally aware of the dangers present."

His eyes danced around, no doubt looking for an escape. "There were guards posted, but I do not know what happened. I was in camp asleep with the others. It was a miracle I managed to escape."

I slowly shook my head as I tsked at his response. "That is not the way I understand the events that occurred. The truth is, you were one of those guards. But you were not at your post, were you?" My words were a deadly whisper on the still night air.

"Whatever you have been told was *wrong*," he spat out. Not only was he sniveling like a frightened child, but the rank odor of fear wafted off him in waves.

"Every one of the soldiers in that camp lost their lives, some more blessedly quick than others," I reminded him.

His wide eyes darted around frantically, but he did not comment.

"You were a part of that company, yet you miraculously managed to survive. In fact, you were the *only* survivor." Standing as I spoke, I towered over the sniveling man, peering down at him with revulsion.

"I have an explanation ..." he began.

Quick as a viper, my hand shot out and hoisted him up by the neck until he stood on the tips of his toes, our faces inches apart. "The thing is, your explanation is irrelevant. You could have been getting your dick wet or saving orphans from a burning building. Either way, it does not undo what was done." With a final squeeze, I released him to stumble backward, gasping for air.

"You cannot kill me. It is against the *law* of the Hunt."

Reaching into another pocket, I pulled out a pair of sharp black talons. "I have put much consideration into that very conundrum. You see, I cannot allow your fate to be left in the hands of another. I have known for some time that it was you who was responsible for the events of that night, but I was forced to wait until the perfect moment to make you pay. Do you know what these are?" In the dim light, I could see the blood drain from his face. "Claws from a Leannan-Sidhe. It's unfortunate you had to encounter such a deadly Unseelie out here in the Wilds. Everyone knows they never leave a man alive."

Still on his feet, he tried to run, but I grabbed him by the collar of his dapper jacket and wrenched him backward. I slid the heavy material down over his arms behind him before whipping him around to face me. When he looked into my eyes, I showed him the imminence of his death, and I relished his terror. It was a fraction of what he deserved, but at least he would not go unpunished.

When I had first learned of the battalion's massacre, I raced to their reported location like a Hell Hound on the scent of prey. It had taken days for word to first reach the commanders. By the time I was told and made my journey, the scene had been scavenged by animals, and flesh sat rotting in the open. For hours I examined every corpse and each trace of evidence in an attempt to explain what had happened.

Tracks led me into the darkest areas of the Wilds, and using powers that no sane Fae would tap into, I interrogated and slayed dozens of Unseelie savages on my quest to find answers. When I finally located the clan responsible for leading the attack, I slaughtered every one of the soulless monsters. Some might say my actions made me a monster as well. I was apt to agree.

Cormac was the final piece of the puzzle.

I had known that the battalion would never have left themselves vulnerable to attack. The Unseelie had been given a way inside the camp. After a long search, I discovered that one soldier had survived, and the picture became clear. Cormac had abandoned his post and left his fellow soldiers unknowingly exposed. There was no other way they would have been so easily dismantled. They were part of the elite guard, trained extensively in all forms of combat and stealth operations. I knew the training well, as I myself had been a member of that guard.

When I looked into Cormac's eyes, I could see the truth of his actions.

He was weak, pathetic.

Before he could grovel, I slashed out viciously with the talon in my hand. The weapon sliced through his flesh, blood spraying from the arcing wound across his chest.

He howled in pain, and I immediately took a second swipe with my other hand across his neck to silence his cries. His eyes bulged and mouth gaped as he fell awkwardly to the ground, hands still bound behind him.

As much as I would have liked to have drawn out his demise, the Wilds were not the place for such an undertaking. However, his death had to look accidental, giving me a perfect excuse to unleash my demons, shredding his body beyond recognition.

What he had said had been true.

If anyone discovered what I had done to Cormac, I would lose what little I had left. I was aware of the risks I assumed by taking the law into my own hands. Knowing justice had been served was worth any consequences I might face. Fortunately, I was good at what I did and had no intention of anyone discovering the truth.

I massacred his corpse until I was sure he would not be able to survive the damage. As Fae, we could withstand a lot of punishment, but we were not invincible. The scene had unfolded perfectly—Cormac had been lured from his camp by a beguiling Leannan-Sidhe, who were known for their siren-like ability to enchant men. Their glamours were not as effective on Fae men as humans, but that was not the only weapon in their arsenal. It was entirely plausible that Cormac had been enchanted by one of the creatures, and once she got him somewhere secluded, there had been no stopping her blood lust.

I removed the shackles, which I would dispose of somewhere they would not be found, and the pressure in my head eased slightly as I stepped back from the body. The coppery stench of blood was rank in the night air. I would need to clear out soon, but I had to take a minute to absorb the fact that my life's purpose for the past two years had been achieved.

Every minute of every day, a part of my focus was always dedicated to finding those responsible for the deaths of the battalion. If I had thought Cormac's suffering would ease my own, I had been sorely mistaken. I felt no different at that moment than I had days, weeks, or months before. The dead were never coming back, and there would always be another monster out there who would hurt good people.

That had been why I was one of the first to follow Arthur when the Hunt came into existence. I could not imagine a better purpose than to have the freedom to track down and punish scum. The Hunt operated outside of the queen's rule—a brotherhood of soldiers placing honor and loyalty to each other above all else.

A great sentiment, in theory, but not always practical.

We lived by our own laws, enforced by our leader, the Erlking. He dictated our targets and moderated our disputes. Not that there were many. Most of my brothers were good men. I would have laid down my life for a number of them. However, sometimes a target presented itself, and the normal protocol could not be followed. Not every situation was black and white. Cormac Doyle was one of those situations. I was not about to leave justice in the hands of another.

Inside my pack were a clean set of trousers and a tunic. There was nothing I could do about my boots, but they would not be a problem. I rolled up the soiled clothing and placed the bundle in my pack before walking away from Cormac and everything he represented about my past.

I would never go back to being the man I was before the war, and I did not want to. I was stronger now, capable of making the hard decisions that lesser men ran from. I never wanted to feel the unbearable weight of regret again, and if it meant breaking a few rules here and there, so be it.

CHAPTER

EIGHTEEN

ASHLEY

My eyes weren't even open before I sensed that something was different. Energy buzzed under my skin, warming me from the inside. I didn't even have to try to coax the magic out; it filled every inch of me.

"Caz!" I cried softly to wake him. "It's back! My magic is back." I sat up and held out my arms in front of me to marvel at the change. Nothing looked different on the outside, but I could feel the shift inside me. The magic was now coursing through me with ease.

Casek watched me, a sleepy smirk on his lips and something akin to pride in his eyes. "That's wonderful, Ash." He reached out his hand to cup the back of mine, turning my palm up. "Concentrate on the feel of the energy. The way it ebbs and flows inside you. Then envision a small flame cupped in your hand. Press the energy toward your hand and manifest the flame."

I did exactly as he said and immediately felt warmth pool in my palm. The skin heated, but not until I puffed an extra burst of power did a flame burst to life. It was small and sputtering, but I'd never seen anything more incredible in my life.

"I did it," I breathed, rolling my wrist around as I stared at the flickering miracle. "If only I could have mastered it before last night." Memories of the horrific scene assaulted me one after the other as reality set in.

The flame blinked out of existence.

My shoulders sagged, but more out of sadness brought on by the memories than from the end of my magical display because, despite its loss, I still felt the same flurry of energy warming me from the inside.

"You may be getting better at summoning the power, but you still don't have the experience to control it. I'd rather events have unfolded the way they did than for you to have burned down the place with us inside." He peered up at me with a glint of humor in his mossy green gaze.

I gave him a playful eye roll. "I suppose you're right, but I would have liked to have kept my dad safe at least." I sobered. "I really need to check on him."

Casek pulled himself upright, his hand weaving into the hair at the nape of my neck to pull my lips against his. The kiss was achingly reverent, making my head spin when he finally pulled away.

"I got a message in the night that your dad was returned safely to his hotel room. Get dressed, and I'll take you over there."

I nodded dazedly, then squealed when he tickled my ribs. "Okay! I'm going!"

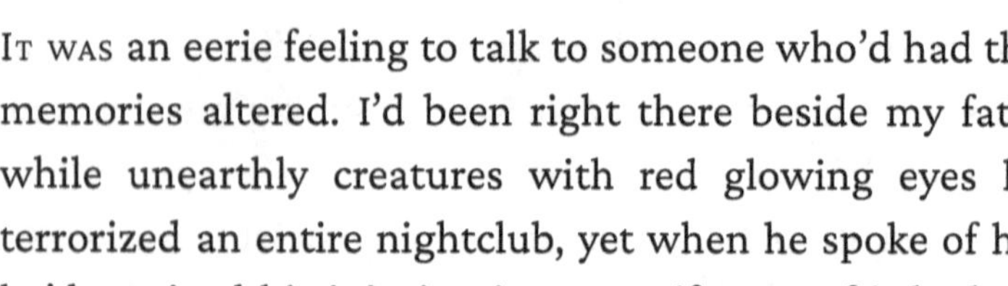

It was an eerie feeling to talk to someone who'd had their memories altered. I'd been right there beside my father while unearthly creatures with red glowing eyes had terrorized an entire nightclub, yet when he spoke of how he'd received his injuries, it was as if none of it had ever happened. He knew he'd been bitten by a dog, but he believed a random stray had attacked him on his way back to the hotel.

As he sat and told me casually about the much less traumatizing event he believed he experienced, I acted surprised and went along with the ruse. A weight lifted from my chest to see him lighthearted and limping about. The extent of my relief surprised me, considering there were times in the past when I'd wished the man dead. I wasn't ashamed to admit it, but I was also glad I no longer felt that way.

"How fortunate there'd been a doctor staying at the hotel who happened to be nearby!" I said, seated next to him on the small sofa in his hotel room.

Dad nodded. "Very fortunate. I just wished I'd gotten his name. Seems like I would have, but I can't for the life of me remember. Maybe it was the pain. Everything that happened is a little fuzzy."

My answering smile quivered at the corners from the swell of my emotions. How was it possible to feel such conflicted emotions so strongly? Relief warring with worry. Gratitude clashing with regret. I was so glad my dad was okay, yet the incident had highlighted how important the reunion had been for me. Had he not come to Ireland, I probably would have insisted for the rest of my life that I'd been better off without him, but that wasn't true. That was fear talking. That was pain. And if I continued to allow those emotions to rule me, my life would be sculpted in their image.

Refusing to forgive my dad wasn't setting boundaries. It was brandishing my hurt and anger like a sword, threatening anyone and everyone who came too close, regardless of the risk they posed. Dad had been sober for five long years. I couldn't even imagine the challenges he'd faced in that time, yet he'd remained in control. He'd more than proven himself. Now it was my turn to meet him halfway.

"I'm so glad you're okay, Dad. I hate that you came all the way here and got hurt." Emotion tugged at my voice.

Dad's eyes reflected a cacophony of his own feelings. "I can take this kind of pain all day. Thinking I'd lost you—that was more than I could handle."

I leaned into him, my shoulder connecting gently with his. Dad's arm lifted to wrap around my back and pull me against his side in the first semblance of a genuine hug that we'd shared since I was a young teen.

Understanding that I still needed to take things slowly, Dad released me with a grin. "I'm probably no good for sightseeing today, but maybe we could do dinner again tonight?"

"That would be great." My heart swelled, filling my chest with warmth. "You get some rest while I get a little work done. We can just go to the pub next door, so you don't have to walk far. Seven work?"

"That's perfect."

He started to rise with me, but I assured him I could help myself out. We said our goodbyes, and I went downstairs to the lobby where Caz was waiting. I told him about the short visit and our dinner plans. As I began to describe my changing emotions about my father, my words fell silent as Casek faded away and a vision presented itself. I was vaguely aware of Casek calling my name but didn't want to risk losing the image if my focus wavered.

I channeled everything I could into the mental image solidifying before me. Yet again, my vision began sharply focused on a head of long hair limp on the ground. This time, the hair was dark brown and beneath the cool gray of cobbled stone. Instead of a beer spilled in the background, the thick red liquid pooling beneath the hair painted an even more violent picture.

It was hard to tell what had happened because I was viewing the scene zoomed in, as if my senses were focused on each small detail. Dark hair. Sticky crimson blood. A green canvas-like piece of cloth poking through the hair. It looked like some kind of tie, but I wasn't sure. I squinted and strained to pull back and see more of the scene. I needed more information.

The image flickered before a slightly more removed perspective flashed before me. It only lasted a second, but it was enough. I knew exactly who the Fear Gorda would try to kill next.

"It's Elle!" I cried, releasing the vision and refocusing my eyes on Casek. "I saw her lying in a pool of blood—it was her brown hair and the green apron she wears at the coffee shop." My words were frantic.

Casek placed his hands on my upper arms to calm me. "Okay, Ash. I hear you. Let's get to the car, and you can tell me everything." His eyes lifted to the hotel clerk behind me before he ushered me outside.

I told him everything I could about Elle and the vision once we were alone. "Do you think he's already got her? My first vision happened a day before the red-headed woman was killed. But the vision about you had been almost in real time."

"There's no way to know for sure. Let's get back to the Huntsman and talk with Lochlan. If the Gorda already has her, there's little we can do. We'll have time to plan if we've been given a day's warning."

Caz raced us back home. As he drove, I typed out a text to Elle, chewing rabidly on my lip the entire way.

Me: You working today?

It sounded so casual, considering the circumstances. I didn't think starting with a text about my vision of her murder would be helpful. I needed to help her, not convince her I was crazy.

Caz and I parted ways at the elevator, though I made him promise he'd tell me the plan as soon as he'd spoken with Lochlan. In return, he made me promise I would not step foot out of the building without him.

Elle hadn't texted me back by the time I was back in my apartment, so I called and left a message for her to call me. Then, I paced.

Knight watched me from his place on the couch, one doggy eyebrow lifting each time his eyes tracked me from one side of the room to the other.

Thirty minutes later, a knock sounded at my door.

I rushed to answer it, freezing when it wasn't Casek on the other side but a dazzlingly beautiful woman with sun-kissed sandy blond hair and warm brown eyes that reminded me of melted caramel.

"Oh, I'm sorry. I was expecting someone else. Can I help you?"

She assessed me curiously as if I was an exhibit at a science fair to be studied and critiqued. That's when I remembered Casek telling me about the Fae woman who had recently arrived. The one with which he'd had some kind of ongoing relationship.

It was my turn to take a more detailed perusal of the woman. My eyes took a sweeping glance down to her feet and back. She wore painted-on skinny jeans with heeled booties and a fitted long-sleeve top with a scoop-neck collar that dipped so low I expected to see nip at any moment.

I didn't want to judge another woman merely based on her attire, but the little green monster stirring inside me made that endlessly hard. And besides, assuming the woman was trouble wouldn't be a crime since Casek had already warned me as much.

"I'm Parisa. I've been in town for a while now and hadn't run into you. I just wanted to stop by and introduce myself." Her words appeared on the surface to be an offering of friendship, but she didn't fool me. Underneath that pot of honey lay a venomous trap. "I can tell that since Casek's been in Belfast, something has formed between you two."

And there it was.

"I don't think my relationship with Casek is any of

your business." I made sure to stand in the doorway, making it obvious the vile woman wasn't welcome inside.

A confident smile spread across her cherry-red lips. "Everything that concerns Casek is my business. He's been mine for a very long time. I've let him dally in the past, but I'm here now to let you know that those days are over."

Yup, trouble. A drama-laden bucket of crazy.

My gut twisted at the prospect of Casek belonging to another woman, and as much as my feminine emotions wanted to wail and rage, my logical side stayed in control. Casek had told me things were long over with this woman, and I believed him. Between my knowledge of him and the vibe I got from her, I didn't buy anything she was selling. "As much as you'd like me to tuck my tail and run, that's not going to happen. Thanks for stopping by, though." I started to close the door, but her hand swung out to stop me.

Her face twisted in a sneer, and she used her height to look down at me intimidatingly. "You'd come between a man and the mother of his child?"

Her words winded me.

She cocked her hip out and waited expectantly for what felt like an eternity before I formed a response.

"You have a child with Casek?"

"I will—I'm pregnant."

She allowed her words to penetrate, stabbing deep into my heart. The pain stole my breath and clouded my thoughts, leaving me helpless to do anything but listen to her words.

"We reconciled while he was in Faery a while back. That's why I'm here now and why you need to walk away from him. Casek and I have a long history together. I know everything about him. Things you couldn't possibly understand." She took a slow breath, her lips thinning, then began again in a softer, more conciliatory tone. "What he's done to you is wrong. If you haven't already figured it out, these men of the Hunt can be callous. I know you're new to our Fae world, but you need to consider that being around the Hunt isn't your only way to learn about being Fae."

This can't be.

He warned me about her for a reason. Think this through.

I took a steadying breath.

Casek wasn't the type of man to cheat, and she had implied they had reconciled. He knew this woman was here in Belfast. If she'd told him about a pregnancy, Casek never would have been in my bed the last two nights. He might have faults, but he wasn't a lowlife. That meant either she hadn't even told him yet or she was lying.

Something didn't add up.

My dad had always said, if it looked like shit and smelled like shit, it was probably shit.

I refused to give Parisa the satisfaction of riding her drama train. First, I would talk to Casek. If he confirmed what she said, then I'd invest in some ice cream and give his car the Carrie Underwood treatment. Until then, I would *not* jump to any conclusions. "You've said your piece, Parisa. Now you need to leave," I insisted with forced calm before closing the door in her perfect face.

CHAPTER
NINETEEN

CASEK

"THIS MAY BE OUR BEST CHANCE TO STOP THIS ASSHOLE," I SAID
to Lochlan after relaying the details of Ashley's vision.

"Agreed, but I'm afraid Ashley will fight us on this one."

"I'm certain she will, but how else will we catch the guy if we don't use the woman as bait?"

Lochlan grimaced. "Hell if I know. These damn creatures are impossible to track." He looked at me, his stare growing curious. "Things seem to be going well between you and Ashley. Think you can convince her?"

"I may hold more sway than I used to, but she and Rebecca are the most bull-headed women on this planet. Neither of them will be bullied into doing anything they don't want to do."

"Of course, they can't object if they don't know."

Lochlan stared at me, giving me the distinct impression that his comment was a test of sorts.

I considered going behind Ashley's back and using her friend as bait without telling her our plan. The idea left an acrid taste on my tongue. I was already lugging around enough guilt about binding her magic. I didn't care to add to that burden.

"Out of the question."

He gave a single approving nod. I'd wondered if he was expecting me to put the Hunt above my feelings for Ash, but as it turned out, I'd had it wrong. He was feeling out my loyalty to Ashley, and he respected my commitment.

Lochlan leaned back in his desk chair. "Then our next step is for you to talk to her. Once we have her on board, we'll work out the details."

"I'll head to her place as soon as we're done. As for the club, it's about cleaned up, and the men are working on damage control. I think it's a little premature to reopen tomorrow, but in theory, we could do it."

"Let's just keep the doors shut until next week. That way, everyone can focus on the more important task of catching the Gorda." He paused, and his eyes assessed me in a way that would have made a lesser man squirm. "I hear Parisa is paying us a visit."

I released a tired exhale as tension coiled in my neck. "We talked briefly. I made the mistake of connecting with her when I was at the palace. She seems to think that meant more than it did. I've explained that she misunderstood, but I'm not sure she got the message."

"Mistake? That's a monumental fuckup."

"Never one to sugarcoat, are you? I'm well aware that I

fucked up."

Our eyes were both drawn to the doorway as Parisa walked in unannounced. "Hello, boys. I hope I'm not interrupting," she purred with a coy innocence she hadn't possessed in centuries.

Lochlan's eyes slid over to me. "Speak of the devil."

Parisa cocked her head and smirked at Lochlan. "That's not very nice. I just came to have a word with Casek, if you wouldn't mind loaning him to me for a moment."

"Actually," I cut in tersely, "anything you have to say to me can be said in front of Lochlan, so spit it out."

Annoyance flashed across her artfully sculpted features before she gave a compliant nod and lifted her eyes to me. "I know you may not be crazy about me being here, but it was important..." She paused, her eyes dancing between Lochlan and me as if she was unsure she should continue. "I had hoped to tell you this privately ... Casek, but ... I'm pregnant." She let the words hang heavily in the air, her chin lifted proudly.

Pregnant.

And if I understood her correctly, she was implying the child was mine.

I was always exceptionally careful and had managed not to knock up a woman in my long lifetime, so my initial surprise quickly morphed to suspicion. Not only was I careful, but Parisa was a Valkyrie soldier above all else. If she had allowed herself to become pregnant, she would have been removed from the guard. I couldn't imagine that would ever be an option for her. All things considered, my gut told me this was a ploy.

I clenched my fists with indignation as I took a step toward her. "You think you can come in here and manipulate me with your lies?" My voice was deadly calm, hardly loud enough to hear, but I knew she'd gotten the message when the color drained from her face. I walked around behind her and closed the office door. "Lucky for us, we have a way of getting to the truth. You didn't know that, did you?"

"What are you going to do? Torture me? You'll start a war if the queen finds out you attacked one of her guards."

I glanced at Lochlan as he rose to his feet and flashed a vicious smile at Parisa. "Not necessary. We have a tool that's far more effective."

Her years of military training kicked in, and her spine stiffened as Lochlan pulled out the Sword of Light. We had recently obtained the ancient Fae relic, but word had not yet reached Faery about our acquisition. The sword gave its bearer the ability to force the truth from whoever was held at its blade. The weapon had been enormously helpful in recent months and would serve as an easy way to determine the veracity of Parisa's claims.

Lochlan motioned her to one of his office chairs, and she reluctantly obeyed. The muscles in her jaw rippled as she clenched her teeth. "I'm not some prisoner you can violate. You'll be sorry if you do this," she hissed in my direction.

I leaned in toward her, restraining myself from the full-on assault my fists ached to dole out. "You're the one who is going to be sorry if that forked tongue of yours was lying. You were sorely mistaken if you expected to walk in here and toy with us."

Lochlan stepped up and thrust the blade's edge up to the soft skin at Parisa's throat. The silver metal began to glow softly, and Parisa's spine stiffened further.

"Are you pregnant?" he asked in a commanding tone.

Parisa's nostrils flared, and air came and went from her lungs in jerky puffs as she struggled against the magic. She held out longer than most, but in the end, she was no match. "*No*," she spat out bitterly, slapping the sword away from her and rising to face me. "You think that mutant trash can fill my shoes? She *can't*, and I told her about the baby, so good luck getting her to talk to you now."

Lochlan lunged between us before I could rip her to shreds, the room instantly prickling with the Erlking's power. "You may hold power in Faery, but over here, you are *nothing*. I have more questions for you. Sit down."

Her red lips tightened into a thin line, and she glanced down at the sword still gripped in Lochlan's hand. "The queen will hear about this."

"I have no doubt. Now *sit*."

She plopped down insolently, and Lochlan returned the blade to her throat.

"Why did Guin send you here?"

"To watch the women."

Lochlan's eyes sparked dangerously at the admission that Rebecca was also under surveillance. "What exactly were your orders?"

"To keep an eye on Rebecca and learn what powers Ashley possessed."

"Tell me all of your orders."

Her lip lifted in a snarl, and her eyes dropped to the

side. "Convince Ashley to come to Faery and work with Guin."

"Why the pregnancy story?"

Her eyes returned to Lochlan with a malicious glare. "To get her to hate you. All of you. If she hates the Hunt, she might be open to leaving Earth." Her eyes slid over to mine, losing none of their venom. "And to remind *you* who you are and who you belong to."

Lochlan's humorless chuckle was a thinly veiled threat. "I thought you were smarter than that, Parisa."

She stiffened, forcing a mask of neutrality back in place. "And I thought you were smarter than these asinine questions."

My gaze met Lochlan's, our minds both going to the same place before he asked his next question.

"Do you know anything about the Fear Gorda in Belfast?"

"No," she spat.

"Did you have anything to do with the Hell Hounds invading the Huntsman?"

Her jaw flexed, neck straining with the effort. "Yessss," she finally hissed before her jaw clamped shut again.

"Why did you send Hell Hounds into our building?" Lochlan's voice was little more than black malice, the sword piercing further into Parisa's neck.

"I told you," she spat. "So the girl would think she wasn't safe."

Lochlan stood perfectly motionless for long seconds as he warred with himself.

"She's not worth it. Just a pathetic minion," I told him.

Parisa's eyes flashed at me, but she didn't argue.

Eventually, Lochlan lowered the sword and pulled Parisa up out of her chair. "I don't care if you are the queen's guard. If I catch you here again, I'll kill you myself. Get out."

Her lips pursed as she lifted her chin haughtily and traced away.

I had to roll my head from side to side to coerce my neck to relax. "Well, shit. We need to ward the building against her, and I'd better get down and talk to Ashley." I hated to think what kind of hornet's nest Parisa had stirred up with her pregnancy lie.

"I'll get with the others on the wards. You go to Ashley. Let me know how we plan to proceed."

I waved in acknowledgment on my way through his office doorway.

"I heard Parisa paid you a visit," I said as soon as Ashley opened her door. The fact that she'd even let me in was a relief.

"Yeah, but I can't say that I believed anything she said. I decided I wanted to hear from you before jumping to any conclusions."

Thank Christ.

"I don't know what all she told you, but she is *not* pregnant with my child. She just showed up at Lochlan's office with the ridiculous claim, but she didn't know we had the Sword of Light. Once she was compelled to tell the truth, she admitted that she'd made up the whole thing. She wants to come between us and find a way to lure you to Faery to become the queen's pet. She went so far as to orchestrate the Hell Hounds attack to make you feel unsafe."

"That *bitch*. She mentioned that being here with you Huntsmen wasn't my only option—as if I'd ever move to Faery." Ash rolled her eyes, and I had to fight back a grin. She'd been given the opportunity to think the worst of me and had chosen to have faith instead. My girl had come a long way in a short amount of time.

Now, for the next hurdle of our conversation.

"After discussing things with Lochlan, we agree on how to proceed, but considering this is your friend's life at stake, I insisted you be included in the decision."

Ashley stilled at the gravity in my tone.

"It's almost impossible to track a Gorda. They're masters at covering their tracks and blending in. If we have any hope of catching him, the answer lies in using your friend as a lure." I decided at the last second that lure sounded less triggering than bait. Even something so seemingly trivial might be the key to gaining Ashley's cooperation.

She nodded. "I figured that's where this was headed. It makes the most sense."

A part of me dropped to my knees in relief, but a wiser, more cynical part of me braced for the catch. "I'm glad we agree," I said warily.

"However," she continued.

Ah, there it is.

"If Elle is going to be bait, then I'm not leaving her side until the threat is over."

My eyes drifted shut as I breathed through my

outrage. Of course, Ashley would insist on protecting her friend. I should have seen that coming.

"Ashley, we'll have safeguards in place to ensure she isn't taken. If you're present, that might scare away the Gorda."

"Then that's a risk we'll have to take. Either way, I'm assured that no harm comes to Elle."

"If we don't take this opportunity, we could miss our chance to catch the guy."

"If this opportunity doesn't pan out, I'll have another vision, and we can try again."

I might as well have tried arguing with the wall. I was never going to win. "All right, but you better follow our instructions to a T. No deviations. No improvisation. Period."

"I understand." She raised her phone to show me a string of texts. "I heard back from Elle. She's out of town visiting family tonight, but she'll be back at work in the morning. I'd say that's a good time for surveillance to begin. She should be safe for tonight while she's out of town. In the meantime, we can plan, and I'm supposed to meet my dad for dinner again tonight."

"I can't believe I'm doing this." I ran my hands over my face.

Ashley pulled my hands down, then pressed her body close to mine and draped her arms over my shoulders. "Thank you for trusting me."

I lifted her in my arms, tugging her head back gently with my fingers fisted in her hair. "Don't make me regret it."

CHAPTER

TWENTY

ASHLEY

"I have to say, you seem to be taking all this rather well. Parisa, your dad, and now Elle being in danger—that's a lot to process." Becca peered at me with wide eyes.

I'd just spent the past twenty minutes calmly outlining everything that had happened since we'd last talked. There was a lot to cover, considering it had only been a day. Ordinarily, the frenzy of developments would have amped up my energy to a frenetic state. Between having a plan in place and getting fucked against the wall by Casek before he left to meet back up with Lochlan, I was feeling surprisingly mellow.

I shrugged. "Just another day here in Belfast, I guess."

Becca snorted a laugh. "Ain't that the truth."

"How's Cat doing? Hopefully, her world has been a little less chaotic than ours."

"She's good. I think, maybe—" Becca fidgeted. "Maybe she's really good."

"Excuse me?" I balked at the suggestive hint. "Has Cat met someone?"

"Sort of, but I could totally be reading into things. It'll be interesting to see how it plays out."

"That's all you're going to give me?"

She pretended to zip her lips shut, then grinned mischievously.

"No. No," I said flatly. "You said no more secrets, and I can tell something is up. It may have nothing to do with Cat, but you've been acting funny lately—not answering your phone and disappearing for hours. I thought we agreed no more secrets between us."

Her brows lifted in the center apologetically. "I know! I'm so sorry. I didn't say anything at first because of plausible deniability. I didn't want Guin to be able to blame you if I got caught. Now that Merlin has your back, it's probably safe."

"Jesus, Bec. What have you done?" My frustration melted into worry.

"Remember Fenodree? The Fae man who helped teach me my powers while in Faery?"

"Yeah?" I asked warily.

"Well ... I sort of helped him escape to Earth." She continued in a rush to explain. "He'd been exiled for ages to this god-awful place, and I just couldn't leave him there. The day we went before Guin to gain our freedom, I made a quick detour and rescued him."

"So you've tucked away this ancient Fae man living off the land in a savage wilderness for centuries somewhere

here in the city?" I understood why she'd done it, but it sounded like a disaster.

"Not here in the city."

"And I assume somehow Cat is involved?" I remembered when the two had been quietly whispering at girls' night.

"Guin has no idea who she is. I knew she wouldn't be followed, and like you said, someone needed to check on him more frequently than I could get away."

My eyes bulged. "*Him*? Is *that* who you were talking about when you said Cat had met someone?"

She put her hands up in a gesture to slow down. "They've only met once, so there's nothing between them—don't get me wrong. There was a crazy intense energy passing between them, and Cat's been awfully eager to help. But like I said, I could be totally reading into it."

I slumped backward in shock. "Wouldn't that be something?"

"Right?" Becca was quiet for a second, her shoulders falling. "I'm sorry again for not telling you. I just wanted to keep you safe."

I sighed deeply. "It's okay. That seems to be the trend lately. I know I should consider myself lucky to have such caring friends." I smiled, though wanly. "Guess I'm going to pretend to get some work done before I have dinner with my dad tonight. I'll probably just end up sitting here wondering what kind of plan the guys will concoct."

"We'll find out soon enough, then we'll nab the bastard."

"Let's hope so. Living under constant threat of attack is getting old."

Becca squeezed my hand. "Go have fun with your dad tonight. We don't know what tomorrow will bring, so we just have to do our best to live our lives."

I smiled softly. "Speaking of living our lives, are you ever going to move your stuff over to Lochlan's place?"

"Ugh," she groaned, rising from the sofa. "Eventually, I guess. It's such a hassle, and you know how much I hate change. I figure I'll get to it one of these days."

I laughed, shaking my head. "Love you, Becs."

"Love you, too, dork." She blew me a kiss. "Talk to you later."

"Counting on it."

She let herself out of the apartment, and I begrudgingly retrieved my laptop and began to work. I worked on and off until it was time to get ready for dinner. Knight disappeared for an hour midafternoon. I started to worry that he'd gotten wind of something happening, but when he finally returned, he was licking his chops and carrying the distinct aroma of buttery garlic bread.

It had been hard to concentrate on anything but food after that.

A few minutes before seven, Casek drove me to the restaurant next to Dad's hotel. He managed to snag a parking spot out front where he could see me through the window, so he agreed to stay in the car. I'd been prepared to have him skulking about in a booth nearby, but this felt less awkward. Dad wasn't there when I arrived, so I got a table and scrolled through my phone while I waited. The minutes ticked by until it was fifteen after, and tension knotted my stomach.

Where was he? It wasn't like he'd been out sightseeing

and might have been delayed getting back. He could hardly walk.

Wondering where my father had disappeared to brought back an onslaught of memories and emotions I preferred to keep buried. Countless nights spent wondering if he'd come home before I went to bed, and if so, would he be half passed out … or worse—awake and livid.

The reminder gave me chills.

I placed a call to him but received no answer. When the server came to check on me, I showed her a picture of my dad and asked if she'd seen him.

"Oh, yeah! I think he was here a little earlier over at the bar." She grinned, glad to be of help without any clue of the catastrophic devastation she'd just unleashed inside me.

Wounds I'd thought were long scarred over suddenly ripped wide open.

How could he? After all this time. After I'd finally let him back in. How could he turn himself over to the destructive malice of his addiction? Was a relationship with me not worth the restraint of temptation?

Questions wrought with a long-familiar agony assaulted me as if I were fifteen again and the past eight years had never happened. It was easy to fall back into the same thought patterns despite years of effort put into forgetting. I felt like the same vulnerable little girl, and Dad was still tearing my heart to shreds.

I could hardly breathe as I sat in that booth. My vision blurred with unshed tears.

Stop. Stop right this instant. You are NOT *that little girl, and you will* NOT *crumble.*

The voice boomed inside my head, giving me something to cling to.

She was right.

I was an adult with a voice and the power to control my life. I didn't have to subject myself to fear and doubt.

Wiping at my eyes, I scooted from the booth and approached the bar. I had to take a deep breath to help still my shaking hand before I lifted my phone to the bartender.

"Excuse me, have you seen this man? I was supposed to meet him, but we may have gotten our times mixed up."

"American, right?" the man asked. "Yeah, he was here not long ago. He had two club sodas, then disappeared without closing out his tab."

Club sodas? "He didn't have any alcohol?" My stomach dipped, swinging like a pendulum from one extreme to the other.

"Nah, just soda."

He hadn't been drinking. Elated relief brought on a wave of dizziness.

I nodded, pulling out some cash and setting it on the bar without looking at the bills. "Here you go. Sorry about that."

Dad wasn't off getting drunk. So what the hell happened to him? Had he gone back to the room and fallen asleep? Collecting myself in a hurry, I walked outside and signaled for Casek to join me.

"Dad was here earlier, according to the bartender, but he disappeared." I continued quickly as a vengeful darkness settled over Casek. "He only had club soda—no alcohol, but he bailed without paying. That's not like him. I don't know what's happened, but I'm worried."

"Let's check his room."

We went next door to the hotel and up to Dad's room. Casek used his magic to unlock the door, but we found nothing inside that gave us any clue as to where my father had gone.

"Let's go back to the pub," Caz suggested. "That's the last place he was seen. Maybe I can track him from there."

I nodded, reassuring myself that this was all a big mix-up. He hadn't been drinking as I'd suspected, so there was no reason to give weight to any other of my unfounded fears.

We walked back to the pub. Casek took my phone with the photo of my dad on display and began to approach the staff. As he spoke to a server, I overheard a man complaining in a heavy Scottish brogue to the bartender.

"I've tried to use the cludgie twice now, and the damn thing's still locked. Either someone's wrecked themselves or it's locked itself with no one inside."

Cludgie? Did he mean toilet? Could my father simply be stuck in the bathroom? It was worth a check. I went back behind the bar to the dark hallway that housed the small washrooms. The women's door was cracked open, but the men's was shut. I knocked.

Silence.

"I'm coming in," I said through the door, then held the knob and prayed my magic would figure out how to do its thing. I'd witnessed the others all use the skill. It had looked easy enough. Fortunately, the ancient lock wasn't sophisticated. I felt the mechanism click as it retracted. The door only opened a few inches before it met resistance. Looking down, I saw a man's leg on the floor. Jeans with white socks and a pair of sneakers I recognized.

No. It wasn't. It couldn't be.

Shoving the door with more force, I peered inside and began to scream.

TWENTY-ONE

ASHLEY

I'D ALWAYS BEEN TOLD HOW PRETTY MY EYES WERE. I HAD HATED
the sight of them for years—avoided my own gaze in
mirrors and used heavy liner to disguise their shape—
because I had my father's eyes. The same shape. Color.
Expressiveness.

Nature had managed a perfect copy-paste when it
came to our cornflower-blue, almond-shaped eyes.

I knew his eyes as well as I knew my own.

I knew how to read them, and I could never mistake
the petrified horror frozen in those turbulent depths. I'd
shoved the bathroom door open and rushed to my father's
side, but there'd been no helping him. His lifeless body
slumped farther to the floor at my touch.

But his eyes.

There was nothing lifeless about them.

How could death reflect such intense emotion?

Shouldn't the absence of life leave a body as peaceful as a blank canvas? No worries or responsibilities. No joy or loss. It was the very definition of lifeless. Yet the magnitude of fear trapped in my father's sightless eyes would haunt me for the rest of my life.

I hadn't realized I'd continued screaming until I was yanked against Casek's solid chest, his body shielding my gaze from my father.

"Shhh, baby. I've got you." His whispered words were the only thing that penetrated the piercing pain lancing through my body.

How could fate be so cruel as to take away my father after I'd only just gotten him back?

One day. I'd had him for one day.

The anguish and frustration welled up inside me until it boiled over in a wailing, guttural howl.

Sorrow gripped every cell in my body, leaving no piece of me untouched.

Somewhere beyond my ability to focus, Casek spoke in a hushed tone. People had gathered outside the bathroom. The police had been called. Life went on. But not for my father. Not for me.

"Why?" It was the only word I could manage. The simple question repeated on an endless loop inside my head. Why would he be taken from me after I'd finally let him back in? Why would this happen? Why hadn't my visions shown me this would happen so I could have protected him?

"I'm so sorry, Ash. I'm so sorry," Casek murmured close to my ear.

Why was he sorry? This wasn't his fault. It was the

Gorda. I was certain of that.

I'd seen the product of his vile depravity before. I knew the look of one of his victims. But this wasn't one of his normal strikes. This was personal. Intentional. He'd killed my father as a message. Why else switch from his normal female targets? Why else attack out in the open during the evening hours? There wasn't even a remote chance this had been a coincidence. My father had been targeted, and the realization was the only thing that helped pull me from the clutches of grief.

An unnatural calm settled over me like ocean waters gone smooth and still before a storm.

When my breathing returned to a normal, steady rhythm, I pulled free of Casek and wiped away the salty remnants of my tears. "We have to stop him. Whatever it takes."

A barrage of emotions passed behind Casek's green gaze before he nodded, then turned toward the door where Lochlan had forced his way through the crowd.

"Can you handle this?" Casek asked. "I need to get her out of here."

Two more Huntsmen appeared behind Lochlan, ushering the bystanders out of the hallway.

"Go take care of her," Lochlan instructed gravely.

Casek guided me through the pub to the car, not severing contact with me for a second until I was buckled into the passenger seat of his vehicle. An ambulance arrived as we were leaving. Not even the bright flashing lights and screeching siren broke through the haze of my numbness. I felt no more human than the husk of a man I'd left on the bathroom floor.

CHAPTER
TWENTY-TWO

ASHLEY

Rebecca met us at the lobby of the Huntsman, enveloping me in a hug. My arms came around her mechanically. She and Casek hovered over me at the apartment. It would have been annoying if I could have summoned the energy to care. Instead, I'd been swallowed by a torrent of injustice and outrage and grief too violent for words. All I could do was keep breathing. Keep my head above the waves and try not to sink.

I spoke without thought. I touched without feeling. I ate without taste.

None of it felt real.

A thick, filmy haze surrounded me, insulating me from the world around me. Dulling my senses. Cocooning me in numbness.

"Ash, honey. Maybe you should get some rest,"

Rebecca suggested after I'd sat wordlessly on the sofa for well over an hour, staring out the window.

"I'm not doing anything until we hear back from Lochlan."

"But Elle isn't in town until morning. Nothing can be done until then."

"I'm not shutting my eyes until I know the plan," I said with more force.

Rebecca nodded reluctantly, eyes briefly cutting to Casek. I didn't care what they thought or how many private conversations they'd had. I wasn't going to sleep until I knew we would be taking action. That plans were in place to stop this monster.

As I sat in the quiet stillness of my apartment, my sorrow and regret mutated into a caustic fury bubbling in my veins.

The senseless killings had to stop.

I'd wanted to track down the Gorda before, but now ... now, it was the only thing that mattered. I would use every resource available to me. Set aside all other responsibilities and abandon the thought of all other pursuits until I'd sent this monster to hell where he belonged.

The acrid scent of singed fabric drifted to my awareness. When I looked down, my hands were glowing amber and had burned clean through my denim jeans.

My eyes met Casek's for an instant. His gaze shone with understanding. He knew what it was to lose someone. To need revenge for that heinous loss.

When Lochlan finally returned, I leaped to my feet. "Did you find any new leads?"

"No. I'm so sorry, Ashley."

Anticipating his response, I gave a single quick nod. "Then we continue with our plan to target Elle. This attack was personal. That fact is indisputable at this point. The Gorda wants me. Considering his targets and my vision, Elle is our best bet."

Casek stepped forward. "You're wrong. Every bit of this is about *me*. You're just an avenue to hurt me."

"Either way, I'm still the focus," I responded tonelessly. "I'll stay with Elle because I'm the one he wants, and he probably won't get close if any of you are present."

"We talked about including you in the plan, but I never agreed to let you go alone." Casek's entire body stiffened in anticipation of a fight.

"I'm not saying you won't be involved, but we all know that bastard isn't going to fall into some simple trap." I paused, an idea formulating. "How far can you trace?"

The two men exchanged a wary look before Casek answered. "A hundred yards, at most."

"What if we used an electronic signal—something I could have in my hand at all times—that I could use to notify you of trouble? You could all be stationed within your trace range but not so close to scare off the Gorda. I'd be inside to make sure Elle is safe. I'm not leaving her alone for a second. Not after the vision I had. Not after..." I couldn't finish the sentence.

A muscle in Casek's jaw bulged, his teeth gritted. "And if something happens to you so that you can't signal for help?"

"Then you'll come for me." I raised my hand to the back of my neck where Casek's mark still resided.

"No," he barked, turning his back to us as he walked to the window. "I'm not letting you do this. It's too risky."

Fury whooshed through my blood, heating it to a boil in an instant. "It's not your place to *let* me do anything." The words hissed past clenched teeth.

Casek whipped around at the sound of my rage and charged at me. "I don't give a fuck about my place. I'd rather lock you and your friend in our basement where I know you're safe than risk losing you."

"*Enough!*" Lochlan roared, his command laced with power. "Ashley, I'd like to speak with you privately. Caz, cool the fuck off while we're gone."

I glanced briefly at Casek, then followed after Lochlan. I'd had a scathing reply primed on the tip of my tongue, but it had fizzled even before Lochlan intervened because of the vulnerability Casek had displayed in admitting his fear of losing me. As the only person in the world who witnessed what he'd experienced losing his sister, I knew better than anyone what he'd suffered, and I didn't want him to go through that pain again.

Lochlan led me back to my bedroom and closed the door behind us, slowly pacing. "Have a seat." He motioned to the bed.

I did as he requested and remained quiet.

"I know you're desperate to stop the Gorda. Your grief is still so raw, and it feeds the fear inside you. These are understandable responses to the situation; however, you don't fully grasp the difficulty of the task. We are truly doing all we can without unnecessarily risking one another. And while the risk may seem worth it when your emotions are so turbulent, this is not the best time to be making decisions."

"That's easy to say when it's not your world being torn apart," I said softly, most of my ire dissipating once I'd left the living room.

"That's not true. Casek is my brother in every way that counts, and the events right now are putting him at risk of grave danger. Not to mention that as Rebecca's dearest friend, you are a part of my family as well. I don't take any of this lightly, I assure you."

The very last of my fight deflated as tears welled in my eyes. "We have to do something. We have to stop him."

He paused his pacing and met my pleading stare with resolve. "And we will, but I need you to be patient. I need your trust."

I nodded, wiping at the first tear to break free.

Lochlan breathed deeply, his gaze dropping before he stilled, then lowered to crouch next to my desk. More specifically, the trash can beside my desk. He gingerly reached in and pulled out a string of woven grass stalks with red paint on the ends. He held them up gingerly between his thumb and index finger as though the grass might bite.

"Where did you get this?" he asked, his tone suddenly pitch black.

"I don't know. I've never seen it before."

"You didn't put it in the trash?"

I shook my head adamantly. "Why? What is it?"

"It's a circlet from a binding—" His eyes cut to mine, and his lips thinned. "A binding spell."

Something venomous slithered under my skin. "What do you mean a binding spell? Bind what?"

"There are all sorts of uses for a binding spell. Who else has had access to your room?"

"No one besides me and Becca and Casek. Knight has been in a few times if you count him."

He clenched the grass in his palm and exhaled deeply again. He didn't like my response, but I couldn't figure out why. What could a binding spell have to do with me?

"It's nothing," Lochlan said, trying to pass off his discovery.

Bullshit. It was most obviously *not* nothing.

Why would the circlet have been in my trash?

If something was bound, it was restricted or confined or locked. What could have been locked away?

The thought had barely formulated when memories of my magic miraculously coming and going sprung to the front of my mind. The night after I'd pushed into Casek's memories, I'd woken without access to my magic as though it had been sealed behind a glass case. Over a week had gone by before Casek had stayed the night with me, and I'd woken to find the block had disappeared. The hum of power had been a constant ever since.

No. He wouldn't have.

"Ashley?" Lochlan said with a hint of warning.

"Tell me it isn't true," I whispered, bringing my tearful gaze to his. "Tell me he didn't."

He rubbed a hand over his face. "I don't know for sure, but I know how worried he's been that your magic would make you a target." He closed the distance between us and lifted my chin to bring my eyes back to his. "I'm going to send him back here for you two to talk. Casek is a good man. Try to remember that." With the rise of his brows, he released me and strolled from the room.

A minute later, I heard the front door click shut, and Casek stepped into the room. I couldn't look at him. I was afraid of what I'd see. Would he admit what he'd done? Could I ever forgive him if he did?

Stealing my powers away from me. Rendering me helpless to fend off the Hell Hounds alone. Making me think I was defective when I couldn't do the simplest Fae magic.

"I want the truth," I said in a hollow voice, eyes boring a hole into the carpet at my feet. "Don't step another foot in here unless every word you speak is the God's honest truth."

He slowly crossed to the window, eyes cast in the distance. "I never expected you to survive Ronan's attack. When I carried your broken, lifeless body to the hospital, I knew there was no chance. At the time, I'd thought it was a shame because I'd seen your tenacity and spark during the weeks before. I appreciated your bold take on life, no matter how much I hated to admit it. When word arrived that you'd been spared and made Fae, I expected you to struggle with the new turn your life had taken. Rebecca had resisted accepting her new circumstances on every level. I thought you'd do the same, but again, I was wrong. I saw it in your face the first time you showed up at the club to get the key to your new apartment. You were invigorated by what had happened and only too ready to leave everything you'd known behind. Your courage and optimism were enchanting. I was utterly captivated yet horrified at the same time. You were so brash, and you had no idea of the dangers around you. Still, you acted invincible whether you had powers or not." He paused, still not looking my way. "I'm not trying to make excuses, but I want you to know where I was coming from. I acted out of fear and a desperate desire to protect you." He quieted and finally turned his eyes to me. "What I did was wrong, and I realized that. The moment I came to my senses, I broke the spell. It terrified me, especially with Durin and Parisa here to witness your incredible gifts, but I freed your magic anyway because I knew it was the right thing to do."

After almost six months of frustration waiting for my powers to emerge, he'd stolen them away again. He'd known how much I wanted my Fae powers, and he'd taken them from me.

I'd been desperately trying to figure out why I hadn't foreseen my father's death. I'd seen Casek being taken, though the vision ended up inaccurate. It had still been a vision. If I'd had full use of my magic, could I have prevented my dad's death?

I couldn't breathe.

Just the whisper of unknown possibilities was suffocating.

Don't forget, Casek was trying to protect you, Ash.

It was true. His intentions were good, but was that enough?

Are you really willing to walk away from him and everything you've cultivated between you because he made a mistake?

It was a fatal mistake, but weren't we all hopelessly flawed to some extent? Look what I'd done to my father.

Yes, I'd managed to find room to forgive him, but what if I'd taken that step years earlier? How much time had we lost to my fear and pride?

Casek had only been doing what he thought was best to protect me. How many times had I wished when my father was at his worst that my mother loved me enough to protect us from his wrath? How many nights had I prayed she'd be strong enough to take us away? To make the hard choice.

Minutes ticked by, drawn and dense with tension as I sorted my thoughts.

When I finally lifted my watery gaze to his, it was free of the blame and anger I'd been so quick to cling to in the past. I wasn't that same girl. I didn't want to be weighed down by her baggage.

"You hurt me." The words were nothing but a fractured breath. "Don't ever do it again."

Casek closed the distance between us, taking my hands and pulling me to my feet. His hands cupped my face reverently as though he held my very soul. Our foreheads came together, our tormented breaths mingling with one another.

"I would never make that same mistake again, but know that I will always protect you by whatever means available to me."

My fingers clenched into fists, clinging to his shirt. "No blood magic. Promise me that one thing, Casek, *please.*"

"How can I make that promise when it might be the only thing that can keep you safe?"

"I don't want my safety to come at that price. If you care for me at all—"

"You know I do," he said gruffly. "There isn't anything I wouldn't do for you, Ashley."

His words burrowed deep into my heart, filling every crack and crevice.

"Promise me, Caz. I've already lost my father. If I lose you, too, I won't … I won't survive it."

Even in the dim light, I could see the torment bright in his eyes. "Don't you see? I'm in the same position. I lost one woman I loved. It would break me to lose another."

My heart stumbled and spun in my chest, creating a wooziness deep in my belly.

Did Casek just tell me he loved me?

I was stunned beyond words. It took three tries before I could make a sound. "Then you'll respect my wishes. I couldn't live with myself if I knew you'd gone to those lengths for me."

With a savage growl, his lips seized mine. Punishing. Demanding. Surrendering.

He poured his soul into that kiss, and I greedily accepted, signing my name on the dotted line of our sealed agreement. I would accept him for exactly who he was, and he promised to keep himself whole for me. It was a covenant upon which our budding relationship could grow. The promise of a future.

"Let's go to bed," he said once my head was spinning and my knees were weak.

I nodded, exhaustion descending at a rapid pace despite the heat of our exchange. My emotions had been shoved through a meat grinder over the course of a few hours, and it had taken a toll.

We undressed in silence. I put on an oversized T-shirt,

and he left on his underwear. I wasn't sure I felt like being touched, but he curved his warm body around mine anyway the instant we were under the covers. His protective touch made it tempting to fall apart because I knew he'd be there to catch me, but I didn't want to. I wanted to be strong and whole and invincible.

"I'm so sorry about your dad, Ash," Casek whispered, his thumb stroking my arm.

My chin quivered. "I'll have to tell my mom, but I'm not sure how. She'll be devastated." The last words were only air as sorrow choked my voice to nothing.

"That can wait. For now, I've got you, and as long as you're here with me, everything will be okay."

I nodded, my breath catching.

Casek was silent for several breaths before speaking again. "Have I ever told you about my family?"

"No." We both knew he hadn't, but it was his way of distracting me, and I was endlessly grateful.

"My father was a type of Fae Lord, and my mother was genteel. They were well suited in temperament and rarely fought. We had a happy childhood. It's why I had no desire to ever stray from the life I'd known. Our country manor wasn't exactly a castle, but it was constructed of sturdy stone and kept us well protected. Raisa and I were left to our own devices most days and ran half-wild with the other local children. Life was simple and as close to perfect as I have ever experienced."

"Did you go to school?"

"We had tutors that would come to the house. The closest thing we had to school was when we started to reach maturity, and we gathered with other kids who had the same elemental gifts to practice our developing powers. They had to be pretty strict because even Fae children who grow up knowing about magic get excited when they can finally access their own powers. I was the worst. The pranks I pulled were atrocious."

"You?" I couldn't imagine Casek as a riotous young boy.

"I wasn't always a brooding assassin."

A soft smile tugged at my lips. "You *can* joke," I teased quietly.

He gave me a squeeze. "Only when necessary."

"Is there anything else I should know about you?" Sleep slurred my words.

"Plenty, and I'm sure you'll ferret out every detail. For now, get some rest, sweet girl." He kissed my temple, and that was the last thing I remembered.

CHAPTER
TWENTY-THREE

"My plan will work if you'll consider it rationally. I'll have Knight with me and will remain in the coffee shop with people around us. You'll be on watch the entire time." Early the next morning, we all sat around the Huntsman conference table discussing our options, which meant I'd been pleading my case to remain with Elle and act as bait.

"And how long do you plan to conduct this operation?" Casek asked. "What happens when her work shift is over? Do you plan to follow her home?"

My mouth opened and closed. I was embarrassed to admit that I hadn't thought that far ahead. After seeing her apron string in the vision, I'd been convinced the threat revolved around her time at the coffee shop. "Maybe I can suggest a sleepover. I know it's not ideal, but Elle is the best lead we have. We can't lock her away any easier than I can follow her indefinitely. Not that I think time will be an issue. After my dad ... the Gorda is making bold moves. He's not going to lie in wait any longer."

"I agree with that last part, at least," Lochlan put in. "Everything points to an imminent attack."

Casek grimaced. "How am I supposed to send you in there with little understanding of your powers and no defense against one of the most vile Unseelie in existence?"

"What if she wasn't unprotected?" Rebecca asked, all eyes turning to her. "I'm not even sure if it's possible, but I was just sitting here trying to think of our options, and it occurred to me that the Druids are able to prevent some Fae powers from affecting them. Lochlan, remember how you tried to use voice manipulation on them when we broke into the British Museum? It had no effect at all."

My pulse kicked up a notch.

"It didn't then," Lochlan conceded. "But I was able to manipulate your boss before I knew he was one of them, and we were leaving for Faery."

Becca bit down on her lips impishly. "Actually ... you didn't. I warned him ahead of time, and he pretended."

He raised a sharp eyebrow and sighed. "Of course, you did."

"Let me get Cat on the phone and see what I can come up with." She lifted the phone to her ear. "Hey, Cat. You somewhere you can talk?" Her mom was suspicious of Rebecca and all Fae, so any conversation they had would need to be in private.

"Good," Becca continued. "I need to ask you how you guys keep from being susceptible to Fae magic." She listened and nodded. "What are the chances we could use that rune? I haven't told you much just because there's not much to tell, but we've been trying to track something called a Fear Gorda. It's incredibly dangerous and has killed several women in the city. We think it's going after Ashley's friend Elle next."

I could hear her audible gasp over the phone. Rebecca's reminder sent a similar jab of pain through my chest.

"We're running out of time and need to catch this guy, but there's little we can do because we can't get near him. His magic is too dangerous. But I was thinking," Becca explained. "If we could help repel the magic like the Druids do, maybe we could get close enough to kill him." She listened to Cat for several beats, the corners of her mouth tugging downward. "Ah, I understand. Well, it was worth asking ... yeah, okay. I'll keep you posted. Thanks, Cat." Becca set down her phone, her shoulders slumping. "She says it's something the elders have to do—some kind of elaborate spell. She doesn't know how it works."

Desperation was a leaden cape upon my back. "We have to do something," I pleaded quietly. "Every minute we sit here is another opportunity for the Gorda to take Elle." My gaze locked on Casek's. "I'm not her, Caz. And this isn't that basement. You'll be there to keep me safe. Please, don't stop me from helping my friend."

The pen in his hands snapped in two, but his eyes never left mine. "I'll give you the daylight hours. If nothing happens by dusk, we bring her to the Huntsman for safekeeping. You can decide whether we tell her the truth or use magic to keep her unaware."

His concession was more than I expected. I nodded with relief. "Okay, I can work with that."

WE SPENT the next hour preparing. I dressed comfortably and made sure I had my knife and pepper spray with me. They were the only weapons I had besides my magic. Knight was brought into the fold and instructed that he would be stationed at the front entrance. The guys felt his absence would look more suspicious than his presence would deter. Plus, they wanted someone within close reach of me. Knight was the most logical candidate.

Once all the obvious details had been worked out, I collected my computer and work bag to take to the coffee shop. The men had already positioned themselves within tracing distance—all but five of the Huntsmen, along with Rebecca, ready and waiting for my signal. I'd been given a small trigger device that I would use as an alarm and promised I'd have it in my hand at all times. One press of the button would alert them to danger. All I had to do now was get in position and wait.

My heart thundered in my ears as I set down my things at a table against the wall and scanned the back counter for Elle. A part of me had been stressing that while we were busy planning, the Gorda could have gone after her in the early hours or even have followed her out of town. But when I spotted her smiling eyes greeting a customer, I heaved a deep sigh of relief.

This is going to work. Elle is alive and well and will stay that way.

I sat down and opened my laptop. I'd planned to pretend to work all day, not wanting to risk missing any danger while engrossed in any real work or mindless internet scrolling. With my back to the wall, no one would be the wiser.

I'd just settled in, eyes stealthfully scanning the small shop, when Elle brought a coffee to a nearby table. As she passed, she waved, and an odd sense of familiarity came over me.

Magic. I sensed magic.

I remembered Becca telling me that the guys had sensed she was Fae from the day we arrived in Ireland. Now that my magic was available to me, could I sense the same thing? She couldn't be Fae. She lived and worked here—but Cat had the use of magic, and she was human. Could Elle be a Druid?

Holy shit, could it be possible?

If she was Druid and knew about the Fae, I could tell her what was going on and not freak her out. She'd understand the danger. Maybe we could come up with an even better trap with her cooperation.

I jumped up and hurried over to her, my heart thudding in my chest. "Hey, Elle! Can I talk to you privately for a minute?" I approached with enough enthusiasm that the poor woman took a step back, her brows arching high.

"Uh, yeah. Let me just tell them I'm taking a quick break. I actually live upstairs if you want to come up for a minute."

"That would be great!" I watched her go behind the counter and get permission for a break, then followed her to a side door that led into the building lobby. "This is really convenient. I didn't realize you lived so close."

"Yeah. When I got the job, I decided it would be easiest to rent from upstairs."

We took three flights of stairs, then walked down the hall to an apartment marked 312. She let me in, closing the door behind us. Her place wasn't at all what I'd expected. She didn't have a single piece of décor on the walls. No photos. No curtains. No flowers. Just bare beige walls. A couch. A kitchenette. Her belongings scattered about the floor.

The place was decent quality, yet it felt desolate. Depressingly baren.

"Sooo … did you want to talk to me about something?" Elle asked, drawing me back from my musings.

"Oh!" I shook my head, forcing myself to focus. "I'm going out on a limb here, and it's a long story, but I've finally got my magic, and I can sense yours. You're a Druid, aren't you?"

She crossed her arms over her chest, her eyes narrowed. "Is this some kind of joke?"

It hit me that I didn't know anything about Elle's family. What if she was a Druid and didn't know? I didn't know much about the secretive Druid sect, but I supposed she could have been born a Druid, then adopted out. Maybe she'd been given rune magic and had no idea.

"No, um. It's not a joke." I tried to figure out how to explain myself when a vision began to take shape before me. Elle and the room faded away as bright white walls came into focus along with a woman, naked and bound in a chair, matted red curls her only cover. I stood behind her, and though I couldn't see her face, I could tell she was still alive and rocking gently the way a child might when calming themselves. The scene was enormously disturbing.

Was I being shown another victim of the Gorda?

Before I could formulate another question, the vision began to fade like smoke, revealing yet another layer behind it. This scene was much darker and even more sinister, if that was possible. I was in a hallway with a door, which approached as though I was walking toward it. Inside lay my father just as I'd found him on the floor of the pub bathroom.

The sight drove my pulse too hard, too fast, pummeling my veins.

No. I don't want to see this. Make it stop.

I desperately tried to turn away. To reject the image before me or close my eyes against its repugnance. But I found no relief against the torturous sight as though someone held my eyes open and forced me to bear witness.

I tried to scream, but no sound emerged.

There was nothing but silence and terror as a parade of spindly black spiders wriggled out from my father's parted lips. One by one, they crept over his body, moving in my direction.

Fear and desperation were poison burning me from the inside out.

I wanted to scream and flail and fight, but I could do nothing. Instead, I listened to my heart as it silently shattered.

TWENTY-FOUR

CASEK

"What the fuck were you thinking? Or were you even thinking at all?" Lochlan cut his eyes to me in a look that was almost as scathing as his questions.

We'd located a vacant apartment on the second floor of the building across from the coffee shop and stationed ourselves discreetly at the window. He'd been more or less silent since we'd arrived, but as soon as Ashley entered the coffee shop, he'd let loose his verbal assault.

He didn't have to explain. I knew exactly what he meant.

"You saw yourself that I undid the spell. That should tell you that I realized I'd fucked up."

"After how long?" he shot back.

"Eight days. It's not exactly a lifetime."

"No, but a lot can happen in that time. She could have been killed."

I stepped closer, bringing my face inches from his. "Don't you think I fucking know that? That's the only thing I've been able to think about for weeks is how much fucking danger she's in. Every woman this bastard has killed reminds me of my failures. How I lost Raisa and how I could lose Ashley just as easily. All I wanted was to avoid something just like this." I motioned to the window. "Yet here I am, hiding away while she could be killed. So if you want to lecture me, go ahead, but you're wasting your breath. I'm already painfully aware of my shortcomings."

His voice was tired but firm when he spoke again. "You know the punishment for the crime you've committed. Blood magic cannot be permitted. How did you even know..." He paused, studying me. "The Gordas you hunted after Raisa's death. That's how you did it, wasn't it? Fucking blood magic."

Silence hung in the air like a hangman's noose.

Now he knew my darkest secret. Not even killing a Huntsman brother could compare to the transgression of using blood magic. With the secret out, my fate would be in his hands.

The toilet flushed from deeper in the apartment, slicing through the tension.

Lochlan had insisted on Rebecca staying at his side during the mission, limiting our opportunity for candid conversation until she'd slipped away. He'd used her brief absence to confront me, and it appeared our time was running short.

"I'm not sure I could exact a punishment on you greater than what you've already suffered." He finally turned his eyes toward me. "You've been my mentor and my closest friend. Knowing what you've done, the powers you used at the risk of losing your own soul, I'm greatly disappointed. Should you ever be tempted to tap into such dark magic again, I will kill you myself." With his judgment delivered, he turned his hard gaze back to the window.

That would be the only warning I would get, and I didn't plan on testing his resolve.

I retreated to my side of the window, peering between the cracked vinyl blinds, breathing a tiny bit easier, knowing the secret was no longer wedged between us.

We had Huntsmen stationed as strategically around the coffee shop as we could manage, considering the close nature of Belfast construction. Ashley hadn't wanted anyone in the back alley, worried it would scare off the Gorda with Knight guarding the front, but I could only make so many concessions. I hated everything about this plan. Not that it was a bad plan. I would have been the first to suggest it had anyone but Ashley been used as our bait. As things stood, I was on edge and ready for a fight. Now was not the best time to confront me.

"Do you guys really think he'll show himself in broad daylight?" Rebecca asked as she returned to the living room.

"It's hard to say what he'll do," I answered. "When things are personal, people become unpredictable."

Rebecca didn't ask any more questions. Twenty minutes passed in agonizing silence.

"It's nine thirty," Lochlan murmured. "Time for her first check-in."

We'd agreed Ashley would text every half hour. I

checked my phone. No message. I gave her one solid minute before I texted her. Two minutes later, she hadn't responded.

"Shit. I knew this was a mistake," I growled. "We're not even an hour in, and she's not following protocol." I tapped my earpiece to talk to the others. "Anyone see anything?"

One at a time, the others reported back with no sightings.

"Let me check with her before we freak out. It'll only take a second." Becca closed her eyes to reach for Ashley's mind in a dream walk. In less than a minute, her eyes opened, revealing solid black irises. "Something's wrong. I can't reach her."

I didn't wait for a second longer. Tracing directly into the coffee shop, I looked around for Ashley, ignoring the confused stares of customers who'd seen me magically appear out of nowhere. I quickly spotted her laptop and bag at a back table. No Ashley.

I honed in on my connection to her and realized she was now above me. That's why I hadn't sensed her location change—she was still in the building, just higher up.

A fissure of relief helped settle my thoughts. I wasn't sure why Ashley would abandon her post, but she wasn't far.

I walked to the counter and motioned for the barista's attention. "Is Elle here?"

"She's on a quick break." The woman smiled and flushed when her eyes met mine. "I think she ran upstairs to her apartment with a friend, but she'll be right back."

"What's happened?" Rebecca called out breathlessly

as she, Lochlan, and Knight rushed inside. Rebecca couldn't trace, and it appeared Lochlan decided not to leave her alone on her way over.

"She's gone upstairs with Elle."

"She went up with Elle, or someone took them upstairs?" Becca asked in confusion.

It didn't make sense. If Ashley had gone up voluntarily, why had she not texted, and why couldn't Rebecca reach her to dream walk?

I looked back at the barista. "Was there anyone else with them?"

"Not that I saw. Is everything okay?" Her eyes darted from me to the others, worry settling in.

I didn't waste time answering her. "Rebecca, how well do you know Elle?"

She stared at me for a second. "Um, I don't, really. We all talked to her over FaceTime at girls' weekend, but otherwise, I haven't met her."

When my eyes cut to Lochlan, his worried gaze mirrored my own. "Could it be?" I asked, the question meant more for me than anyone else.

"There's only one way to know for sure," Lochlan said in a lethal murmur.

I turned back to the petite woman behind the counter. "What's her apartment number?" This time when I spoke, my question was layered with magical command. I didn't want to waste time arguing with her about what she should and shouldn't tell a stranger.

"I don't know, but it's on the third floor."

As soon as the words were out, I bolted for the front

entrance. I had no concrete evidence, but my gut screamed that Ashley was in danger.

CHAPTER
TWENTY-FIVE

ASHLEY

My head ached fiercely. Stabbing pain radiated from the back of my skull, churning my empty stomach. I turned from where I sat and vomited to my side, my body heaving its rejection of what I'd just experienced.

"I'm impressed," came a female voice across from me. "I can't say that I've ever encountered a creature who could fight their way free like you just did."

I cracked open my eyes and peered at Elle. She sat on the ratty sofa across from me, her eyes bright with intrigue.

My mind grappled to catch up. I'd thought I was having a vision, but had it been an attack by the Fear Gorda instead? Why were my hands shackled? Why wasn't Elle more upset?

I scooted down the wall away from the stench of my vomit. "Fight their way free of what?" It was the best I could come up with. My mind felt so sluggish. Any mental strain at all shot stabs of searing pain through my skull.

"Of me, silly."

I looked at her again, this time more attentively. She wore a vile grin on her lips, and the glint in her eyes was nothing shy of depraved.

The Elle I'd thought I'd known had shed her skin and revealed the revolting truth of her nature.

"You're him," I breathed. "You're the Gorda."

How could we have been so wrong? When she'd first started killing women, before the Hunt knew the Gorda's mission was personal, they'd assumed a male was behind the deaths because that was the normal nature of a Gorda. Lure in the opposite sex and feed off them. But if Elle had been trying to throw off the Hunt from the beginning, what better way than to target women instead?

I clenched my eyes shut from the sting of bitter frustration.

"This isn't how I saw things unfolding, but it will suffice. And it's such a relief to have a decent meal. You can't know what it's been like feeding from those pathetic humans. Hardly a taste, and they crumble."

Elle wasn't just a monster; she was evil incarnate.

What was her plan for me? Use me to get to Casek, or did she have something more practical and infinitely more terrifying in mind? How long could a Fae victim survive her brand of torture? How long had Casek said it had taken him to find Raisa? Weeks? Months? I could never withstand the misery. Elle would shred my mind, piece by piece, until I was a shell of a being.

It would be a fate so much worse than death.

Her feminine chuckle scraped over my skin and slithered down my spine. "No matter how much time we have together, you can bet I'll make the most of it." She'd sensed my fear and reveled in the taste of it.

"They'll find me, you know. And once they do, they'll kill you." I spoke softly, the words as much for me as they were for her. As I did so, I slowly slid my right hand closer to my jacket pocket. My knees were pulled up to my chest, helping to hide my movements. The iron cuffs on my wrists kept me from using magic, but I'd stashed the alert device in my pocket. I scrunched the fabric in my hand, unable to get my shackled hands in the pocket itself without drawing attention to my movements.

"Looking for this?" Elle held out the small square fob with a single alert button. "I took the liberty of checking your pockets while you were ... occupied." She lay the device on a table next to a phone, which I now realized was mine. "And as for your *friends*, I've had no problem evading them for this long. I'm sure they won't be an issue."

I tried not to let her words bother me, but it wasn't easy. She had me shackled and hidden away before I'd been able to signal for help. I hadn't texted, so they'd figure out something was wrong, but would Casek's mark help him locate me, or would the iron cuffs block our connection?

Despair licked at my ankles like a rising tide.

I refused its advances. In the months since I'd first stepped foot in Belfast, I'd survived worse, and I'd survive this as well.

"Did Morgan send you? Is that how you knew where to

find him?" I wanted to keep her talking to buy them time but also to gain as much information as I could.

Her eyes narrowed. "Who's Morgan?"

"You don't ... you don't know Morgan? The Fae sorceress who was opening portals and trying to overthrow the queen?" If she hadn't been helped by Morgan, how the hell had she made it here from Faery?

"Can't say that we've met, but I like the sound of her," she mused.

Maybe it was a mistake to believe her, but I could have sworn she was telling the truth.

"Well, you missed your chance. She's been defeated."

Elle shrugged.

"How did you get here if not with Morgan?"

Her eyes flitted briefly away from me as though she suddenly realized she wasn't sure how she'd gotten here. "It doesn't matter how."

"I was told Gordas blend well, but your ability to assimilate was impressive." It was the truth, but I also figured a little petting of her ego couldn't hurt.

"All in only five months. Long enough to become invisible and learn everything I needed to know," she preened.

"It was risky to approach me, though."

"Not really. Our gift as a Gorda is access to the mind so that we might know what will cause the most fear. We can't see everything, but I could sense your magic was trapped. I decided to test my theory and spoke with you. When you showed no signs of sensing who I was, I tested your ability to withstand my feeding. It was only a tiny taste, but it was the best I'd felt in months."

"The spiders in the sink," I whispered. It seemed so

obvious looking back, but I'd been clueless at the time. What other visions had occurred during the week my magic was bound? "And the scene of Casek being taken." I'd wondered why the vision was wrong, but it hadn't been. I had seen exactly what Elle had intended me to see.

I was stunned.

When Casek had confessed to binding my magic, I'd assumed his spell had mutated my visions, but that wasn't the case. His binding had worked. Any type of vision I'd seen during that week had been fed to me by Elle, and I'd been clueless.

Her grin was revolting. "When you told me the Huntsmen would all be gone, I'd thought it was the perfect chance to lure you away. How better than to use your own misguided feelings against you?"

"I thought Gordas had to have physical proximity to feed. You weren't anywhere near me."

"Wasn't I? Your lights were the only ones on in the building—the perfect beacon. I used the fire escape to sit outside your windows, providing me perfect access."

"But if you had planned to lure me away, that would mean you knew I had visions and were trying to use them against me. Show me a vision I feared and hope I acted upon it."

"I told you, I can sense the greatest fears in everyone. Yours was the inability to master your magic. I sensed your fear that your visions wouldn't help you save my victims. It would have all played out perfectly had there only been one or two of you. With that beast constantly at your side, I had to keep my distance."

I'd been played from day one. It was no wonder the

Huntsmen were so wary of Gordas. They truly were formidable opponents, and if I didn't find a way to free myself, I would learn the true meaning of suffering.

The same way my dad had.

I glared at her, tears clouding my vision. "Why? Why take my dad from me? He was totally innocent in all this." My throat cinched tight with pain and anger.

Elle shrugged. "If I've learned one thing in life, it's that no one is innocent enough to escape fate. Sometimes, you're just in the wrong place at the wrong time. He was an easy way to hurt you. Your pain is Casek's pain. That was enough for me."

A hatred too ugly for words corroded my insides.

I desperately wanted to lash out. I needed to do whatever I could to hurt this monstrous person before me who had caused so much devastation, yet I couldn't. I was powerless in my iron cuffs. The only thing I could do was swallow down the vile acrimony and buy myself time. I had to keep her talking.

"Why are you doing this, Elle?"

I rolled my ankle around in my boot ever so gently, trying to discern if the knife I'd stashed inside was still present. It was hard to say. Even if it was there, I wasn't sure how I could use it to escape, but I'd still rather have it than not.

"I'm a Fear Gorda. It's right there in the name," she said callously.

"That's not what I meant. Your attack on us is personal. Why?"

She scowled. It was the first sign of any true emotion, and in a way, it was encouraging. Where there was hate, there could be love. She wasn't a mindless predator. Redemption wasn't a possibility—not in my eyes—but if she had a sliver of conscience, there was the hope of escape.

"I don't suppose Casek told you about how he massacred my entire family?" She spat his name like poison on her tongue.

"He told me he hunted a clan of Gordas. After they killed his sister."

She sneered. "One woman. They took one woman, and he killed them all. Well, almost all. He didn't scour for survivors enough to find a single terrified little girl hidden away by her mother in a secret panel. He went from house to house on a killing rampage. I watched through a tiny crack as my mother and father were interrogated and torn limb from limb." Her eyes glazed over as though the centuries-old memory still held her tight in its clutches.

Meanwhile, I grappled to understand how I felt toward this broken woman. She'd taken my father from me. She'd brought unending torment to countless victims, yet that was her nature. She hadn't asked to be born a Gorda. Elle had only been an innocent child when she witnessed her family being slaughtered. In a way, she was just as much a victim as the others. Her circumstances weren't an excuse, but I found that she was worthy of my pity, if only a little.

"None of this will bring them back," I whispered.

Her eyes pierced me with pure hatred. "I was a *child* left alone in the Wilds. That man took *everything* from me."

No, there would be no redemption for Elle. Her loathing had consumed her completely.

"So what is your plan? You want to hurt Casek by hurting me?"

She lifted her knees to her chest, mirroring how I sat. I had to remind myself not to buy into the vulnerability the position implied.

"Once I learned the identity of the man who'd slaughtered my clan, I learned everything I could about him. I needed to know him to make him suffer as I had. All my information was consistent—Casek was solitary aside from the Hunt. He had no ties. Nothing and no one he cared about that I could take from him. When I finally made it here to Earth, I watched him myself from a distance and confirmed it was true. The best I could do was taunt him until you came along. I always tried to watch when they uncovered my victims. I loved to see the frustration on their faces. One day, you appeared outside a pub, shivering and wide-eyed. He was instantly enraged. The second I saw his reaction to you, I knew you were perfect. You would be my revenge."

Her head turned toward the door as soon as her words ceased.

"What is it?"

"*Quiet,*" she hissed.

I wanted to jump up and scream for help, hoping someone would be in the hallway, but my vision blurred, and my head swam.

No, not again. Please, not again.

I pushed to my hands and knees, desperately fighting for consciousness. I could barely see. The weight of my leaden body was nearly impossible to support, but I pushed forward, crawling toward the door.

I needed to get out. I had to escape.

The effort to move took all that I had. When I reached the door, I barely managed to crack it open. I had to lean against the wall for long seconds as I recovered my strength. I had to keep going.

Nudging the door open more fully, I glimpsed the freedom of the hallway only to collapse in agony at the sight of my dearest friends bloody and lifeless before me. Rebecca. Knight. Casek. Cat. Lochlan. Liam. They were all there. Broken and strewn about the hallway like ravaged dolls.

I screamed. And screamed. And screamed.

CHAPTER
TWENTY-SIX

CASEK

"Caz, *stop!*" Rarely did Lochlan order me with such resounding conviction.

As much as I wanted to race up the stairs toward Ashley, his command triggered years of training, drawing me to a quick halt. "What is it?"

He motioned for me to wait and turned to Rebecca just as the other Huntsmen filtered into the lobby. "You're going to wait here with the rest of the men. I won't hear any arguments."

"We don't have time for this shit," I snapped.

Lochlan ignored me, waiting for Rebecca's reluctant nod. "You men listen for word down here. I want two on the back side of the building and two surveying the street on either side."

The men quickly split up, and Lochlan joined me on the stairs with Knight at his side.

"I know you feel this is urgent, but it's just as important that we don't fuck this up. We need to be prepared for the possibility that she can ensnare both of us at once and the likelihood we'll encounter wards that will keep us out."

I listened to my Erlking and friend but just barely. The need to get to Ashley was a living thing clawing beneath my skin, demanding I ignore everything and *run*.

"This is a Gorda we're dealing with, so there is no way to prepare. All I want is to get Ashley back. We can deal with the Gorda later." Done being patient, I resumed climbing the stairs two at a time.

Once we reached the third floor, I slowed, peering around the corner into the hallway. I could sense Ashley's proximity. The need to go to her grew stronger than ever.

With no obvious signs of danger, I crept forward. "You two stay here." If this was a death trap, we didn't need all three of us taken at once.

The stairs were at the far end of the building. Each side of the hall housed four units. At the opposite end, a window provided access to the fire escape. Ashley was in one of the apartments, but I didn't know which one and wouldn't until I got closer.

One slow step at a time, I worked my way down the hall. I made it past the first two sets of doors when one creaked open behind me. I looked back and saw a flash of blond hair.

Ashley.

Gun in my hand, I pressed the door open to get a better view inside and froze at the sight of Ashley tied to a chair in the center of the living room. Her head was tilted to the side, blood dripping from her nose and mouth, and her eyes bulged wide with terror.

No. How could this be? How could we have been too late?

I rushed inside and cupped the porcelain skin of her face. She was cool to the touch. "*Ashley!* Jesus, *fuck!* Come back, baby. Don't do this to me."

My chest constricted so tight I thought my ribs would crack.

I didn't care, though. Let my entire body break into pieces if it meant an end to this torment.

I pressed my cheek to hers, my hands trembling, and unleashed a tsunami of pain in a roar that barreled from deep in my chest.

"*Casek!* Caz, can you hear me?"

I suddenly became aware of a stinging on my cheek. When my eyes opened to see what had happened, Ashley's image blurred and morphed until it was Lochlan before me, blue eyes glowing with alarm.

"What the fuck is happening?" I asked, rubbing my face.

"She had you ensnared. You made it fifteen feet down the hall, then stopped. I called you, but you didn't answer. You didn't move a muscle like you weren't even there."

Thank Christ, it wasn't real.

I breathed through the adrenaline and coaxed my body back from the grips of panic. "She knows we're here then," I murmured, trying to regain my bearings. "She can trace away at any time, but then she'll lose her hostage." I paused, looking at where I stood now versus where Lochlan had said I'd stopped. "You were able to get to me safely without her attacking you?"

He gave a sharp nod. "I can't say for certain, but I suspect she can only ensnare one mind at a time. Was that your experience before?"

"I hunted alone, so it was an issue I never faced." So little was known about the Gordas because it was so rare for anyone to survive an encounter. "What if we test that theory, and one of us occupies her while the other goes after Ashley? If she switches targets, then we also adjust."

"It could work," Lochlan agreed. "I'll need to go first. You're the only one who has a read on Ashley's location."

I hated the idea of turning over my Erlking to the Gorda, but as long as it was temporary, there would be no lasting effects. "Let's do it."

"As soon as I stop, you find her. Don't worry about me."

I dipped my chin in agreement and watched as Lochlan boldly charged down the hall. He made it about as far as he'd said I had before his steps slowed, and he stilled like a machine whose batteries had failed.

Hang on, Ash. I'm coming.

I decided to trace to each door. It took a second to orient myself and regain the feel of my bond, but it was still faster than running down the corridor. Within seconds, I'd reached the last door and confirmed that I could sense Ashley inside. However, as we'd suspected, I could also sense a substantial ward protecting the perimeter.

Shit. There was no physical or magical force I could create strong enough to overcome this type of ward. Not on short notice.

All of a sudden, Knight nipped at my hand.

I squatted down to meet his golden gaze. "There's a ward I can't get past."

He pawed silently at the ground, then used his shoulder to nudge me aside.

"Can you get through the ward?" Hope surged in my chest.

The giant white wolf pressed his ears back and crouched, head low before springing through the door as if he weren't corporeal. As if he were a living ghost.

The sound of Ashley's cry hung in my ears. Then Knight's savage growl dissolved into a whimper, but only after sharp claws raked across the inside of the door. It was the sound of his scratches mutilating Elle's ward and breaking the spell.

I slammed my shoulder into the door and burst inside. My eyes locked on a young woman sitting casually on the sofa as though she didn't have a care in the world. She lifted her hand, wiggled her fingers in a coy wave, then disappeared.

"Casek!" Ashley pulled herself upright just in time for my arms to seize her tightly against me. "I knew you'd find me."

"Always, sweet girl," I whispered into her soft golden hair. "Always."

Knight shook off his disorientation and stood at the same time as Lochlan barged into the room behind us. I reluctantly released Ashley and turned to Lochlan, who was now communicating an update to the others and calling them to us.

"She's traced away, but she didn't have time to properly cover her tracks."

Lochlan shook his head. "It's too dangerous. Let her go."

"Fuck that," I shot back. "She wants me, then she'll get me. We end this now." I stormed to where she'd been sitting and chanted the necessary words to follow her magical footprint. This type of spell could only be performed within minutes of a person tracing. If I didn't act fast, I'd lose her, and I was done being hunted. She likely didn't expect me to follow her. With my gun ready, it would take one quick shot, and this war would be over.

Ignoring Lochlan's roars behind me, I clasped my gun in my hand and let the magic take me.

CHAPTER
TWENTY-SEVEN

ASHLEY

I HADN'T STOOD BY AND WATCHED A SITUATION UNFOLD SO helplessly since I'd lived under my parents' roof. I swore to myself years ago that I'd never again be a bystander. That I would speak up and protect the people I cared about.

My oath was all but a distant memory as I stared at the spot Casek had occupied seconds before.

He'd left. He was going to take on Elle all by himself.

I had to do something. I had to *think*.

"They can't get far, right?" I asked Lochlan, who had finally ended his irate string of curses.

"Correct. We can only trace short distances." He closed his eyes and shook his head. "I can't sense him through my bond as Erlking. If I can't touch his consciousness, I have no lead on him."

My hand flew to the back of my neck. "What about my mark? Could it work?"

263

Lochlan's eyes sparked bright blue. "It should. Even iron can't sever the connection of a mating brand."

I ignored the bit about mating and closed my eyes, focusing all my energy on sensing Casek. The second I felt him, I bolted for the door and flew down the stairs. I didn't care about my shackled hands or my lack of a weapon. I paid no mind to Lochlan and Knight barreling after me. All that mattered was getting to Casek. I had to help him.

We passed several Huntsmen coming up the stairs. I tore past them, vaguely aware of Lochlan shouting orders to fan out. He'd called them from their posts once he and Casek had infiltrated the apartment, but that was before Casek had gone rogue after Elle. Confusion hardened their already fierce expressions, but there was no time to explain.

I continued to the lobby. Once on the ground level, the pull led me to the back of the building. I wasn't sure of the best way out, but the coffee shop likely had a rear exit, so I went back through the door Elle had used to lead me upstairs and tore through the kitchen toward the marked exit.

What followed next took all of ten seconds but felt like a lifetime.

I exploded out the door into the cobblestone alley. Elle stood not twenty feet away, her back to me. She was walking, hand extended with a knife clutched in her grip. Casek knelt across from her. His gaze was a foggy green forest, murky and isolated from the world.

She had him in her clutches and was moving in for the kill.

"*No!*" My scream was so animalistic, so savagely feral, I didn't recognize my own voice.

Elle whipped around, her vicious stare colliding with mine.

Pain lanced through my skull as she sank her mental talons deep into my psyche, but before I lost myself to her madness, a streak of white blurred past me.

A snarl of gnashing teeth resounded off the stone walls around us, along with a high-pitched shriek. Woven together, they painted a vicious picture that played out in living color as my sense returned to me.

Knight had lunged for Elle's neck but caught her shoulder instead. She struggled to stay upright, unable to trace away with his jaw clamped tightly into her flesh.

However, as with any attack on a Gorda, he could only last so long before he, too, fell victim to her mental torment. But this time, when his movements turned weak, and it looked as though she might break free, a gunshot exploded through the air.

Elle flew backward to the ground, her body unmoving. Where her face had been was now a gory mess of blood and tissue and bone, the green tie of her apron poking through her thick hair spread on the cobbled stones.

Casek stood not far away, gun outstretched.

He never took his eyes off her.

Though she lay motionless, and it was obvious she wouldn't be getting up anytime soon, he marched forward and emptied the remaining bullets into her body. Only then did his eyes seek mine.

I ran to him, my shackled hands reaching up and over his head to hold myself tightly against him.

"It's okay, baby. You're safe now," he whispered close to my ear. "She won't hurt anyone ever again."

I shook my head, sobs beginning to overwhelm me. "Not me ... you ... so worried." Each statement was accented by heaving breathless sobs of relief. I hated crying. It was the quicksand of emotions, dragging a girl down until she couldn't see straight. I tried to avoid it at all costs, but nothing was to be done about it in this instance. All the emotions I'd grappled with in the preceding days came at me all at once. I was nothing but a tiny reed, desperately trying to survive the flood.

The vibration of a masculine chuckle was the life vest I needed. I clung to the sound, letting its warm density fill me until I was grounded again.

"We did it, Caz. We stopped her." I lifted my hands back over his head to release him, able to stand on my own again.

"We did—all of us together." His fingers wove into my hair as he pulled me in for a kiss. "Now it's time to get these shackles off you. The only time you should ever be in cuffs is when you're in my bed."

I was suddenly a tad unsteady again.

A flood of warmth heated my cheeks as we turned to face the others. Lochlan stood with a growing group of Huntsmen circled around the body. They all listened intently as he spoke. I had no desire to hear. I was done. All tapped out and ready to retire my superhero cape.

For today at least.

Knight sat not far from the group, his doggy tongue lolling out the side of his mouth. If it weren't for the traces of blood marring the jowls of his snowy white fur, he would have looked perfectly docile.

It was a good thing he wasn't.

We'd needed his ferocity today. Merlin's guard dog had been indispensable.

Casek's gaze followed mine. "If he hadn't been able to pass through Elle's ward, I don't know how we would have gotten to you."

I gave his hand a squeeze before releasing it, then walked to Knight, squatting to wrap my arms around him. "Thank you, buddy. You really saved the day." My voice quivered with gratitude.

Knight licked my face in one long slurp from chin to forehead.

I laughed, almost falling back on my behind.

Casek clasped me under the arms, helping me back up to my feet. "Come on, let's go home." He motioned to Lochlan before leading me around the corner toward the main street. Once we got back to the Huntsman building, he took me to the basement and removed the shackles in a workshop-type room full of tools and supplies.

"What will they do with her?" I asked, rubbing the raw skin on my wrists. I wasn't sure why I wanted to know. I was glad she was dead, but that didn't erase the tragedy of the entire situation.

"She'll burn. It's the best way to ensure she can't ever return." He lifted my hands in his and placed a single delicate kiss on the underside of each wrist.

The air emptied from my lungs.

He was being so incredibly sweet, but I needed to talk

about what had happened. I needed to tell him what I'd learned.

"She was there when you killed the Gordas," I said softly.

A shadow darkened his gaze. "I figured that was likely the case."

"She was so damaged, Caz. I know her kind is a different breed already, but she was so broken. It sounds crazy to feel sorry for her after everything she did, but it was heartbreaking, in a way."

"I don't think it's crazy. Our ability to empathize is what separates us from her kind. It's what makes you such a loyal friend and a formidable enemy." The corners of his mouth hooked upward.

I fought a smile. "You're being awfully sweet. It's a little unsettling."

Casek sobered, his eyes locking with mine. "I could have lost you today, Ash. No more games or denials. You're mine, and I'll give you sweet every damn day if that's what it takes to keep you by my side."

My heart expanded to twice its normal size, straining against the confines of my rib cage.

I adored this man—all of him. His brooding silences and playful smirks. His ferocity and bravery. His compassion and generosity. I wanted every part of him, especially those darkest parts that first drew my attention.

Peering at him from beneath my lashes, I drew my tongue along my lip. "And what if I don't want sweet?"

The hunger in his answering gaze threatened to swallow me whole.

"You'll take what I give you," he informed me in a

husky murmur. "After almost losing you, though, I'm in the mood for sweet. Later, when the memories aren't so fresh, I'll show you just how dirty I can be."

"Okay," I breathed, drunk on his words.

He spun me around, bringing his lips close to my ear from behind. "Upstairs, Ash. Before I lose it and fuck you here in the workshop." His hand gave my ass a sharp swat, spurring me into action.

Even sweet from Casek had a touch of cayenne, and that was just the way I liked it.

I walked to the elevator, practically purring with anticipation. Casek didn't disappoint.

CHAPTER
TWENTY-EIGHT

ASHLEY

By seven that evening, I was told all that remained of Elle were unpleasant memories. My relief that the entire situation was resolved cast enough joyous light to outshine the sliver of remorse I'd had over losing a friend. Her friendship had been a farse, but the loss was still felt, even if only briefly. By the time we all gathered that night around the conference table to check in and discuss the day's events, the only grief remaining was all for my father. I wasn't sure I'd ever fully escape the shadow cast by that loss. I didn't necessarily want to, either. The fact that I grieved for him at all was evidence that I'd had my dad back, even if only for a day.

"Is there anything else we need to cover tonight before we adjourn?" Lochlan asked the group.

I cleared my throat, feeling all eyes swivel in my direction. "I don't know if it means anything, but there was one thing that Elle said that made me curious. I asked her if Morgan had helped her cross worlds, and she had no idea who Morgan was. She was emotional enough that I believed she was telling the truth. Could she have gotten here using one of Morgan's portals without encountering Morgan?" During Rebecca's dealings with Morgan Le Fay, I hadn't been present and had no idea how the portals worked.

Lochlan's face hardened as he met Rebecca's equally severe gaze.

"No, that's not possible," Becca explained. "The portals could only be opened briefly, and Morgan couldn't be absent while Elle or any other creature passed through."

"If she didn't have Morgan's help, how else could she have gotten here?" My question hung heavily in the air around us.

Lochlan was the first to comment. "She could have found a way on her own, though it's unlikely. Merlin or someone of equal strength could have managed the feat, but again, the likelihood is low that she could have found someone with such capabilities willing to send a Gorda to Earth. Aside from those options, the only person who can circumvent the queen's wards would be the queen herself."

"That doesn't make any sense. Why would she do that?" One of the men asked.

"I'll admit it's unlikely, but she was behind the Hell Hounds attack," Lochlan noted. "If she could send one caste of creatures after us, it would be wise to consider she was behind the other as well. Elle got here somehow, and we'll need to figure out how it happened."

"It's almost impossible to get anyone to turn on the queen." The man grimaced.

"I'd agree with you if it weren't for the sword. Get our hands on the right people, and we can force the truth."

Everyone nodded in agreement.

"Anything else?" Lochlan asked.

Rebecca placed her hands on the table and sat forward. "I was going to mention this at some point, but in light of what was just discussed, I want to emphasize the importance of solidifying our ties to the Druids. I can't help but wonder what we could learn from them. Would the protective runes they use aid us in capturing someone as dangerous as Elle? I'd prefer to have access to every tool available."

"That will take time," Lochlan said. "I encountered staunch resistance when I met with them."

"I know. I guess what I'm saying is, don't give up. I think there's a lot we can learn from one another."

"I'll keep that in mind." He tipped his head toward her. "Now, if there isn't anything else, I think we've all had a long day."

Quiet murmurs filled the room as everyone stood and dispersed.

Casek followed me as I left. I wasn't sure what our plans were for the night but didn't ask while others were around us. When he took the elevator with me to my floor, my chest warmed. We'd been together all afternoon, so I had half expected us to spend the night apart. Our relationship was new, after all.

"You making sure I get home okay?" I teased, falling back on humor when under the pressure of uncertainty.

"Fuck if I'm sleeping away from you when I know you're right here in the same building."

Excuse me while I mop up my melted heart off the floor.

"I guess that makes sense," I whispered as I opened the door.

My cheeks had to be as red as the damn shirt I was wearing, judging by the heat radiating off them.

Before I could close the door behind us, Casek stopped me. Stalking close so that his enormous frame caged me against the wall, he braced his hands on either side of me, leaving just enough space between us to tease me with his delicious body heat.

"You *guess* that makes sense?" Each word was a devilish challenge.

He leaned down, still keeping our bodies apart, and scraped his teeth along my neck.

My entire body erupted in goose bumps.

"I mean ... that sounds ... good. Yeah, that sounds good," I said, my own words suddenly jumbled and breathless.

He trailed the bridge of his nose along my jawline before raising his lips to ghost across mine. My lips parted in anticipation, but instead of ending the delicious torture with his touch, he turned his face away.

"Knight. Out." The command sliced through the silent apartment.

"But where will he go?" I fought a smile. I knew Knight could take care of himself. I just wanted to see what Caz would say.

"Don't care." He turned his face back to mine. "He's not staying here and listening to the sounds you'll be making tonight."

"Oh," I breathed.

Casek's eyes turned molten. "Yeah ... *oh.*"

Behind us, Knight lumbered off the sofa and then harumphed as he moseyed out the door.

I couldn't help but giggle, though it died quickly when I looked back at Caz. He hadn't lost an ounce of his intensity. If anything, his desire flared so brightly that its flames licked angrily at my skin.

"I have a bone to pick with you," I said softly, lifting my palms to rest on his broad chest.

He didn't say a word, so I continued.

"Today, when we were coming after you, Lochlan called the mark on my neck a *mating* brand." I raised an eyebrow.

"And?" he challenged.

I'd brought up the subject but was suddenly speechless. I'd half expected him to brush off the wording or claim it had been the only option to protect me.

"Um..." I fumbled. "It just sounded like ... *more* ... than I realized. I wasn't sure how to take it."

"It's there because you're mine. If I'd been honest with myself, you were mine the second I sank inside you. I didn't tell you the truth about the mark because I knew it was fast, and I knew you might not take it well. Yes, it was a little underhanded. Do I care? Not even a little, so long as it's my name you wear. And because I want you to know that I'm yours as well, I want your mark on me the second you learn how."

I was stunned.

Normally, talk of commitment made my skin crawl with the need to escape. Casek was different. The thought of binding myself to him felt like the ultimate way to arm myself against the world. With him by my side, I could do anything. Survive anything.

Everything about our relationship seemed so fast, yet how could I deny myself something that felt so right? I'd spent my adult life running. I didn't want to run anymore. I wanted Casek.

"I think I'd like that," I said, my fingers curling into his shirt.

"Good, because I want everyone to know nothing can come between us. *Nothing*." His lips finally claimed mine in a kiss so deep and demanding and fervent that I no longer knew where I began and he ended.

He lifted me in his arms, slammed the door shut, then carried me to the bedroom. His hunger was so ravenous that we could have been apart for weeks rather than hours.

My clothes were off in a heartbeat, discarded at my feet just as thoroughly as my doubts and reservations.

Casek took both my hands in one of his, lifting them high above my head, then grinned. "*Now* it's time to get a little dirty."

EPILOGUE

ASHLEY

5 Weeks Later

"That's wonderful news, Mom! I'm so proud of you." I grinned over the phone, feeling more like the parent than the child as my mother shared news of her permanent job offer at the local college back home. She'd impressed the administration so much during her interim position that they'd invited her to stay on full time.

The weeks since Dad's passing had been incredibly hard on her. I'd visited for a week to help with the funeral and be at her side, but even my presence did little to lift her out of the depths of despair. For the first time since receiving the news of his death, I could hear a pulse of excitement and hope in her voice.

"I'm so relieved, and I've adored teaching. Now that summer school is over, I'll have a couple of weeks to prepare for the fall semester. I feel like maybe I'm settling into my new normal. I hate to say that in a way, but I suppose it's necessary."

"Dad would have wanted you to be happy. And I know he would have been thrilled for you."

She was silent for a beat, and I feared her grief had taken hold, but when she spoke, it was happiness that rattled her voice. "I'm just so glad you two were able to reconnect. He was so happy when he called home that first day. I wish you could have heard him talk about how proud he was of you and how much he loved you."

It was my turn to choke back emotion. "The memories of those couple of days will stick with me forever." I paused, my throat constricting. "I'm sorry it took me so long to forgive him. I know that was hard on you both."

"I have so much more to be sorry for than you do. I know I should have left during those years. I was weak, and I couldn't bring myself to forget the man I knew he could be."

"It was hard for me to separate the addiction from the man, but I think I get it now. I thought maybe I'd come home again in the fall for his birthday." I knew Mom would struggle, and I wanted to be there for her. It was a new sensation for me. The resentment had eaten away at my compassion for years. I hadn't cared how Mom was feeling because I'd felt like she hadn't cared about me, but I knew that wasn't the case. I didn't agree with her choice to stay while he was still drinking, but that didn't mean she didn't also care about me. The addiction had infected the entire family. She'd done the best she could.

"I'd really love that. Okay, this wasn't supposed to be a sappy call." Mom laughed through her tears. "It's late here, so I'll let you go. Take care, baby girl."

"Love you, Mom."

"Love you, too."

I smiled as I set down my phone, though no one was around to see it. Becca had finally moved all her things to Lochlan's apartment, and I hadn't seen Knight in three days straight. I hadn't expected him to live here forever, but his absence still stung. I'd gotten used to having the furball around.

My place felt a little empty without either of my room-mates, so I spent most of my time at Casek's apartment. Tonight, I'd come home to get ready for an evening at the club. Full hair and makeup required more than the basic toiletries I kept upstairs at his place.

An hour later, I was almost ready when a knock sounded on my front door. I threw on my robe and answered to find Becca on my doorstep with a beaming grin.

"Hey! I got ready early and thought I'd sit with you while you finished up."

"Daw, just like the old days!" I gave her a quick hug and pulled her inside. "I'm glad you're here because I can't decide which dress to wear."

We walked to my bedroom, where I'd laid out two dresses on the bed.

"Not even close. The blue one. You look amazing in blue."

"I do, don't I?" I said, giving her a wink with a blue pulse of light behind my eyes. I'd been diligently practicing my magic every day. The physical aspects like fire and tracing were much easier to improve upon than my mental gifts. Learning to control my visions was hard when I never knew when one might appear, which wasn't all that often. I'd had two in the past five weeks. One involved Knight's disappearance, though I hadn't understood until he was gone. The other revolved around a failed batch of cookies I should have known better than to attempt to bake.

Apparently, my visions weren't all about life and death.

It would have been helpful if Merlin had come around to give me some pointers, but we hadn't seen or heard from him since he named me as his apprentice.

"Okay, I think I'm ready." I checked out my reflection in the mirror, doing a little spin. "Is Cat coming tonight?"

"She's out of town visiting family. It was a little odd. She didn't tell me she was leaving or anything, but apparently, she goes on a trip like this every summer. I guess she forgot to mention it."

"That's too bad. I haven't seen her in ages. We'll have to do a girls' night when she gets back."

"Definitely," she grinned, joining me in front of the mirror. "You ready to get up there?"

"Let's do it." We grabbed our clutch purses and left my apartment, taking the elevator up to the club level.

When we stepped into the large open room scattered

with the first arrivals of the evening, my eyes were instantly drawn to Casek across the room. As if he'd been waiting for us to arrive, his steely gaze was already honed in on me and hungrily devouring every inch of my body. The outside world fell away, and I abandoned Rebecca and cut across the room like a hot knife through butter.

Casek had been stationed by the back hallway that led to the bathrooms and offices. He leaned against the wall, wearing a tailored suit perfectly fitted to his large frame. The only thing more arousing than the sight of him was the knowledge he was all mine.

"Hey, handsome," I greeted coyly.

He grabbed my hand and pulled me against him. "I've never seen anything so fucking gorgeous in my entire life." He spoke in a rasp close to my ear. "Dance with me."

I stilled, pulling back to see if he was serious.

"I didn't think you danced." Not once in almost eight months of knowing him had I ever seen him dance. Not on the dance floor nor alone in the privacy of his apartment. The only dancing Casek performed was the horizontal sort.

"Only in exceptional circumstances," he whispered. His piercing eyes said, *and everything about you is exceptional.*

I had to remind myself to breathe.

Casek took both of my hands and pulled me toward the middle of the room. I raised my hands to the back of his neck, loving the way his skin heated when my fingers connected with my brand. I'd made it a priority to learn how to reciprocate his mark. It had been weeks since I'd performed the spell, but a giddy smile still crept across my face every time I saw the delicate black lines on him.

The dance floor was empty. It was too early for a crowd, which suited me just fine. No distractions. I preferred to give all my attention to the way my body molded perfectly against his. To the sensual way he moved in rhythm with the pulsing beat.

Casek could definitely dance.

I should have known better than to doubt him. He'd shown me countless times in private just how well he could move.

For one song after another, Casek tempted and teased until my body hummed with an electric need so blinding, I feared I might embarrass myself on the middle of the dance floor.

As one song transitioned to the next, I pulled away, my cheeks flushed. "I think I need to run to the restroom for a minute." My dazed, breathless words brought a knowing smirk to his lips.

However, instead of letting me leave, he pulled me back against him. One hand behind my head guided my lips to his, the other lifted beneath my dress to cup my sex discreetly enough that only someone watching closely would notice.

He used his magical touch to light my body on fire, his mouth devouring my shocked cries.

The orgasm was instantaneous.

Fireworks incinerated my veins, molten heat liquifying my bones.

I had to cling to his shoulders to stay upright, too

intoxicated to even care that I'd just had my first public orgasm.

When I'd regained my senses, Casek helped steady me until I could stand on my own.

"*Now*, you can head to the restroom."

Completely sex drunk, I nodded and teetered off.

Once inside the 1920s-era Hollywood glam ladies' room, I sank onto a tufted velvet ottoman to regroup.

Holy hell, can that man disorient me.

A Cheshire grin crept across my face as the door to the restroom flew open.

"Who is that man, and what have you done with Casek?" Becca's warm brown eyes were wide with astonishment. "I didn't even know he could dance!"

"Me either." My cheeks began to ache from the intensity of my smile.

Becca sat across from me and began to speak, but the room grew dark around the edges with the telltale signs of a vision. Knowing I was safe to immerse myself in what I was about to see, I allowed the image to materialize before me without struggle. I was too high on dopamine to practice control at the moment.

From dark to light, white walls materialized in front of me. It was a familiar scene—the exact same setting as I'd seen when Elle took me prisoner. Later, I'd assumed the entire vision had been a product of her manipulations, but that wasn't the case. Elle was gone, and the vision had returned.

The red-headed woman I'd seen before sat in her chair, naked and rocking. Her back was turned to me, but this time, her head swiveled toward me, and my blood ran cold at the sight.

The young woman was Cat, only her eyes didn't shine with their normal brilliance.

They were empty—utterly lifeless.

She wasn't dead, but it was as if all the life had been sucked from her, leaving her an empty shell. The sight was horrifying.

When my eyes refocused on the room around me, Becca gaped at me, eyes wide with worry. "Did you have a vision?" she asked in a hushed whisper, her olive skin looking suddenly pale.

I nodded, my hands tightly clasping one another. "It's Cat. She's in terrible danger."

Thank you so much for reading *Venom & Vice*!
The *Of Myth & Man* series contains a total of four books, of which *Venom & Vice* is book 2.

In book 3, Blood & Breath, Cat finds herself deep in the clutches of a forbidden love affair. Fate has brought them together in a way neither expected, but forbidden love comes with a price. Will the two find a way to overcome or be lost to one another forever?

In book 4, Siege & Seduction, Morgan Le Fay teams up with a sworn enemy to help her achieve a life-long desire, uncovering truths about the villainess that will change everything. *Siege & Seduction* ties together the four previous books in a romantic adventure full of jaw-dropping twists and heart-stopping heroics you won't want to miss!

Make sure to join my Facebook reader group and keep in touch!
Jill's Ravenous Readers!

ACKNOWLEDGMENTS

When I wrote the very first version of *Curse & Craving*, I had no intention of continuing the saga. If it wasn't for my sweet friend and beta reader Brandi, Ashley's story might never have been told. Thank you, Brandi, for all your input and speed-demon reading skills!

To my endlessly patient husband, my deepest gratitude. For every time you read, re-read, and then re-read again to help me through the writing process. You are a superstar, and your input is invaluable.

To Sue, I thank you for all your developmental editing genius. You told me the things I didn't want to hear and made them sound like no big deal, giving me the confidence to keep going. This book has survived a major metamorphosis over time, and you got that ball rolling.

To Jenny, thank you for making my words sound intelligent. The polish you add to each of my manuscripts makes all the difference in the world.

To Megan and the many hats you now wear for me, thank you for everything! For answering my texts after hours and speed reading on short notice. For your encouragement, ideas, and eternal positivity. You help make this process manageable, and that's no small feat.

My list could go on and on. I'm a very lucky lady to have such a phenomenal support system surrounding me. Thank you to each and every one of you!

About the Author

Jill Ramsower is a life-long Texan—born in Houston, raised in Austin, and currently residing in West Texas. She attended Baylor University and subsequently Baylor Law School to obtain her BA and JD degrees. She spent the next fourteen years practicing law and raising her three children until one fateful day, she strayed from the well-trod path she had been walking and sat down to write a book. An addict with a pen, she set to writing like a woman possessed and discovered that telling stories is her passion in life.

SOCIAL MEDIA & WEBSITE

Release Day Alerts, Sneak Peak, and Newsletter
To be the first to know about upcoming releases, please join Jill's Newsletter. (No spam or frequent pointless emails.)
Jill's Newsletter

Official Website: www.jillramsower.com
Jill's Facebook Page: www.facebook.com/jillramsowerauthor
Reader Group: Jill's Ravenous Readers
Follow Jill on Instagram: @jillramsowerauthor
Follow Jill on Twitter: @JRamsower

GLOSSARY OF TERMS

Below are a number of the important terms and characters from *Venom & Vice* and the *Of Myth & Man* series thus far. I have included pronunciations as I would say the word, not pronunciations as the dictionary would offer because I have no idea how that works.

Arthur—Powerful Fae General who broke away from Queen Guin and formed the Wild Hunt.

Battle of Tirath—Battle where the Seelie forces were outnumbered and lost many lives during The Great War.

Beltane—The day halfway between the spring equinox and the summer solstice (early May). One of the naturally occurring days when the veil between worlds is the thinnest and the availability of magic is greatest. The Druids celebrated the day with bonfires and used ashes to ensure the protection of their crops and livestock.

Bergresar—Ancient, evil Shadow Fae.

Blood Magic—An ancient, dark magic that requires the use of sacrificial blood. Used too many times, blood magic eventually creates a bloodlust in the user so intense he or she is reduced to a state of mindlessness in the search of blood. This condition is considered a flagrant violation of the laws of nature by most Fae, and thus the use of blood magic is often punishable by death.

Brownie—Small green-skinned Fae that lives peacefully in homes, often known to clean and sometimes steal items for itself.

Cormac Doyle—Soldier who abandoned his post during a special mission in The Great War against the Unseelie.

Draug (*drog*)—Shadow Fae creature that can dissolve into shadow and is drawn to finding jewels and other treasure.

Druid (*drew-id*)—Descendants of the people who were taught the use of rune magic by the Fae.

Elders—Druid leadership council made up of 11 district members, one of which is elected as the chief elder who presides over council meetings.

Erlking (*earl-king*)—The elected leader of the Wild Hunt.

Faery—A world with latent magic that can be accessed from Earth via portals.

Fae—The inhabitants of Faery, also known as Faeries.

Fenodree (*Fen-oh-dree*)—The Fae man exiled to live in the Shadow Lands because he broke Seelie law by marrying a human woman.

Gally Trot—(aka Knight) The name given to Merlin's k-nine companion by the Fae.

Glamour—The use of magic to change one's appearance.

Guinevere—Queen of the Seelie Fae.

Hellfire—Unnatural green fire that burns through anything it encounters. One of the only know beings to wield the substance is the Nuckalavee.

Hell Hound—Unseelie creatures usually found in pairs. They are roughly the size and look of a large Earthen dog but have red glowing eyes and violent temperaments.

Lambton Worm—Dragon-like aggressive Unseelie Fae who lives primarily in water but can survive on land as well.

Leannan-Sidhe (*Lee-an-an shee*)—Vampire-like Unseelie that uses glamour to lure Fae or human prey. They feed their magic through the draining of their victim's blood.

Mab—Extremely powerful Queen of the Unseelie killed by her twin brother Merlin.

Merlin—Eccentric Fae sorcerer.

Nukalavee—Shadow Fae that is so ancient and malevolent that it is believed even the mention of its name brings bad luck. It is known for its unique ability to create Hell Fire, and can manipulate dreams among its numerous dark powers.

Oberon— (aka Alberich) The leader of the Wild Hunt and foster father to Lochlan.

Phooka (*poo-kah*)—Small Unseelie about the size of a young child usually found near large bodies of water.

Portal—Magical doorway between worlds.

Red Cap—Vicious Unseelie known for cannibalism and wearing caps soaked in the blood of their victims.

Rune—Magical symbol used in spells.

Seelie (*See-lee*)—The Fae who live peaceably under the Seelie Queen's rule; most of the Seelie possess light magic.

Shadow Fae—The inhabitants of the Shadow Lands. Not technically Fae, but became known as such after their world became joined with Faery.

Shadow Lands—A dark and dangerous place believed to have been joined with Faery in an ancient cataclysm of worlds. The landscape steeped in perpetual darkness appears barren, and its inhabitants are a vicious face of beings who possess dark magic.

Sight—The ability to see through a Fae glamour.

Sluagh—(aka The Unforgiving Dead) A host of malevolent souls of deceased evil Fae.

Sword of Light—(aka Excalibur) A sword crafted by an ancient species able to imbue iron with magic. The sword is also known as "The Answerer" for its ability to force any at its blade to tell the truth.

The Great War—Early in Guinevere's reign, the war between Seelie and Unseelie.

Trace—The ability to transport instantly from one place to another.

Twilight Realm—A temporal plane between worlds that can only be accessed with a combination of light and shadow magic.

Unseelie (*Un-see-lee*)—The Fae who refused to be governed by the Seelie Queen and are thus forced to live in the Wilds of Faery. They tend to be vicious and solitary creatures.

Wild Hunt—The group of Fae men who separated from the Seelie kingdom when the Erlking Arthur had a falling out with the Seelie Queen Guinevere. They are self-governed warriors with no lands of their own and who choose to roam in search of prey to hunt.

Wilds—The uncivilized parts of Faery outside of the Seelie kingdom inhabited by the animalistic Unseelie.

www.ingramcontent.com/pod-product-compliance
Lightning Source LLC
Chambersburg PA
CBHW050816190726
48286CB00007B/1886